Praise for

"Hilarious."

—*New York Times*

"Poignant and wickedly funny."

—*Vanity Fair*

"The funniest book you'll pick up all year."

—*Daily Candy New York*

"Witty."

—*New York Daily News*

"A laughing look at everyday calamities."

—*New York Times* Book Review

"Hilarious, cathartic."

—*People*

"Charming."

—*InStyle*

"Winning."

—*Slate*

"Meet the Carrie Bradshaws of the birdie world."

—*Elle*

"Hopelessly hysterical."

—*Boston Herald*

ARE YOU GOING TO

★

KISS ME NOW?

ARE YOU GOING TO
★
KISS ME NOW?

Sloane Tanen

sourcebooks
fire

Copyright © 2011 by Sloane Tanen
Cover and internal design © 2011 by Sourcebooks, Inc.
Cover design by Cara Petrus
Cover images © Win Initiative/Getty Images; Henrik Sorensen/Getty Images

Sourcebooks and the colophon are registered trademarks of Sourcebooks, Inc.

Published by Sourcebooks Fire, an imprint of Sourcebooks, Inc.
P.O. Box 4410, Naperville, Illinois 60567-4410
(630) 961-3900
Fax: (630) 961-2168
teenfire.sourcebooks.com

Library of Congress Cataloging-in-Publication data is on file with the publisher.

Printed and bound in the United States of America.
VP 10 9 8 7 6 5 4 3 2 1

For Brooke and Bubble

Another Day in Hell

One of the most surprising things about being stranded on a desert island is how difficult it is to live without a mirror. I never realized how dependent I am on my reflection as an affirmation that I exist. I also never realized how dependent I am on shade…and sunscreen. After three days, my arms and legs are completely covered in freckles. I can only imagine what a fright my face must be, not to mention my hair. The experience is oddly liberating until I remember that "they" can see what I look like. This makes me cringe. But I can see what they look like too. And believe me, that's more important.

It's funny how we have all these preconceived notions about experiences we've never had and people we've never met. Like, if I asked you how you'd feel about being marooned on an island somewhere off the coast of Madagascar with five celebrities, you might think it sounds romantic and glamorous, right? I know I would have. In fact, coincidentally, my best friend Jordan and I used to play a game called "Three Huts" where there are three imaginary huts on an island and in each one there is a different famous person who would serve a specific purpose.

For example, in Hut One is the celebrity you'd most want to hear talk, but you don't get to say anything back. I'd usually put Stephen Colbert in Hut One because I figured I'd need someone to make me laugh and/or keep me informed about what was going on back in the real world. Shia LeBeouf is funny, too, so he's my Hut One stand-in.

In Hut Two is the person you'd want to have listen to you, but she can't talk back. This was always the hardest hut to choose because I could never come up with a celebrity who might be selfless enough to stop thinking about herself long enough to actually listen to what somebody else was saying. Now, if I was only on the island for a couple of days, I'd definitely stick Audrina Patridge in there so I could tell her what an idiot she is and how egregiously she's overestimated her importance in the world. But, if I needed somebody to really listen to me, I'd go with the fat girl from *Hairspray* because she seems nice and like she wouldn't judge me. Plus, if she turned out to be boring, I figured she could always just sing.

And in Hut Three, of course, is the celebrity you get to make out with, but there can be no conversation. I rotate among Johnny Depp (even though he's kinda old), Chace Crawford, and Taylor Kitsch. I always figured if Huts One and Two were a bust, I'd just hang out in Hut Three 24/7. How bad could that be, right?

Well, speaking from the perspective of somebody who's currently in the unlikely position of actually being stranded on an island with five and a half celebrities, I can testify that I will never again fantasize about being in a hut with anybody famous, for any amount of time, ever again! Granted, I didn't get to choose my fellow castaways, but at this point I'm pretty convinced that all "celebrities" should be caged in Hollywood and confined to the pages of *US Weekly*. And, BTW, if you're there, God, it's me, Francesca, and I really want to go home.

PART ONE:
WHAT KIND OF AN IDIOT WOULD DO SUCH A THING?

"I'm never going to be famous. My name will never be writ large on the roster of Those Who Do Things. I don't do anything. Not one single thing. I used to bite my nails, but I don't even do that anymore."

—Dorothy Parker

Earlier, Bored in Lake Oswego

I should start at the beginning, four months ago, on the night of the senior prom. I wasn't a senior, or a prom person, so the fact that I hadn't been invited wasn't bothering me…much. I mean, I didn't want to go, but it would have been nice to be invited.

"Stop hunching," my mother said, as she blew through the front door, precariously balancing a messy stack of patient files and her bottomless pit of a purse.

I was watching *The Mayans* on the History Channel and chose to ignore her. In retrospect, I realize I should have helped my mom unload, but after a full day of texting Jordan, the fingers on my right hand were crampy.

"Why do you go out of your way to make yourself look unattractive, Francesca?" my mother asked with a faint air of disappointment. "You could be such a pretty girl if you just presented yourself a little."

I remember thinking this was pretty funny because I never *tried* to look unattractive. In fact, I spent a lot of time applying my various lotions and potions, but the effect was clearly lost on my mother—and most everyone else, for that matter. That said, I suppose it was better to look like I was trying to look bad and succeeding than trying to look good and failing. As far as I was concerned, the grunge look was classic. I took pride in my flannel shirt collection. I'd rather die than show up at school dressed like my sister. I mean, maxi dresses and gladiator sandals? Unless it's 44 BC and your name happens to be Calpurnia, it's not a good look.

I'm not ugly or anything. It's just that curly red hair and freckles aren't exactly the high school standard of hotness. In a world where Scarlett Johansson is considered the ultimate in female beauty, a face that reads like a can of fish food hit the fan doesn't stand a chance. I'm sure one day being "exotic" will be an advantage, but at Arthur Eddington High, blending in always felt like the way to go.

And really, what did my mother know? She and my sister Emily were catalogue pretty with golden skin and ever so slightly wavy blond hair. I, on the other hand, was the spitting image of my dad. My mom and all the old ladies thought my flaming bush head was just terrific, but they didn't have to live with it. It was exhausting having to wake up an hour early just to blow dry and flatiron it into some form of normalcy. Like I said, I put plenty of time into looking like I didn't care what I looked like. Not that my efforts paid off. By the time I got to school, it was always in a puffy ponytail with little frizzles sprouting around the crown like pubic hair. Red pubic hair. Jesus.

"Well?" my mother said, looking at me.

"Well what?" I asked, still staring at the TV.

"What do you think?" she said, moving closer.

"About what?"

"My hair," she said indignantly. I looked at her.

"What about it? It doesn't look any different." Which was true.

"They took off five inches, Francesca," she cried, stroking the blunted ends like a lost limb. "How can you not see the difference?"

"Oh, wow," I said, opening a box of dry cereal. "I barely recognized you. That's something."

"Francesca!"

"C'mon, Mom, it's not exactly an extreme makeover." My mother's hair was way too long that morning, and it was still way too long, especially for someone her age. I mean, wasn't there a decency rule about that kind of thing?

"You never notice things, Francesca. For an aspiring writer, you're not very observant."

"Well, Mother, did you notice that I made soup for the week or that the garage door is now working?"

She paused.

9

"It is working, isn't it?" She stopped to think. "Ha, I pulled right in. You finally fixed it."

"Finally?" I squawked. "For a psychotherapist you could be a lot more sensitive."

"You're right, sugar loaf," she said absently as she started digging through her hobo bag. "What would we do without you?"

"Cute hair, Mom," Emily said as she swung into the kitchen wearing an avocado face mask and her running clothes. She was getting ready for her big night as prom queen. Blech. Is there anything more mediocre than the mores of a high school prom? My mother gave me a triumphant smirk.

"Thank you, Emily," she said. "Francesca didn't notice." I shoveled a fistful of dry cereal into my mouth.

"Are you kidding? It's huge," Emily chirped, smacking me on the shoulder as she grabbed one of the apples from the fridge. Emily has always been of the school that People Thrive from Positive Encouragement. I've always been of the school of Never Trust Anyone Who Works on Commission.

"Maybe you could even go to here," Emily said, holding her fingers at my mother's collarbone and looking at me. "I think you'd look fantastic like that, don't you, Fran?" She took a bite of her apple and waited for my response.

"Yeah, that'd be really outstanding," I mumbled, not looking at either one of them as I texted Jordan.

J:

Where are you? In addition to Emily's endless duties as captain of the track team and the swim team and senior class president, apparently she's now a stand-in for my dad. Gross. And Mom is lapping it up. I have got to get away from here. I mean, just because I don't join groups or give pep talks to girls in latex and swim caps doesn't make me defective, does it? And besides, I'm too busy grocery shopping and cooking for them to join anything but the Super Savers Club.

I pressed send and watched Emily play with my mom's hair. I would never do that. Touching totally freaks me out. Seriously, didn't Emily find it exhausting being so affectionate and upbeat all the time? I preferred being "reserved" and "withholding," the two adjectives my mother most often employed to describe my personality. I watched my mother smiling as Emily lifted her hair into a mock ponytail. She looked old, and I suddenly felt sort of sorry for her. I decided to channel Emily and see how it felt. After all, my mom was in a humiliating mid-life crisis. Her husband just left her. I was her daughter. The least I could do was offer up some beauty tips.

I put my phone down and gave my mom the once over.

"I don't know," I said, "I'd cut it to your jaw line and maybe do a color rinse to cover all the gray. At least you'll look a little younger." Channeling Emily felt pretty good.

11

"Francesca!" my mom yelled.

"What?" I said. I was staring at my mother, who was pretending to be mad even though she really wasn't.

"Fran's just cranky because nobody asked her to the prom," Emily said with uncharacteristic bluntness.

"Oh yeah, you really got me there, Em. If only I could get poked with a cheap carnation before being whisked off to a Radisson hotel by a bunch of drunk idiots in rented penguin suits. I can't believe I'm being denied this great American tradition. I'm so sad."

"You can say that again," Emily laughed before trotting back upstairs.

"Your mask is cracking!" I shouted after her in a lame attempt to have the last word.

Truth be told, I really was in a foul mood that afternoon. And it wasn't just my general resentment about having to take care of my flighty mother and spoiled sister. Maybe Emily was right. Maybe I was mad about not going to the prom. Most of the juniors weren't going, but the worthy ones were, and that included my best friend, Jordan.

Jordan Singh and I have been best friends since sixth grade. We both do well in school with minimal effort, and we both vehemently oppose team sports or anything that smacks of school spirit. She's one of the few people who actually likes reading as much as I do who isn't a sci-fi loser. In fact, Jordan's verging on popular—but that's due more to the way she looks than to her personality. Despite the fact that she's totally gorgeous and cheerful and has a normal family, her inner geek is alive and well, and for that I love her. Aside from my father, she's the only one who gets me. And that's worth putting up with my being virtually ignored when the two of us are in the company of boys. Ever since eighth grade, when Jordan suddenly filled out, I've felt like her flatland mascot.

Whereas I'm pretty in an Isla-Fisher-stuck-her-finger-in-a-socket kind of way, Jordan's gorgeous like a young Eva Mendes or Padma Lakshmi. People stare at her when we go shopping or go out to eat, and there's always some guy giving her his phone number. It puts me in a horrific mood even though I know it's not her fault. She's just totally boy crazy and loves the attention. Last year, Jordan dyed her glossy dark hair red, and a modeling agent approached us in the mall about having *her* try out for a hair commercial. I freaked. I mean, I hate my red hair, but it's my thing, and it must come with side effects like crispy texture, fish-white skin, and freckles. It's just not OK to take the color and pair it with silky strands and a beautiful copper complexion. That's cheating. I explained this to her, in softly hysterical tones, and she dyed it back the next day. Our friendship remains intact. Like I said, she gets me, and she loves me, even though I can sometimes be what she calls "a little abrasive."

Finally a message came in.

Fran:

Sorry about your mom and Em. It's like a bad reality show over here. The ENTIRE family is here "helping" me get dressed. My dad is lecturing me on female dignity while my mom keeps trying to cover my prom dress with a hideous, sequined pashmina. Ugh. I mean, did you think the neckline was "plunging"? Aunt Rani says I look like an American tart. Ha. Wouldn't that be an excellent name for a movie? It could be about an Indian woman who opens a bakery. We should write it together. Why don't you come over and rescue me?
X, J.

J:

Can't. Having dinner with my dad. If he shows. American Tart sounds worse than a Vince Vaughn Christmas movie.
F.

In lieu of the prom, I was having dinner with my father. I'd totally been on my dad's side since "the separation," but lately he'd been acting like a real ass. He only called us about once a week now, and every time I went over to the restaurant he seemed really uncomfortable. What a cliché. It had been over six months since he left, but my mom was still under the impression that he was coming back.

My mother was clueless like that. I mean, he had a new girlfriend. Her name was Chandra, and let's just say she wasn't exactly challenging Madame Curie in the brains department. That said, she was thirteen years younger than my mom, and she didn't dress like a Santa Fe lesbian potter. I was still clinging to the hope that my dad would get bored with Chandra's Mercury-in-retrograde chatter, but ever since I saw the matching yoga mats in the back room of the restaurant, I'd had my doubts. The image of my dad doing yoga is as unattractive as my working out to the *Pilates with Ashlee Simpson* DVD I spent eighteen dollars on last month. There's also the *Buns of Steel* video I liked to watch while sitting on my bed working my way through a log of Starburst. Whatever. At least I had the dignity to confine my dreams of a better me to the privacy of my own bedroom.

After Queen Emily and her entourage finally left, my mom went upstairs to get dressed for dinner with my aunt. I was still outraged that my mom let Emily spend $350 on a dumb, slutty prom dress. The woman was obviously racked with guilt for driving my father out of the house with her ankle-grazing hemlines.

I was doing homework in the kitchen and waiting for my dad to pick me up. "Doing homework" meant reading the *US Weekly* I'd stashed in my backpack after school. My plan was to wait by the back door so I could sneak out as soon as I heard my dad's old Volvo pull into the driveway. I knew he didn't want to deal with my mother. I suspected her flare-ups were the reason he'd stopped calling the house.

I pulled out the magazine and the Skittles I'd hidden in the pantry and waited for the sound of his car. If my mother had any idea that both my allowance and my salary from the library went to buying candy and tabloids, she'd seriously kill me. The fact was, my love of candy was trumped only by my passion for gossip mags. Nobody knew. Not even Jordan. I mean, she knew I read them on occasion, like everyone else, but she didn't know that I read all of them, every week, and that I knew on which days of the week each one was delivered to the grocery store. I could have happily done nothing but read tabloids all day. And if I didn't have money to buy them, I'd log on to PerezHilton, TMZ, or the NeverBeenScooped site.

When I was finished with the mags, I'd roll them up and stuff them in the bottom of the trash outside so nobody would find them. I was addicted and ashamed. I hated all those celebrities, and yet I envied how special they got to be. It wasn't fair. I mean, nobody cared that I let Andy Blank touch my boob last Saturday, so why did I care if Miley Cyrus got drunk at the CMAs or if Zac Efron wore eyeliner? But I did care. A lot. Maybe I secretly wanted to be famous because I felt underappreciated at home.

Maybe I suffered from low self-esteem. I could have psychoanalyzed it to death, but what was the point? All I knew was that my fascination with all of it was disgusting and topped the list of the many things I truly loathed about myself. It just didn't go with the package I was trying to present to the world. It wasn't easy reconciling my innate sense of superiority with my inexplicable crush on Ryan Seacrest.

The cover of *Star* was a beaming Heidi Montag with what looked like another botched boob job. "Yes, I had plastic surgery again!" the headline read. I felt a quiver of excitement. And to think it was readers just like me who made this bimbox famous. Shameful. I was studying Heidi's askew nipples when I heard my mom's voice.

"When is your father supposed to be here?" she asked, coming into the kitchen in a ghastly long sack dress I'd never seen before. She also had on purple eye shadow that was obviously meant to complement the dress but merely screamed, rather than whispered, "I was born at Woodstock." I cringed but didn't say anything. I prayed my dad would be late so he could be spared this week's episode of *What Not to Wear*. And to think she was giving *me* tips on how to present myself. Ha.

"Seven," I said, sliding the magazine under my trig book as I typed a message to Jordan. I knew she'd already be in the limo, but I figured she could read it later.

J:

Lord, you should see what my mom's got on. I mean, wouldn't you think my dad leaving her for a 26-year-old pastry chef would have inspired her to abandon the prairie skirts and clogs to the decade from which they were born? Talk about a beauty rut. My God. And how about a little Botox, lady? Pamela Anderson and Madonna are working mothers, and you don't see them running around looking like background singers from A Mighty Wind.

I hit send.

"I honestly don't know how you maintain your GPA," my mother nagged. "You're always on that phone. It's not healthy. What about human contact? Who are you writing to all the time? What is there to say?" This nagging was a monologue I heard about three hundred times a day. I was just relieved she hadn't seen the magazine. Texting is an affliction of my entire generation, so whatever. "Mother, the point is I *do* maintain my GPA, so don't worry about it. Just go. Have fun."

J:

When is my mother going to LEAVE??? She's so obviously stalling. Next she'll ask me if I have a boyfriend or if I'm doing drugs. Isn't it obvious that I'll never have a boyfriend? And wouldn't I be in a good mood at least some of the time if I were doing drugs?

"Are you going with someone, honey?"

"No." Ugh. I hated the expression "going with." I mean, going where, you know?

"Are you smoking marijuana?" she asked with a contrived tilt of her head. I couldn't help but wonder if that worked on her patients. "I thought I smelled marijuana the other day in the pantry."

"Jesus, Mother! No."

"All right, Ms. Sunshine, I'm off then," she sighed, grabbing her keys.

"Buh-bye," I waved her off, thrilled at the uncharacteristic haste of her exit. But, of course, that was foolish of me. She turned around and looked at the red Skittles bag.

"Why are you eating candy before dinner? You really shouldn't eat that processed crap. You are what you eat." She had a point—looking as she did like a bowl of lentil soup.

"OK, I'm processed crap," I said, popping a handful in my mouth.

"Don't be fresh, Francesca. Those are fattening and have zero nutritional value."

"You think I'm fat?" I suddenly felt like the girl from *Hairspray*.

"No, you're beautiful. But you have to watch out for junk food. Why can't you eat more like your sister?"

"Oh my God, you think I'm fat!" I yelled.

I had put on a little weight, but I was hoping nobody had noticed. Leave it to my mother, the therapist, to find the open wound and squeeze some lemon juice on it.

"I'm not getting into this with you right now," my mother said, closing the door on the only conversation I was interested in having with her.

"Fine." I was pissed. I thought about throwing up the Skittles, but it was too gross. I couldn't do bulimia. Anorexia maybe. I'd waste away to seventy-eight pounds and would have to be taken away. Then she'd really feel guilty about what she "did" to me. Unfortunately, I'd never really been the eating disorder type. I'd have to find another way to exact my revenge. In the meantime, I decided to wait until my mom left and then throw the half-eaten bag in the trash and pour Windex in it to avoid temptation. Jesus. Maybe I was the eating disorder type.

"OK," she said, "I'm off. Call me if there are any problems." She hesitated a moment, obviously wondering what else she could bug me about before she left. "Did you finish studying for your history final?" she asked, hand on the doorknob.

"It was last Tuesday, Mom. Just go already!"

She looked guilty. Like she should have known and was losing track of everything and everybody.

"I'm sorry I didn't ask about it," she said. "How was it?"

I realized this was a golden opportunity to ask for twenty dollars, but I really just wanted her to leave.

"Easy," I said. It always was.

She smiled and moved in as if to give me a kiss before heading out the door. I flinched.

Just then, the kitchen door opened. Great. I hadn't heard the car in time.

"Hiya," my dad waved, poking his head through the door and smiling sheepishly. His posture was stooped and guilty.

"You don't knock?" my mom hissed. "You don't live here anymore, Jon." Lucky him.

My dad shifted. "Sorry." He said this with as much conviction as a two-year-old being forced to apologize for dumping sand on another kid's head in the playground.

"Let's go." I popped out of the chair and headed toward the door.

"Let's," my father smiled gratefully.

"How's the frosting maker?" my mother asked casually. This was easily her most cringe-worthy moment since their separation. So it was going to be that kind of a night.

"Chandra's fine, Melissa. And she's not a frosting maker, she's a pastry chef…and she has a name."

"Right. Chandra the pastry chef. I keep forgetting that that's a real job," my mother snorted, "or a real name." My dad ignored her and turned back to the door. Did she not get how transparent her sarcasm was? I mean, did she honestly think being such a witch was going to make him reconsider his decision to leave in the first place? I felt sorry for my dad.

"Jon, we need to talk about Emily getting a credit card before she leaves for college." I could almost taste her panic that he was getting away.

"Fine, we'll talk about it next week," he answered, motioning for me to go, go, go. I glanced at my mom and noticed that her face was suddenly all puffy and red, and I could see beads of sweat forming around her temples. God, please don't start crying, I thought. Her desperation was tragic. I mean, the dress, the eye shadow, even the haircut. Did she really think the combined effect was going to wow him into thinking he'd made a big mistake leaving her brand of babe behind? As if. My father just looked like he wanted to get out of the room.

"It's always next week with you, Jon."

"All right, Melissa," he mumbled, rubbing his forehead. "I want to take Francesca to dinner now. I will call you Monday, and we can talk about everything you're angry about then. You're not the only one having a hard time, though I know how much it completes you to see the world that way."

"Oh," my mother laughed shrilly, "are you having a hard time, Jon? What part, exactly, has been hard on you, Jon? Is it hard to align your chakra with Chandra, or is it hard to live with the guilt of abandoning your family? What's the hardest part, Jon?"

I expected my father to fly into a rage, but all he said was, "Melissa, you don't know the first thing about Chandra's chakra."

Chandra's chakra? Did my dad actually say that out loud? I let out a weird peal of laughter from somewhere in the back of my throat. They both looked at me, and I slapped my hand over my mouth and shut my eyes. The last thing I wanted to do was upset my dad.

"What are you laughing at?" my mother shouted, her rage filling the room. Her face was the color of my hair.

I looked at them both staring at me with concern, and I started laughing even harder. And I couldn't stop.

"You think this is funny, Francesca?" she yelled. My head was now buried in my lap as I convulsed in a squatting position on the floor. Yes, Ma'am. I thought it was really funny.

"What's the matter with her?" my dad asked.

"It's just a nervous reaction," my mother said. "Your leaving has been particularly hard on her," she added, and then asked me to wait outside by the car so she could speak to my father alone. My dad rolled his eyes. I was still laughing but couldn't help thinking that her using me to get alone time with my dad was disgustingly sad and transparent.

From Hero to Zero

I t was so nice to have that hour alone with my dad at the restaurant. We drank ginger ale and ate French fries with mayonnaise. For the first time in months, I realized how sad I was that the only person in the house who ever understood me wasn't there anymore. I missed him. The worst part was that I couldn't really blame him for leaving. I do love my mom, but she's a nag, and her anxiety levels about everything from mortgage rates to mosquito-transmitted West Nile virus are beyond exhausting. I could only imagine what she was doing to her patients. Maybe my dad found her neuroses charming the first twenty years they were married, but the novelty had clearly worn off.

Since he'd gone, my mother and Emily spent a lot of time man-bashing my dad. Mom was really working the dutiful, abandoned wife routine, and it was totally bogus. If one thing was clear to me, it was that my mother and Emily had driven my dad away. For this I would never forgive them. It seemed like they were always mad at him for one thing or another, and when they weren't disappointed in him, they were ignoring him. I mean, could you blame the guy for wanting out?

The fact that my dad actually had the balls to leave was the shock of my mother's life. And now that he had a new girlfriend, she was in a panic that maybe he was the best thing she'd ever had and she'd blown it. And she was probably right. If only she were a little less narcissistic, a little less globally neurotic, a little more of a caretaker. And while I wasn't naïve enough to think he and my mother would be getting back together, that night, at least, it felt like our relationship was going to be OK despite their problems. Over the last few weeks, he'd been so removed I wasn't sure what was happening. I was scared he was leaving all of us, and I wanted him to know that I was on his side. I wanted him to know that we were the same. I didn't want to be associated with my mother, or Princess Emily, for that matter.

"I fixed the garage door this afternoon," I said, trying to engage him in an area of common interest. Ever since I could remember, I'd been following my dad around the house, watching him change light bulbs, fix the sprinklers, paint the house, and cook dinners.

"Yeah?" he lit up. "What was wrong with it, broken roller?"

"The power wasn't on," I laughed. He laughed, too, and pounded my hand on the table affectionately.

"I miss you, Bam," he said, eyes filling up with water. "I miss my brown-eyed deer."

"Me too." I didn't say anything else for fear my voice would crack. He hadn't called me Bambi in a long time.

"Have you been cooking, or are you all living on Lean Cuisine now?" he asked, trying to change the subject.

"A little of both. If I don't have time to go to the market and make something, we order in. You know how it is."

"It's a lot of responsibility for you, Fran. I'm sorry. Why don't you stop by the restaurant on your way home from school, and I'll ask Ramon to have something prepared that you can take home?"

"Like she'd ever go for that. Anyway, it's fine. Once Emily goes to school, it will just be Mom and me, and it'll be more manageable. Right now, what I need is a break from both of them."

"I can't say I don't understand," he laughed guiltily.

I was about to ask him the big question I'd been ruminating over since he left. I wanted to move in with him for a while. Maybe just for the summer. I was on the verge of asking him when he ruined everything…forever.

"Franny," he said, leaning across the table and putting both hands over mine. I looked at the mingling of our freckles and, for once, didn't hate my hands.

"Yeah, Dad?" I said, imitating his serious face and smiling.

"I need to tell you something, and I need you to be OK with it. I haven't told Emily or your mother yet." He was looking at me like I was an adult, and it was making me uncomfortable. I stopped smiling.

"OK," I said, instinctively pulling my hands away and putting them in my lap. He stared down at the back of his empty palms and told me that dumb, new-age Chandra was pregnant. Then he told me that they were going to get married as soon as my mother agreed to a divorce.

All I remember after that is my dad trying to catch my arm as I ran out of the restaurant. I left my backpack on the seat. I could hear him calling my name as I ran down the highway as fast as I could. My legs were spinning so fast I felt like I was on a bike. In retrospect, I can only imagine what a sight I must have been to the cars blasting past me in a blur. When I finally stopped, I was three miles out of town, in front of the only place I knew was safe: Jordan's house.

● ● ●

"What can I get you to eat?" Jordan's mother asked, sitting on the edge of Jordan's bed the next morning. Her hair was tied back in a tight knot, and she was wearing a gorgeous blue sari. I think everyone over the age of forty should wear saris. They're the perfect combination of good style and maximum coverage. What more could you want at that age?

Mrs. Singh is a stay-at-home mom expelled from the

1950s. She cooks breakfast, lunch, and dinner for her family every night of the week. She doesn't drive, and the house is so clean you could brush your teeth with the toilet water. My mom could learn a lot from Mrs. Singh.

"Nothing, thanks." I looked at the clock and noticed that it was 8:45 in the morning. "Oh my God, I'm late," I cried, jumping out of bed in a panic. Jordan's mother reminded me it was Sunday. Jordan was at SAT prep until 3:00. That she actually went to SAT prep the morning after the senior prom was so Jordan. I was sorry she was gone but glad it was Sunday. I sunk back into her crisp, white sheets and began to reconstruct the last fifteen hours of my life.

"Don't worry, Francesca," she said soothingly. "I called your mother last night, and she knows you're here."

"I wasn't worried," I mumbled. And it was true. I couldn't have cared less what my mother thought about anything at that moment. She was responsible for driving my dad to Chandra. And then I thought of my father with a new baby. If he could forget us all so quickly and just start a new family, maybe he wasn't who I thought he was at all. At that moment, I really detested both of my parents. I felt like puking.

"Your father was very concerned. He went back to your house after you left the restaurant. He was waiting there when I called to tell your mother you were here."

"My mom must have loved that."

Mrs. Singh didn't say anything.

"Did he tell her?" I asked.

"Tell her what?"

"That he's having a new baby?"

"I don't know, Francesca. I think so, perhaps." Her unlined face got a little pinched between her brows. "Your mother's going to pick you up after work." My mother saw patients on weekends too.

"Like I care."

"This must also be hard on your mother," Mrs. Singh said, searching my face for traces of empathy. I made sure she found none. She stood up and grinned. "OK, Francesca, I have a splendid idea. Why don't you relax while I make you a grilled cheese with tomato, basil, and honey. I saw it on *Oprah*. Gayle gave it five stars. Sounds good, no?"

"It sounds weird," I said, smiling. I was kind of hungry, and everything Mrs. Singh made was good.

She laughed and got up, and I started to wonder what I was going to do in Jordan's house all day without my backpack or cell. Then she handed me a stapled brown bag that she said Jordan left for me. After she left, I opened the bag and saw it was the week in tabloids plus a *Seventeen* and a *Vogue*. And a pack of apple Jolly Ranchers. You had to love that girl. Of course, I'd already read all the magazines, except the *Seventeen*, so I started to peel through it with the sort of enthusiasm I generally reserved for *People*. *Seventeen* was definitely not my thing, but it was a hundred times better than nothing.

After sifting through countless articles on "the new plaid," pap smears, and applying self-tanners, I saw one of those "My Life" essay contests. The subject was "Living with Loss," and the prize was VIP tickets to a secret "celebrity event," publication of the winning essay in the April issue of *Seventeen*, and a partial academic scholarship. I liked the idea of attending a screening in L.A. with Robert Pattinson, a published essay would be just the thing to dress up my college application essays, and a partial scholarship could mean attending the college of my choice. Adios, Lake Oswego. I noticed that the deadline for submissions was the next day. It was perfect. I had no time to overthink it.

I'd never had any delusions about my writing, but I'd been told on more than one occasion that I was good. I don't mean to sound conceited, but it's true. I'm creative and I like telling stories—in print. I'm much more interesting on paper than in person. Everyone has always assumed I'd grow up to be a writer, including myself. I just rarely got around to writing anything other than text messages. On the rare occasions I kept up with my journal, the contents were so depressing they could have had me committed to a psychiatric ward. I mean, it's not like I ever recorded anything good that happened in there. The few times that something pleasant happened in my life—and I do mean few—the last thing I was doing was writing down how great I felt. There were Little Golden Books for people who liked that sort of thing. So I'd developed a bit of a flair for expressing my particular brand of teenage angst. It was all very emo.

Anyway, seeing as I had nothing to do for the next seven hours, I decided to write "Good-bye Father: A Daughter's Loss" by Francesca Manning. I wrote the long-winded, sad-sack piece of catharsis on Jordan's computer. It was hilariously bad, but I felt much better having written it all down. I filled out the contact information and set up a new email address so nothing could be traced back to me online. I emailed the file to *Seventeen*.

• • •

"We need to process this as a family," my mother said, reaching for our hands and glaring at my father. It was Sunday night, and the four of us were sitting around the kitchen table. My mother was purposefully sitting in what had always been my father's seat. He looked appropriately displaced.

"I agree," my dad said. "I was just waiting for the right time."

"Like the night after my high school prom?" Emily cried, her voice filled with an atypical bitterness that somehow lifted my spirits. Her eyes were puffy and red.

"That wasn't my intention, Em. You know that."

"How can you do this?" she asked my father, tears streaming down her swollen cheeks. "It's disgusting. How can you just abandon us all and start a new family? You're a cliché! You should be ashamed of yourself."

"That's good, Emily," my mother said, encouraging her with a stroke on the back. "Let it out."

It was hard not to laugh when my mom said things like "let it out." I marveled that she had real patients who paid her real money to deliver such drivel. We all listened to Emily weeping for a few minutes before my mother tossed out another chestnut of psychiatric hogwash.

"Fran?" my mother whispered gently. "Is there something you'd like to say to your father? This is an open dialogue."

I shook my head. I didn't dare make eye contact with him. I knew if I made eye contact with him I would start to cry. And if I started to cry, the whole conversation would devolve into some horrific family therapy session. I was in no way ready for that kind of "dialogue." Honestly, I just wanted him to go away. I wished all of them would just go away.

"It's OK, Fran," my dad said. "We can talk about this."

I opened my mouth, but nothing came out.

"She doesn't want to talk to you," Emily said after a long silence.

"Fran," my father said. "Please."

"You're having a baby?" I finally asked, staring at the linoleum counter as I traced imaginary figure eights with my forefinger.

"Yes," he said.

"Then there's nothing to say. You've made your choice."

"Francesca," my dad mumbled, choking on a sob he tried to smother with a cough, "please understand that you girls are not being replaced. I'm sorry for the pain this causes you, but I deserve a chance to be happy too. I love you girls. Nothing changes that. I am not abandoning you."

I could hear my mother taking long, meditative breaths.

"There is nothing in this world more important to me than my relationship with the two of…"

"I have to take a shower," I said, cutting my dad off as I slid my chair out from the table. I wasn't interested in his excuses, and I certainly wasn't going to tell him I under-stood what he was doing.

"Francesca," he pleaded, reaching for my hand.

"Let her go," I heard my mother say as I ran up the stairs to my bedroom. If my father could behave however he wanted to, with no thought about how his actions might affect me, I saw no reason why I had to give him the big, daughterly OK. He was on his own.

Sixteen Going on Seventeen

When I received the call from *Seventeen* six weeks later I thought it was joke.

"Is this Francesca Manning?" a woman's voice had asked on the other line. It was a hot June day, and I'd called in sick at the library. Nobody was around. My mom was at work, Jordan was in Colorado with her family, and Emily was visiting our cousin in California as a graduation gift before leaving for college in the fall. I was studying a picture of Uma Thurman without makeup on the cover of *Star*. I considered saying no. Whoever was calling, it wasn't anybody cute, and I was busy.

"Who's calling?" I asked.

"This is Courtney Gallagher from *Seventeen* magazine."

Seventeen magazine? I sat up. With all the drama following my dad's big news, I had completely forgotten about the essay. It felt like years since I'd written that schlock. And I seriously blocked out that I'd actually sent it in.

"This is Francesca."

"Congratulations, Ms. Manning, you've been selected as the winner in this year's nonfiction writing contest."

"Very funny, Jordan," I said, deflating.

"I'm sorry?"

"Jordan?"

"Excuse me?"

"You're not joking?"

"Joking? Is this Ms. Manning?"

"Jordan?"

"Who is Jordan?"

"Are you for real? I won? Are you serious?" I asked, allowing myself to feel excited. I was momentarily forgetting that the prize was having the essay actually published for the entire world to see. I kind of felt like I might start to cry, but I managed to get a grip.

"We all loved your essay about your father's death and the comfort you found in books. It was very moving."

OMG. It all came back to me in a flash. I'd written the essay as if my father had died in a car accident. It was so much easier to write that way, and I was so mad at him about the baby I half wished it were true. Jesus. There was even a passage about *A Tree Grows in Brooklyn* and how both Francie Nolan and I could only blossom into adults—yes, I used the word *blossom*—once the burden of a difficult but beloved father had passed. Holy shit. I'm dead meat, I thought. I wondered if I should admit this lapse into fiction to Mrs. Gallagher, but then I remembered the celebrity event and the academic scholarship part of the prize. Visions of R. Patz and Stanford clouded my common sense.

"Thanks," I said. I was looking at a picture of my dad taken two days ago at his forty-sixth birthday party. I started to think about all those authors being publicly flayed on *Oprah* for faking their memoirs and panicked again.

"Um, Mrs. Gallagher—"

"And the theme," Courtney Gallagher continued, "is perfect for encouraging literacy in developing countries where loss and recovery is a day-to-day trial." She interrupted me before my feeble attempt at coming clean could be finished.

"Thanks. So where am I going?" I joked, envisioning Gwyneth Paltrow and me macro-cleansing together in her London flat or Justin Timberlake and me presenting "Best Kiss" at the MTV Awards.

"Africa," Mrs. Gallagher said, and she didn't sound like she was kidding either.

"Excuse me?"

"I'm getting the idea you didn't receive the email sent out to the finalists last month, Ms. Manning?"

"I didn't," I admitted, remembering the email account I'd set up and never bothered to check again. "I didn't even know I was a finalist."

"Well, no wonder you sound so surprised! You were

selected from a very competitive pool." She sounded like she was going to burst.

"Wow," I said, mimicking her enthusiasm while imagining the disappointed pool of my worthy and honest peers.

"Well then, in addition to the partial scholarship to the college of your choice," she continued, "you'll also be going on a celebrity tour of Madagascar and other regions of East Africa through GLEA."

"GLEA?" I asked.

"Girls' Literacy East Africa," she patiently explained. "It's a branch of UNICEF."

"Oh."

"The winner documents the entire trip for *Seventeen*," she continued. "Writer's dream, right?"

"Does this mean the original essay won't be published?" I asked, feeling a wave of relief wash over me.

"Of course not! Your essay will be prominently featured in our April issue along with your diary of the GLEA tour."

Crap. I could feel a raging case of hysterical hives brewing under my skin. I reluctantly gave Mrs. Gallagher my mother's work phone number and email so they could discuss the details regarding my passport, inoculations, travel, and accommodations. I remembered thinking that it was typical that the one good thing that had ever happened to me was about to condemn me forever. What was the matter with me? They'd ship me off to juvie for sure. My father would never speak to me again. Even Jordan would be horrified to discover that her best friend was a liar and an imposter. And then I had an idea.

"I know this is sort of unusual, but I wonder if you could not discuss the subject of my essay with my mom?" I asked Gallagher. "Maybe you could tell her it was a fiction writing contest or something?"

"I can't do that, Francesca." She paused suspiciously. "Why don't you want her to know about the beautiful essay you wrote? I'm sure she would be very proud of you."

"It's not that I don't want her to know. I just don't want to tell her yet. She's still really raw on the subject of my dad's dying, and I don't want to upset her," I lied. "I'd like to show it to her once it's published. That way I can surprise her without having to deal with the psychological fallout beforehand. It might upset her now."

Gallagher paused again and, much to my surprise, agreed to simply tell my mother that I requested that the subject of the article remain confidential until publication. That would do. I could figure something out between now and then.

Once I'd managed to postpone my inevitable exposure as a swindler, I could focus on the larger issue at hand—that I had to go to Africa with famous people. I couldn't help but feel this was some karmic revenge for my secret tabloid fixation. I mean, I wanted to put something fancy on my college application as much as the next girl, but I didn't want to travel to Africa with Spencer Pratt for the privilege. I was more of a hide-in-the-hall-and-judge-people-behind-their-backs sort of girl. And what would my dad say when he found out I'd killed him off? I was pretty sure his new baby would never do something like that. I mean, what on earth had possessed me to enter a writing contest for *Seventeen* magazine anyway? How completely cheesy. I didn't want anyone reading my writing. And I certainly didn't want to go to Africa with a bunch of celebrities. I could barely talk to my peers in the school cafeteria. Seriously, I could barely talk to Mrs. Gallagher. And what was I going to do without Jordan? I rubbed my phone like a worry doll.

On Not Getting Papped

I went to the bathroom one last time before the plane landed at John F. Kennedy airport in New York. *My thighs look distinctly thinner*, I thought proudly as I balanced myself over the lavatory toilet. It seemed my fear of being outed as a fraud, coupled with my anxiety about the actual trip, had combined in the not unwelcome outcome of a nine-pound weight loss. Between that and my frequent trips to the bathroom at home, my mother was totally convinced that her little lecture about junk food had indeed driven me to bulimia. All I could think of in the days before I left was that it really was too bad I was going, as I'd finally gotten a little leverage in the family. I swear my mother likes me more when she's worried about me. It gives her maternal vomit-outs a place to land.

I turned on my phone the minute the plane landed in New York.

There was a message from Jordan.

F:

Are you there yet? Tell John Mayer to stop calling me. It's annoying and I have a boyfriend. I hear Brad Pitt is pregnant with Viennese quintuplets. Does he look chubb?

J.

Starcasm. Jordan didn't share my hidden fascination with pop culture. She genuinely didn't care how much Kate Bosworth weighed. I admired her for this and tried to mimic her casual tone.

J:

Who cares? Just landed in NY. Not even off the plane. Stand by.

F.

Of course I did care, and the prospect of meeting everyone was exciting but was also giving me diarrhea. That said, I read *US Weekly* and comforted myself with the fact that A-listers didn't fly commercial—in groups. I was pretty sure J-Lo flew private, and I certainly wasn't going to be intimidated by fringe actors. Tara Reid could suck it. I took out my phone to jot down some notes. My assignment was to document my impressions of the experience for *Seventeen* from take-off in New York to landing at Dulles, two weeks from now. I was holding my thumbs above the keyboard, but I couldn't think of anything to say. I was thinking of that animated movie *Madagascar*. Maybe those crazy refugee animals would be on our flight.

When I got into the terminal at JFK, the first thing I saw was a man in a gray suit holding up a white sign that read "Francesca Manning." I looked around stupidly as if there might be another Francesca Manning on my plane. I walked over to him and introduced myself, forgetting the bright pink laminated name tag I'd been forced to wear by a representative from *Seventeen* at the airport in Portland. I blushed. A name tag. How mortifying. He nodded silently. I nodded back.

"Bags?" he asked. I nodded again. He nodded. Weirdo. He wrestled my carry-on bag away from me, and I practically chased him down an escalator to baggage claim. I felt like I was in a Kafka novel standing next to him as we both stared silently ahead at the carousel going around and around. My bags came out about twenty minutes later, and Mr. Chatty put them on a cart.

We started walking again. And we walked and we walked and we walked. I struggled to keep pace with him. I assumed we were going to the Admirals Club (where I knew the VIPs wait—I was feeling VIP-ish), but I never saw the club, and so the endless walking continued. I turned to ask Chatty where we were going, but his grave-yard expression put me off. And then I saw that we were leaving the airport. This made me edgy. I followed him through two glass doors, and we were outside, immediately enveloped by hot, steamy New York breath. My eyes closed against the sun as it reflected off the white pavement. Just as I thought things couldn't get any weirder, I opened my eyes and noticed a lone, unmarked black sedan waiting at the curb with a suited driver leaning on the passenger side. He raised his hand in a halfhearted salute. And all I could think was: *I'm going to die.*

Newspaper clippings of teenage abductions and prostitution rings flashed through my head. I started to sweat. "Your car, Ms. Massing," Chatty Guy said.

"Manning," I corrected, panicking. "I thought we were flying out of JFK?"

"No, Teterboro."

"Teter who?"

"Teterboro," he said again, like this cleared anything up.

As if in some choreographed ballet, Chatty slid the baggage cart to the driver, who began silently loading my luggage into the car trunk. When he was done, he walked around and opened the back door for me. As I slid into the cool, cushy back seat—complete with magazines and chilled water—I thought of the million times I'd seen news stories about young girls getting into cars with strangers and thinking what kind of idiot would do such a thing. Apparently, that would be me.

My heart was beating through my chest, but I was too embarrassed to say anything. I cut to a fantasy where Diane Sawyer was interviewing me about my abduction.

DS: How did your captors manage to get you into the black town car, Ms. Manning? Was there a struggle?

ME: No struggle, Diane.

DS: So what happened? she'd ask, her voice brimming with television concern.

ME: I just followed a strange man in a gray suit who told me to get into the car with another strange man in a gray suit.

DS: And why did you get into the car without a fight?

ME: I didn't want to make a scene. And the car had air-conditioning.

DS: So, just to clarify, you followed a strange man through a crowded airport and then got into a black car with another strange man because you didn't want to make a scene and because the car was well air-conditioned?

ME: That's about the size of it, Diane.

I'm a role model for young girls everywhere.

I took out my phone. Perhaps I should tell someone my whereabouts just in case.

J:

Music Express Limo, License plate number 2K159.

F.

After I sent the text, I did my best to settle in and enjoy the ride. For all I knew, this was perfectly normal, and really, I was quite comfortable. I pressed the window and lock buttons just to make sure they worked. They did. I crossed my fingers and closed my eyes. The driver asked if I'd like to hear the radio, which I took as a good sign. I didn't think a molester would be so polite. Just in case, I dialed 911 and suspended my finger above the Send button.

After about an hour in the car, we pulled into what looked like yet another airport. From a distance, I saw low-level white buildings punctuating the sprawling asphalt at regular intervals. It looked like a minimalist village out of the Twilight Zone. There were no people, but I did see some planes roasting in the sun. Big planes, small planes, and even some helicopters. The driver made a sudden left, and I saw a crowd of men with cameras hovering around a sole town car much like the one I was in. Paparazzi? I took a deep breath. Maybe I wasn't being abducted. Maybe I'd get papped!

I smashed my face to the tinted window to see who was in the car. All I could see was the driver getting out and opening the back door. The cameramen started going absolutely nuts. I heard the paparazzi yelling but couldn't make out the words. I watched them make a tight circle around whoever had emerged as she moved slowly and awkwardly toward the hangar entrance. The group stopped, cameras flashed, the group moved. Repeat. It was like watching lions trap an antelope on the Discovery Channel. All of a sudden, a plump, frantic, middle-aged woman burst out of the hangar doors barking and pushing her way through the pack. There was another brief pause during which I could make out a girl's voice, then more cameras flashed, there was some applause, and then the two women dashed inside the hangar. All I could see was the back of a knotted, big, black-haired head perched on a wee-tiny body. The cameramen let her go, shuttled back to the curb, and waited for their next victim. Me.

My heart was about to blow through my chest as our car inched up. My throat was so dry the sides of it were sticking together. I took one of the conveniently placed mini water bottles and drank it in one gigantic gulp. Or so I thought. Half of it dribbled out of my mouth onto my gray Anthropologie shirt. That was exactly why I preferred flannel. Jesus H.

"Here we go," my driver said as he came around and opened my car door. I was staring into at least thirty enormous camera lenses. Talk about a deer in headlights. The name Bambi had never seemed so fitting. Everyone was screaming as I forced myself out of the car. It was terrifying. The noise was deafening. I can't believe I ever thought being famous would be fun.

And then, as I stood to face the crowd, the cameras and the yelling all stopped at once. Seriously, I could have heard a bird taking a leak back in Portland. One camera clicked, and then I heard a guy say, "Shit." And then silence. "Who the hell is she?" an angry voice called from the mob. Nobody responded. I clutched my phone with a sweaty palm. I wasn't pap-worthy. It was deathly quiet. Fifteen seconds earlier, I had thought there must be nothing worse than being famous. Now I realized the only thing worse than being famous was *not* being famous. I had disappointed fifty people I'd never even met just by virtue of my being a nobody. I might as well have stayed at home for this.

The mob parted for me apathetically as I walked toward the hangar. They went back to drinking their coffee and smoking and behaving the way they do when "nobody" was around. Then I remembered my bags. I turned around and saw the driver carrying them behind me, laughing with the cameramen. Were they laughing at me? If I looked like Jordan they would have at least *thought* I was somebody— or that I was on the verge of becoming somebody. And just like that, the familiar self-loathing began. I tried to think of one part of my body that I liked, and all I could come up with were my calves. They're muscular and lean, but even my calves have freckles on them, so they're flawed. I get that looks don't matter, but I also get that they do…more than anything sometimes. I felt like crying.

Mercifully, a black limo pulled up to the curb, and all the parasites resumed their position screaming at the car.

I knew I should walk into the hangar and hide, but I didn't. Something made me stop to see who it was. When the door opened, I had to squint my eyes because what I saw was so mind-blowing I started to wonder if this whole thing wasn't some crazy dream.

"How are the wife and kids, Joe?" Cameraman One shouted as the totally legendary Joe Baronstein stepped out of the car and turned to face the cameras.

He was so much shorter than he looked on film, and he was older and fatter too. But it was him, and it was almost like he was made of magic dust. I'd been looking at that face for as long as I could remember. Joe Baronstein had been in show business for maybe twenty years before I was even born. Like Tom Hanks and Robin Williams, he got his start on TV. He played a teenager named Squiggy Small on a hit series in the 1970s called *Small Secrets*. I had the misfortune of seeing it once on Nick at Nite. It was a comedy about a psychic family living in a little Texas town. And there were musical numbers! Yes, a musical comedy about a family of Texan clairvoyants. Can you imagine anything so dreadful? And I thought *The Partridge Family* was bad. My mother still refers to it as the best show in television history, which really says it all.

Joe was the only cast member from *Small Secrets* to go on and have a career. He made a few independent movies before being propelled to super stardom in the mid-1980s playing Matt Spacey, a hard-ass New York City detective looking to end the war on drugs. He then had a long run as king of the cop thrillers, and I swear he's been in like every great movie I've ever seen. I don't know what happened to him—maybe he just got old—but about three years ago, he started making one bad movie after another. Seriously, his last few movies were abysmal at best. That said, he was still an A-lister. If Robert De Niro still had cache after *Meet the Fockers* and *Rocky and Bullwinkle*, Joe Baronstein was in no immediate danger of not getting the good table at the Ivy. Those older stars got free passes. And anyway, despite Joe's recent box office failures, he looked like a happy guy.

The camera guys formed a sort of respectful half-circle around him. He spoke as if he were standing behind an invisible podium. He'd clearly been doing this circus show for years.

"They're great, Lew," Joe responded beaming. "Adelaide's playing my daughter in *Hoggalicious Two*. She's a natural." Joe was as friendly as could be. I was still reeling from the fact that Joe Baronstein was standing three yards away from me and that he actually knew these guys' names. He called him Lew. I was dying to text Jordan, but I didn't want to miss anything.

"How's Jonah's European tour?" another photographer shouted out.

"Great," Joe said, smiling tightly. Jonah Baron (he

dropped the "stein") was Joe Baronstein's illegitimate son. He was in a hugely popular Christian boy band called the Born. Personally, I don't know anyone who downloads Jesus tunes onto their iPod, but obviously such people exist because Jonah Baron is one of the most successful teen icons in the world.

"No offense Joe, but we don't think of you as a humanitarian. Why the GLEA tour?" another guy asked as he pushed his way to the front.

Joe laughed, and his face crinkled up exactly like it did in the movies. Before Joe could answer, another paparazzo interrupted with a question.

"It's rumored DiCaprio pulled out of your next project because he felt you were poisoning the environment with your private planes and excess fuel usage."

Joe laughed again. "You believe everything you read in your magazine, Norman? That's ridiculous. Leo and I are fine. Look, once and for all, I'm a professional pilot. If I wasn't an actor, I'd be flying commercial airliners." He paused and then continued. "In my line of work, private jets just make financial sense when people have busy schedules and wish to use their traveling time for work or wish to limit travel delays and so gain more working time. And, finances aside, private aircrafts are often the only efficient method of traveling to cities and regions not serviced by major airlines."

His speech sounded painfully rehearsed.

"So, you're flying these guys over to Africa today?" a lady photographer I hadn't noticed until now asked.

"You bet," Joe responded.

A gasp from the crowd.

"Why not?" he asked as casually as if he'd ordered the pasta instead of the fish. "We save time and money using my Boeing. I've piloted her on a fifteen-city, 35,000-mile tour. I've logged over seven thousand hours flying time. I'm an Ambassador-at-Large for Virgin Atlantic." Did he always talk like this? If I hadn't been so freaked out by what he was actually saying, I'd have been asleep. And wasn't he being just a little defensive?

The guys burst out in applause and barraged Joe with questions. *This* was a story. My feet were lead. Joe Baronstein was flying his plane, *my* plane, all the way to Johannesburg? Don't get me wrong, I thought the guy was a good actor and all, but I'd have been much more comfortable with a pilot who wasn't worried about the dismal premiere of *Hoggalicious Two* a month from now. I was certain nobody had told my mother about this.

I managed to sit down on one of two wooden slat benches just outside the terminal door. I was paralyzed with fear and heat. Just two feet behind me, through the glass, I could see the inside of the hangar. It was a sparsely decorated waiting area with the black-haired girl and what looked like her entourage taking up about half the massive room. I still couldn't make out who she was, but I was afraid of her, and walking in there alone was out of the question. My phone rang. I scrambled to turn it off but not before seeing it was Jordan. I switched it to vibrate and sent her a quick note.

J:

Joe Baronstein is flying us to Johannesburg! No, I'm not kidding so don't ask me if I'm kidding. I'm going to die a virgin.

F.

I felt a blast of icy air as I looked up and saw Joe Baronstein walking through the automatic doors. As he got closer, I had to restrain myself from jumping up and giving him a hug. Between all the movies and the magazines, I really felt like I knew the guy. I'd seen him in bed, chasing down bad guys, water-skiing in Hawaii, eating fries and burgers with his kids. Really, my sense of intimacy was totally creepy. He paused and looked right at me.

"Hiya," he said with a wave and walked inside.

I guess we weren't friends after all. Honestly, I can't think of anything quite as dismissive as a "hiya," but I guess it was polite. If I looked like Jordan, he would have said "hello" and probably introduced himself. Stop it, stop it, stop it. My phone vibrated.

F:

Are you kidding? I'm calling now. Pick up.

J.

I turned it off.

Another limo pulled up, followed by what looked like a red version of my mother's gray Prius. Both cars opened their doors simultaneously. The flashes and screaming started up again. It was hard for me to see anything from my bench, but I figured that standing on it for a better view might make me look a tad too eager. Surprisingly, the cameramen all seemed to have turned their lenses away from the limo and onto the Prius. They were all backing up, giving whoever was in the car a wide berth.

From the limo emerged a chubby young guy with a big head and white, spiky hair, wearing khaki shorts and a crisp purple Izod. His walk was inappropriately diva-licious considering his reception was about as warm as mine. He had an unobstructed walk to the hangar. Apparently, nobody wanted to take his picture either. He was pulling four piled-up pieces of neon-yellow luggage, and he had a long brown cigarette dangling casually from his lower lip. There was a big bulge in his pants pocket that I assumed was a cell phone from 1999. At least, I hoped that's what it was. He did look sort of familiar, but I couldn't place the face. I thought he must have been one of those chameleon-type

53

actors who are so respected because they're not so easy on the eyes.

"Hi!" I said cheerfully, as he walked past me, staring at the pavement. He shot me a dirty look. Strike two. He looked like a younger, gayer version of my uncle Allen. Maybe he was a flight attendant.

There was such a scene over at the curb that I was simply dying to know who was in the Prius. Whoever it was would have to pass me on the way in, so I just sat and waited. I reached into my pocket and took my phone out to jot down notes before I transferred everything on to my laptop. Maybe I could capture some of my first impressions before I forgot how it felt. I had decided that if I made the *Seventeen* diary truly spectacular, the magazine would feel compelled to run it, even after they found out that Jon Manning was not in fact dead but practicing sun salutations with Betty Crocker in Lake Oswego, Oregon.

My thumbs were paralyzed. What could I say? It was too much to absorb. I pretended I was typing anyway. I instinctively understood that gawking like a fan wasn't a good move. Appearing to look busy and uninterested was the way to go. I thought of Heidi Montag and that stupid, camera-ready smile she always had on. Nobody likes her. People definitely like you better if you're not available.

And, by the way, the fact that I knew so much about

celebrities did not, in fact, mean that I was starstruck. I just enjoyed seeing a little cellulite on America's unofficial royalty. Who didn't? I mean, if you think about it, celebrities are the most overrated, self-absorbed, indulged, and superficial group of people on the planet. Sure, they're living the fabulous life, but at what cost to their soul? I didn't envy them, I pitied them.

And then I heard the voice rise from the crowd. That magic, unmistakable voice. "Oh my *god*," I said out loud—even though I meant to say it in my head only. I dropped my phone. An evil, guttural snicker erupted behind me. I whipped around. It was the Izod boy, staring down at my empty lap, smoking a cigarette and drinking a cup of coffee. I didn't know how long he'd been standing there. I was sure he had gone inside. Why would anyone voluntarily stand in this heat drinking hot coffee?

"Who *are* you?" he asked, in the most condescending tone I'd ever heard from anyone under the age of twenty. He exhaled, and a hateful, Joker-like grin crossed his pointy little face. He looked about twelve.

"I'm a writer…for *Seventeen*," I said, with as much confidence as I could fake. "Francesca Manning."

"Is that so?" he smirked, giving me the once over. "How old are you?"

"Sixteen."

"And you're a staff writer at *Seventeen*?" he asked.

"Well, I won an essay contest, and the prize was—"

"Ahh," he said, interrupting me mid-sentence. "That's sweet." It seemed he had the information he came for, and he looked satisfied that he could now place me firmly below him on the feeding chain.

"Chaz Richards," he said, introducing himself and giving me a sidelong appraisal as he waited for the impact of his name to sink in. He took a deep drag on his cigarillo.

"Who?" I asked, knowing full well who he was, but if he thought I was giving him that satisfaction, he had another thing coming.

"Mmm, hmmm," he smirked, "I s'pose you've got absolutely *no* idea who I am, right?" looking at me knowingly and taking out his BlackBerry. So that's what was in his pocket.

"I'm sorry," I said.

"That's for sure," he snapped back.

Chaz Richards (aka Dicole Richie) is only eighteen and has a celebrity blog that's all but wiped out the popularity of *US*, *OK!*, *People*, and *Life & Style*. Maybe not quite, but you get the idea. It's updated every five minutes with the most current, juiciest, and most banal celebrity gossip. And it's usually wildly unflattering, which is why it's so popular. It's like celebrity bloopers with a running commentary by Howard Stern. You know, Fergie tripping in front of the Waverly Inn, Britney's bald baby baker, Marcia Cross trying to pass off a wig as her real hair. Great stuff. And, rumor has it, he's always got the story first, which is why his blog is called Neverbeenscooped.com. I can't imagine how he gets all his minute-to-minute updates, but I always found following Hollywood in real time to be a terrific homework procrastinating device.

"Are you coming on the trip?" I asked, confused at how the most hated celebrity blogger could have managed such a thing.

"Of course I'm coming. You think I'd miss an opportunity to see Milan Amberson sweating in a third world country? I'd sooner cut off a toe. But seeing as you don't know who I am, I guess you wouldn't understand how important it is to me."

"But how?" I asked, trying to deal with the fact that I was actually having a conversation with Chaz Richards, that I was trying to pretend I didn't know who he was, *and* that I was pretty sure he just said Milan Amberson was coming too.

"Don't ask stupid questions," he said. Ouch.

I tried to think of a non-stupid question when I heard that voice…again. No mistaking that gravelly, masculine tone. There was *no* way he was coming on this trip. OMG. Talk about A-list. This was nuts. It was Cisco Parker! Cisco Parker is a heartthrob of the variety that transcends both age and gender. He was only eighteen, but my mother, father, and Emily were all fans. He was on a wildly successful TV show on Disney for two years (playing a singing possum), before hitting the big screen, playing everything from Captain Marvel, to a schizophrenic, to Alexander the Great, to a college kid with a crystal meth addiction. I don't know if he's a great actor, but he's great looking, so who cares. When I was twelve, I had posters of him wallpapering my room. OK, I still have one, but it's inside my closet door.

Cisco Parker hadn't done one single interview since he tried to slug David Letterman for calling him ubiquitous. Apparently, he didn't know what the word meant and thought he was being insulted. Ouch, ouch. Anyway, he'd managed to leave that embarrassing episode behind, along with his Brother Possum/Disney persona. From what I'd read about him over the last few years, he seemed to be modeling his life after Sean Penn, whom he worshipped. No interviews, lots of do-gooding, and much paparazzi beating. He seemed like a pretty cool guy. OK, I can admit it. I still sort of had a crush on him at that point. Everybody did. I mean, *gorgeous* doesn't even begin to cover it.

The camera guys were desperately trying to get a comment out of him, but he seemed to be pushing his way through, just grunting the occasional, "Yeah," or "No, not today." Like Joe Baronstein, he was much smaller in person than he looked on film. It was almost like looking at a perfectly crafted, pint-sized copy of the original. One of the guys shouted something about him promising to give a statement, and I saw Cisco put down his bag (yes, he was carrying his own luggage—just like *us*) and face the crowd. He gestured with a sweep of his hand for them to back away a bit, which they did, immediately. I found his command of the crowd impressive. He seemed older than eighteen. In a good way.

"One statement," he said. It was so quiet I could hear Chaz blowing smoke rings behind me. Cisco took a sip of his Red Bull and started talking.

"For GLEA, girls' education is a top priority. Our objective in taking this trip is to raise awareness for quality education for all children, and we believe that a focus on girls is the best way to reach that goal. It is also the key to reducing adult illiteracy in future generations. All children and young people have a right to literacy, and it is important that governments provide for children's and young people's literacy development in the context of supportive schooling. As public personalities, or 'celebrities,'" he air quoted, "it's our responsibility to bring attention to these issues and to use whatever influence we have toward the greater good."

I was kind of speechless. He was good. I'd always comforted myself that it didn't matter that a guy like CP would never like me by telling myself that he was most assuredly a big swinging idiot. But he didn't sound like an idiot. His speech was articulate without seeming practiced and sincere without seeming like a PR stunt. He was fantastic. He picked up his bag, and the guys started crowding him and shouting questions at him.

"Is it true you and Georgina are over?" one guy shouted. I cringed. Poor Cisco. After his incredible speech, all the reporters wanted to know about was his supermodel girlfriend, Georgina Malubay. No wonder he hated the press so much. That said, I wanted to know if he was still with her too. I really did. She was one of those models it's hard to hate because she seems so happy and grateful for her success. She was part Hawaiian and only sixteen, like me. And let's just say that our ages, and maybe our height, were the *only* things we had in common. I knew it was hugely pathetic that I knew so much about him and his gigantic girlfriend. Cisco ignored the question, but his face looked pinched. And then there was an onslaught of lame questions that had nothing to do with Africa or literacy programs.

"How does Georgina feel about Milan Amberson going on the tour with you?"

"Are you concerned about Milan's reported drug abuse and her latest DUI?"

"Is Georgina concerned about you being in such close quarters with Eve Larkin?"

I was reeling from the names Milan Amberson and Eve Larkin but cognizant enough to hear Cisco's response.

"Am I concerned?" he barked in the face of one camera guy who was standing too close for his own good. "Am I concerned? What I'm concerned about is that our polar ice caps are melting. What I'm concerned about is the continued violence in war-torn Afghanistan. What I'm concerned about is the fact that you're poisoning the environment with your filthy cigarettes and that you're wearing leather fucking shoes, man." With this, Cisco yanked the cigarette out of one reporter's slack-jawed mouth and poured his Red Bull all over another guy's brown tassel loafers. He pushed the paps aside and made his way through the stunned crowd of reporters. Honestly, the moment trumped the classic scene in *Good Will Hunting* when Matt Damon asks his rival how he likes them apples. It was a movie moment, and, if I hadn't seen it with my own eyes, I would never have believed it. Maybe it was a little self-righteous, but trust me, it worked.

Cisco walked by Chaz and me without a word. I was sure he wasn't being rude. He was upset. I was flooded with maternal instincts I didn't even know I possessed. Come lay your head upon my breast, Cisco, and together we can heal the world. Chaz looked at my lovelorn face and sneered.

"Get it together, honey. It ain't never gonna happen—especially with that hair."

How rude. I'd even had it professionally blown out. True, but so rude nonetheless. "I know," I said. "I just, he's just, he's so…"

"Pretentious." Chaz offered.

"No, he's just so real." I squeaked out like a huge idiot. This Chaz guy clearly brought out the worst in me. He laughed in my face.

"And you're not exactly the poster boy for Pantene," I added, looking at his gelled 'do and trying to center myself.

"Oh, snap!" Chaz said mockingly, patting his spiked hair and sneering at me like a gob of poop he just scraped off the bottom of his shoe. He tossed his cigarette with a flick of his finger and walked inside without another word. I grabbed my bags and followed him into the icy hangar.

The Gerber Baby's a Crazy Lady

The black-haired girl I saw earlier was Eve Larkin, and OMG she was the size of a lima bean. Her head was like a gigantic bobble bouncing on her tiny shoulders. I thought her neck might snap from the sheer weight of the thing. Her shining dark hair was parted severely down the middle and caught into a tight knot at the base of her slender neck.

I fished around for my glasses so I could get a better look. She was sitting next to a large window looking provocatively at herself from under her lids. Her features, while not exactly pretty, were expertly played up. Her green eyes were framed with heavy black eyeliner, and her small mouth was flawlessly defined in a vampire red, which matched the polish on the nails of her little hands. Her nose was so small and precise I was pretty sure it was more decorative than utilitarian. Her powdered skin was a blueish white that was so dense it looked like she was carved out of marshmallows. The effect, coupled with what looked like ten thousand dollars' worth of cashmere, made her look like a very expensive and strange little doll that had been sitting on a dusty shelf untouched for too long. I was trying not to stare, but there was something riveting about how fragile she seemed in person. She looked over at me, and we both quickly looked away.

Considering the fact that she was only nineteen, there was something surprisingly depressing and dated about her. Like Christmas decorations in mid-January. It was almost as if she were a stale version of her childhood self. The lights were on, but they were faded and dull.

Eve Larkin hadn't made a movie in about four years. She was huge until she hit puberty. She was the Gerber baby, the star of the Broadway re-staging of *Annie*, and an Oscar winner all before the age of thirteen. After she won the Oscar for *Trading Phoenix* when she was just twelve, her career tanked. She made a series of bad movies, and then she vanished. I think she moved to England to "pursue an education" or "work on the stage" or some such pretentious crap. I'm not really sure what happened. I remember her as a rosy-cheeked blond, but she'd gone sort of Spanish goth with that jet-black hair and heavy eye makeup. The only reason I was able to recognize her was because she'd been all over the papers in recent weeks for burning down her London flat when she fell asleep with a candle burning. The whole building, which happened to be historic, went down. She'd had some kind of psychotic break after the incident. Rumor had it she'd been drunk at the time of the fire. This didn't make her too popular with the neighbors or the British people in general. So she was slumming it back in America.

I watched her as she sat so quietly and strangely, like a little woodland creature, bundled up in a white cashmere poncho with her knees drawn to her chest. She was still shamelessly staring at her reflection while simultaneously engaged in a hushed conversation with the chubby woman who had rescued her from the paparazzi earlier. There seemed to be about five other people all working for her in some capacity or another. I turned my phone back on. There were seven messages from Jordan. I ignored them and typed.

J:

Cisco Parker, Chaz Richards, aka Dicole Richie, Eve Larkin… and Milan Amberson!!! I am so freaked out. Get me outta here, man.

Do not call me. I can't pick up!

F.

My phone rang immediately. I turned it off again.

Eve was now staring blankly into space as her "people" ran damage control. It was amazing how cautiously they all moved, as if Eve were a psychopath to be flattered and smoothed into tractability.

I moved in a little bit closer. Nobody seemed to notice.

"*Teen Vogue* wants to do a cover," the chubby manager mouthed excitedly as she held her hand over the phone.

Eve shook her head.

"Let me call you right back, Beth," manager lady said as she hung up and sat down next to Eve with the air of a patient mommy about to explain to her daughter why it's important to share.

"This is what we *need* now, Eve," she said as she stroked Eve's arm maternally. "They're moving Blake Lively to October so you can be September. Nobody just moves Blake. Anna wants *you* for September."

"No, Yvette. I cannot stomach a photo shoot on the beach in a floor-length gown with a 'Best Years of My Life' cover line. Not after what's happened. It's not tasteful. It's inappropriate," she said in a stilted British accent. She's from San Diego, BTW.

"Nobody turns down *Vogue*," Yvette said.

"It's *Teen Vogue*," Eve reminded her.

"Don't take this the wrong way," Yvette pleaded, "but this is not an everyday opportunity for us at the moment. You *need* this. This is why you are back in the States. This is why you are going on this trip. This is what it's all about."

"Why do they want to do it? I don't even have a film coming out. It's salacious. No, Yvette, leave me alone," Eve said like a motorized wind-up.

"It's a fashion shoot, for God's sake. To celebrate your arrival back in the country," Yvette said.

"It's because I killed that dog in the…" Eve trailed off, staring into space again.

"Please, Rebecca Gayheart ran over an entire Mexican family and you don't see her on the cover of *Vogue*."

"*Teen Vogue*," Eve corrected her again.

I couldn't help but laugh at her. She was relentless. I must have laughed out loud because Eve and Yvette both turned to look at me and then began to whisper. I slunk back to my corner near the window and opened my phone. Another message from Jordan.

> F:
>
> Well don't call me either. Leighton and I are getting our eyebrows waxed before lunch with Shia at Taco Bell.
>
> J.

Not that I was watching, but after getting himself some coffee from the bar area, Cisco returned to his couch and started taking a stack of books out of his shoulder bag. He was making a neat pile on the coffee table in front of the couch. I wondered what he was reading. Despite myself, I felt sort of in love with him. He looked sensationally effortless in his faded jeans, "Keep It Green" T-shirt, and flip-flops. Generally I found flip-flops a disgusting choice for a man, but his feet were really too perfect to be hidden in something as banal as a shoe. His toes presented themselves like vanilla profiteroles. I tried not to drool.

Joe Baronstein walked over to Cisco with another man who, blessedly, appeared to be a copilot (thank the Lord, sweet Jesus), and they all shook hands. Joe was almost deferential to Cisco, which I found surprising, considering their age difference. I mean, Cisco was the same age as one of Joe's kids. They talked casually for about five minutes, until Cisco's cell phone rang and he excused himself with a perfunctory slap on Joe's aging back. Joe grimaced.

Cisco hung up, tossed his phone on the couch, and walked over to Eve. She sort of stiffened at his approach and then revealed a tight, oddly lipped smile. Collagen much? She stood up and extended a bony little wrist in his direction. He took her hand and graciously kissed her on both cheeks. Light and warmth rushed into her cold face. Then he whispered something in her ear, and she laughed like a French guinea pig on helium. The sound was atrocious.

I admired Cisco's confidence. I mean, yeah, he was Cisco Parker, but she was Eve Larkin. Even if nobody cared about her at the moment, she did have an Oscar, and that was more than Cisco or Joe could say. Did they know each other, or was this their first meeting? I couldn't think of any movie they'd ever been in together, but she'd been in so many for so many years, who knew? She smoothed down her already pin-straight hair in a surprisingly girlish and self-conscious gesture. And then, just like that, he turned around and walked back to his "area." Not that I could blame her, but she watched him walk away for just a minute too long. Obviously, she thought he was cute too. As she sat down again, her slim hands, with their perfect red nails, folded nervously on the cover of a script. The expression on her face at that moment was one of sour bitterness.

Joe, Cisco, and Eve were all at opposite ends of the hangar. Maybe it was my imagination, but they seemed to want to be as far away from one another as possible. The antisocial vibe surprised me. Did they all hate one another or what? I just assumed celebrities were all friends. Maybe Hollywood was like high school, with its own private code of social conduct. Chaz was typing frantically on his laptop. Maybe he knew something.

Then, in what could only be described as the single greatest moment of my teenage life, I saw Cisco Parker walking over to *me*. He was making rounds, and I guess I was next. I backed up on the window for support. I suddenly had a desperate need to pee. I could hear my heart beating in my brain.

"Hi Francesca, I'm Cisco Parker," he said, extending

his firm, tan hand. As if I didn't know who he was! His humility was so refreshing.

"How did you know my name?" I asked, feeling grand. Cisco pointed to the name tag I'd had pasted to my chest— since Portland! Ugh. I was mortified. No wonder Chaz was so disdainful.

I peeled it off and tried to smooth away the rectangular ghost the sticker had left behind. Cisco smiled. I was lost in his teeth, which stood at bright, white attention like a perfect pack of large peppermint Chiclets. I had never seen such teeth. Were they real? I looked over at Chaz, who was chuckling to himself but still typing. I offered Cisco my freckled, white paw and somehow coughed up my reason for existence.

"It's nice to meet you, Francesca," he said, and it really seemed like he meant it. "Congratulations on the contest. I look forward to reading your article."

God, he was such a gentleman. I looked over at Chaz, who was smiling and typing like Satan's secretary. And then Cisco turned to the group and shouted to nobody in particular:

"When are we leaving?" Everybody looked at one another, wondering who was in charge.

"We're waiting on Ms. Amberson," copilot Ted Montgomery, who also had a name tag, answered. "She should be here momentarily."

"Oh no," Yvette muttered from the corner.

"She hasn't even left Soho House," Chaz piped in excitedly, still looking at his computer. His team was obviously on the job. I noticed that Eve's pale face was now purple with rage.

"You didn't tell me *Milan Amberson* was coming?" Eve snapped at Yvette with disgust. "Are you insane, Yvette? I can't believe I let you talk me into this horror flick of a PR stunt. I can't stand the sight of you." Her accent was ratcheted up. Now she sounded like Dame Judi Dench.

"I knew you'd never agree, and this trip is exactly what we need now, Eve, more than a thousand *Vogue* covers."

"We?" Eve asked sarcastically. "I'd like to see your lazy, fat ass get on a plane with me for a change," she snapped. "And it's *Teen Vogue*, for the last time, so stop congratulating yourself."

"Everybody loves you, Eve, everybody just wants…"

"That's enough!" Eve interrupted, holding up her hand.

"Look, you need to get away from here and let this business with the fire cool. Build up your public image before…"

"Don't mention the fire!" Eve shrieked, cutting off Yvette's speech and startling everyone in the tri-state area.

"I'm sorry. It slipped out. It won't happen again." Yvette looked terrified.

Eve's balloon head was now buried in her hands. I wondered

if maybe it would pop. Yvette tried to comfort her, but Eve swatted her away like a bug.

"She's having a mimosa by the pool," Chaz announced gleefully, as if this was the very best bit of news in the whole world. "Milan," he clarified, surprised by the roomful of blank stares.

"Who is *he?*" Eve hissed to Yvette.

"Chaz Richards," Yvette whispered, cowering like a bad puppy.

"From Neverbeenscooped? Jesus Christ!" Eve growled, dragging her small hands down her cheeks. "For the love of all fuck, Yvette. Is Britney Spears in your ass pocket?" She stood up coolly and walked out of the room. Yvette rolled her eyes and motioned to two of the other "people" to go after her. On her way out, Joe Baronstein gently caught Eve's arm to slow her and turned to the rest of us.

"Let's give her an hour," Joe said. "We've got time."

"Speak for yourself, Joe," Eve barked at him as she shook his hand off her little arm and continued out of the room.

"Just an hour, Eve," Joe said apologetically. Seeing them side by side, I remembered that they had been in *Afternoon Rain* together. He played a cop, and she was his daughter who had been kidnapped. So they did know each other.

Cisco excused himself and walked back over to his books. My legs sort of gave out at that point, so I allowed myself to slide down the glass and sit on the cold floor. I grasped for my phone. Waiting for Milan would give me time to pull myself together.

Flying High

Not that anybody was paying attention, but I was still doing my best to act like this was a day like any other in my fabulous life as a grungy, suburban mall rat. This involved wiping the drool off my mouth as I plopped myself down into the gorgeous, buttery leather plane seat. Really, the inside of the plane was the nicest room I had ever been in. It was like a five star hotel with wings. It only had ten seats but felt huge. It had plush beige carpet, seats that swiveled around and converted into beds, private televisions at each station, and hand-polished wood-grain detailing. My butt was like cheese on a twice-whipped baked potato as it melted into the imported leather.

Cisco was sitting in the first seat on the left, four seats in front of me. I was thrilled I'd get to look at the back of his beautiful head for the next seventeen hours. His books were arranged artfully around him. Was he reading them all at once or showing off? Eve was sitting to the right of Cisco, two seats behind him. Her phone was ringing relentlessly. She wasn't answering. She was swaddled in her huge white poncho, staring fixedly at the seat in front of her. Finally, she sighed and picked up the phone.

"What?" she asked rudely. She kept glancing over at me like I was ET, and I guess I sort of was in this crowd. Chaz foolishly sat down across the aisle from Eve but promptly moved to the seat behind her at Eve's not-so-friendly request of "You cannot be serious."

Chaz put away his laptop and was compulsively sifting through what appeared to be a bunch of meditation CDs. After Joe announced that we would be making a few fuel stops, Chaz took out a bottle of prescription medicine, which he was shaking nervously. He kept looking at his watch, so I assumed he was trying to determine at what point he should take a pill for maximum effect, given the uncertainty of our departure time. I wasn't sure whether he didn't like flying in general or he didn't like the idea of Squiggy Small being our pilot, either. I was in the back of the plane. Clearly, the hierarchy was already in place, but I was happy enough, as I knew I had a great view of the entire goings-on before me. We were still waiting for Milan, who was now three hours late.

J:

The flight attendant keeps walking up and down the aisle making fish eyes at Cisco and asking us if we want champagne. Chaz is on his third glass. I'm drinking water by the gallon, hoping I don't break out before we get to Africa. I've already peed three times since we boarded, which makes me happy that my seat is in back and I don't have to advertise my incontinence problems to Cisco Parker.

F.

I hit send and went back to the bathroom. My Droid vibrated almost immediately.

F:
Do you think I care about your acne prevention techniques or your bathroom breaks? Jesus Francesca. That's the best you can do? C'mon.

J.

I was suspending myself above the toilet, busily admiring my thighs, again, when I heard Joe come out of the cockpit and announce that Milan had finally arrived and that we'd be leaving in ten minutes.

A moment later I heard a loud crash. As I opened the lavatory door, in the aisle, sprawled out on the floor in front of me, was what I assumed was Milan Amberson. She was facedown, encircled by long, fried platinum hair. From where I was standing, I could see a good two inches of dark brown roots. She was wearing leggings, a fur vest, and three-inch heels, one of which was broken off and in her left hand. The contents of her bag were splayed all over the place: pills, gum, little bottles of vodka, tampons, an iPod, a latex glove, Purell, two half-empty water bottles, condoms, three tabloids (two of which she was on the cover), a few loose cigarettes, a lunch cup of tapioca pudding, cereal, mascara, an umbrella, a few stray credit cards, receipts, super glue, and about fifteen dollars in loose change.

"Stupid, stupid, shtupid shoe!" she slurred as she attempted to lift her head and gather her belongings. I couldn't believe it was really her. She looked like a joke. Black eye makeup running down her face, blotchy residual spray tan, and what looked like an attempt to apply lipstick smeared halfway across her cheek. But she was pretty gorgeous anyway, with her olive complexion and sprinkling of good freckles across her upturned nose. These were the kind of freckles guys thought were cute. Not the kind that, like mine, looked like beef Bolognese exploded in the microwave. And you could seriously cut ice-cream cake with her cheekbones. Her lips were like Angelina Jolie's baby sisters. Chaz had snapped to attention and was attempting to help her off the floor. I stood there awkwardly, wondering what to do. Eve was clutching the phone to her ear and had a look of absolute horror on her face.

"Oh my God," I heard Eve whisper into the phone. "Amy Winehouse is here."

"You OK?" Cisco asked Milan, glancing at the floor but not moving.

"I'm great, Cisco Barker…I mean Parker," Milan slurred as she pushed Chaz away and motioned for me to help her instead. I did. She stood up, barely, and fingered her vest.

"Fake fur, Cisco!" she announced, proud and loud.

"Good man," he said without even looking at her. He was totally not into her. I loved that! She snorted.

I was busy shoveling her crap back into her purple snakeskin Balenciaga bag as she watched me with detached interest. Then she spotted Eve.

"Hi!" she said excitedly, hanging on to the back of Eve's seat for balance. She extended an unsteady hand. "I am such a huge fan."

"Nobody appreciates waiting three hours for you," Eve frowned, recoiling, as she looked Milan up and down. Milan withdrew her hand.

"I am soooooo sorry. Really. So sorry, Ms. Larkin. I was working late last night and…" Apparently her train of thought, or her excuse, abandoned her. I doubt Eve appreciated the "Ms." She was only a year older than Milan. Anyway, Eve had turned away from her and was whisper-yelling at Yvette again and rapping off a list of demands: no photographs with Milan, chilled Pom juice in the hotel room, no talking with the locals unless there was a camera crew, no questions about why she left England, a masseuse upon arrival.

"Whatever," Milan said as her eyes glazed over. She seemed to be having a flashback as she collapsed into the nearest seat, which happened to be across from Chaz. He smiled bashfully, like she just asked him to the prom or something. She looked at him suspiciously. I handed her the purse.

"Thanks," she said, without looking at me.

She started rifling through her bag and then turned to me sharply.

"Did *you* take my Klonopin?" she asked.

I shook my head.

She dug around some more and pulled out a bottle from which she fished three different-colored pills. Then she took out the mini vodka. She looked over at Chaz, who was staring at her.

"What are you looking at?" she snapped.

"You afraid of flying too?" he asked.

"No."

She swallowed the pills with the vodka chaser and took out the *US* and *OK!* As I said, she was on the cover of both. Eve looked back and rolled her eyes.

"Can I smoke in here?" Milan asked, looking around.

"No," Cisco and the flight attendant said in unison.

"No," she repeated mockingly, imitating them like an eight-year-old and tossing the loose cigarette back in her two-thousand-dollar bag.

"Sweet Jesus. I'll never forgive you for this, Yvette," I heard Eve whisper into the phone again. Her face was consumed with anger and pride.

Milan was one of those people who would be profoundly tragic except for the fact that she's actually talented. Her first few movies were fantastic, and this kept everyone hoping she'd get her act together. In *Cheating*, there was something really raw and fresh about her portrayal of a fish out of water in a cliquish Southern California high school. And she was hilarious in *The Naughty Corner*. I guess what set her apart was that she was a good comedian, which is a rare gift. A few years ago she had the easy charm of a young Cameron Diaz, but she was driving her SUV into Mischa Barton Town. It could have been that crazy, look-alike stage mother, the manager dad who tried to steal her money, the premature cover of *Vanity Fair*, or the Greek heir boyfriend who dumped her for Mary Kate Olsen, but somewhere it all went wrong. She'd been on the cover of the *Enquirer* so many times I felt like she must be forty by now. She wasn't even eighteen! She did look older, though. And she certainly didn't go out of her way to make a good impression on this group. Now here, mother, was a girl who looked like she was going out of her way to look unattractive. Not that it was totally working.

● ● ●

"And the vegan casserole with edamame, Mr. Parker. Can I get you something to drink?" the stewardess asked

Cisco as she laid out his fancy entrée. Her name tag said "Erin."

"Do you have green tea, Erin?"

"Of course."

"And I'll have another Red Bull, please," Cisco added.

He'd had about four Red Bulls since we left New York, and we were only three hours into the flight at that point. His bladder control was impressive. I keep waiting for him to use the bathroom so I could pretend I was so absorbed in my book that I didn't even notice him.

He had seemed to be on the same chapter of *The Fountainhead* for almost an hour and a half. There wasn't a lot of page flipping from what I could make out. I figured he was starring in the film version and therefore studying the text carefully.

Eve ordered the sushi, of which she ate two pieces before pushing the plate away in disgust. She'd been reading scripts with a scowl on her face for the last hour. In between scripts, she compulsively lathered an expensive-looking moisturizer onto her face and neck. Milan was passed out cold. Apparently her scuffle with Erin, the flight attendant, had taken a lot out of her. It was hilarious and went like this.

"Ms. Amberson, can I get you the sushi platter or the ravioli?"

"Fried chicken."

"We don't have fried chicken today."

"Well, that's what I want. My assistant called."

"Yes, but we received the request twenty minutes before take-off."

"Are you incompetent? Is it that hard to make fried chicken?" Milan asked.

"We simply can't accommodate last minute requests."

"He got his hippie platter," Milan said, pointing in Cisco's general direction.

"Mr. Parker's people requested a vegetarian meal days ago."

"Well, what's the point of a private plane if I can't get fried chicken if I want fried chicken? I work so hard, and all I want is a goddamn plate of fried chicken, and you'd think I was asking for foie gras." She pronounced *foie gras* "fwas grass."

Eve helium-laughed.

"What are you cackling at?" Milan turned, startled by the horrific sound of Eve's laughter.

"It's *foie gras*," Eve corrected in a perfect French accent. She smiled radiantly, revealing slightly too-small teeth.

Milan's face turned pink, but she didn't say anything.

"Just get me some cereal…or pudding."

"Would you like All-Bran or Grape-Nuts?'

"I'd like Apple Jacks."

"We don't have Apple Jacks, Ms. Amberson," the stewardess replied wearily.

Milan looked at her like she had an IQ of forty-five. Then she started digging through her crazy, huge handbag and finally pulled out two small boxes of Kellogg's cereal. I kid you not. She held them in front of Erin as if to say, this is what the word *cereal* means. One was Froot Loops and the other was Frosted Flakes. And I thought the latex glove was odd.

"*Cereal*," she said, tossing the Frosted Flakes at stewardess Erin. "I'll have these in a bowl, assuming you have one of those."

Erin nodded and walked away to prepare Milan's Frosted Flakes. That Milan actually got away with speaking to people like that was astonishing.

Milan ate the cereal and then asked for a bowl of ice cream. Unfortunately, that was the last we heard from her. She was out cold.

Chaz Richards and I both had the goat cheese mixed salad and the spaghetti Bolognese, which was absolutely delicious. I was careful to watch Eve pull out her table so that I would look like I knew what I was doing when the stewardess came over to me. We all got tablecloths, real silverware, and hot nuts. My Coke was filled with big ice cubes and served in a real glass. No plastic here.

There was a huge selection of movies and TV shows. Considering it was Joe's plane, I guess it wasn't surprising that *Small Secrets*, the musical psychic show my mom always talked about, was among the choices. I decided it was now or never. I couldn't figure out how to use the personal video player, and I knew embarrassment wasn't a good enough reason to be bored for the next seventeen hours. I asked the stewardess to help me set it up. Chaz gave me a look, but I didn't care. If he thought I was buying him as a world-class jet setter, he was crazy. I saw him fumbling with it too.

The opening credits to *Small Secrets* were like a bad *Saturday Night Live* skit about inbreeding. People were basically river-dancing in kerchiefs and denim overalls. Surreal was the only way to describe it. That people ever took this crap seriously is just crackers. Thank God I wasn't alive in the '70s. I watched in disbelief as the cast members, including a twenty-five-year-old version of Joe Baronstein, "swung their partners round and round." I cringed. I mean, this show was a hit? My mom lusted after this guy? This guy was flying our plane?

I Love You, Joe Baronstein

By the time we got to Johannesburg, I'd watched the boxed set of *Small Secrets: Seasons Two, Three, and Four* two times and was feeling like Joe Baronstein was qualified to do anything—dance, act, sing, fly, perform surgery…whatever. I even downloaded the fantastic soundtrack on to my Droid. Joe worked a fiddle like nobody's business. It was like hillbilly rock. I was digging it. When he came out of the cockpit after landing I clapped impulsively. Everyone turned to look at me. Thank God Cisco joined in the clapping; he must have thought I was politely applauding Joe for landing us safely on the African continent. Everyone glared at me as they reluctantly joined in the awkward round of applause. I got paranoid that Joe *knew* I had been watching the show. Oy. Then they all went back to their Blackberries and iPhones. I took the opportunity to check in with Jordan.

J:

Do you think Joe Baronstein might possibly leave his wife for me? Is a thirty-eight-year age difference too much?

X, F.

Eve Larkin had been applying makeup since Joe announced our initial descent into Tambo Airport. It was really, *really* early in the morning, and I couldn't figure out who she thought would be looking at her in South Africa at 5:00 a.m. Fool that I was.

Milan woke up after a series of vigorous shakes on Erin's part. I really didn't envy her job.

"What?" Milan snapped, turning her back on Erin and burying her face in the seat she'd never bothered reclining.

"We're in Johannesburg, Ms. Amberson," Erin said with a great amount of tact, considering the episode with the fried chicken.

"Great," Milan growled facetiously. She looked furious to have been woken up, despite the fact that she'd been asleep for almost fifteen hours. She fished through her purse and dug out a few pills that she swallowed dry. Then, ignoring the "fasten seat belt" sign and Erin's protests, Milan got up to go to the bathroom while the plane taxied to the terminal. She came back with her face cleaned up a bit. Her hair was in that sloppy knot that only gorgeous girls can pull off, and her eyeliner was back where it was supposed to be. Her lips were naked, but they were lightly stained from whatever she had on the night before. I caught Eve looking at her enviously. Though Eve was exquisitely finished, her beauty was labored. Milan's was natural.

Cisco had all his stuff packed up except for *The*

Fountainhead. He was still engrossed as the rest of us stood up to exit the plane. He had a highlighter and was painstakingly tracing passages. His lips moved a little as they followed his eyes slowly across the page. I was fascinated. Chaz and Milan were staring too. Chaz's lips were upturned in a Cheshire cat–like grin. Milan looked dazed and bemused.

Outside, the air was surprisingly cool. It felt great after the long flight. Joe led our motley crew reluctantly inside the gate, where we were met by an army of bodyguards and a UNESCO representative named Mogens Netzumi. He thanked us all for our participation in the Education for All program, which, thanks to people like us, he explained, had benefited more than ten thousand illiterate youths in less than two years. I was feeling awfully important.

Once we got inside the terminal, I understood why Eve had been applying makeup. There was a throng of photographers. All I saw were huge cameras and blinding lights, and everyone was screaming and shouting. I felt much too tired for this again. Cisco gave the exact same speech he gave in New York, which went over really well, again. He even did the air quote thing, which made me realize it was rehearsed after all. Eve gave a short but intelligent statement, and Milan just smiled and answered questions about her personal life. I don't know why, but I was surprised that people in South Africa would wake up this early to ask Milan Amberson if she was having a lesbian affair with her psychiatrist's daughter. I somehow imagined they'd have better things to do. Then it occurred to me that most of the voices sounded American or British, which led me to believe that these people had actually flown here from other countries just to take a picture of Cisco, Milan, Joe, and Eve at the airport. I hoped they got paid well.

"Did we honestly fly halfway across the world for this?" Eve whispered to Joe bitterly. Milan was getting a lot of attention, and I sensed Eve wasn't happy about it. Joe had his arm around Eve's shoulders, and her arm was around his waist in a show of fake camaraderie for the paparazzi. He laughed off Eve's question, and they both smiled for the cameras like old pals.

"Guys, guys," Cisco interrupted heroically, "we're here to raise awareness about illiteracy in Africa, not Ms. Amberson's personal life. Everyone's briefed on that already, no?"

The photographers laughed, and Milan looked at Cisco with a mixture of gratitude and resentment.

Chaz and I just stood back like two golf caddies at the World Open. I could tell he was trying to keep a distance from me—like my anonymity was contagious—but there was no pretending we weren't together in our nobody-ness. This became even more apparent when there was a sudden burst of excitement and all the photographers nearly trampled the two of us in an effort to reach a very blond, tall, skinny, young guy carrying a guitar case and heading in our direction. He was surrounded by security as well. Joe muttered something under his breath before breaking from our group, and the two hugged in what can only be called the world's most awkward embrace. The photographers were going C-R-A-Z-Y. It was Jonah Baron.

Like I said, Jonah Baron was a teen idol who just happened to be Joe Baronstein's illegitimate son. They were both so famous in their own right that their relationship wasn't the first thing that came to mind when you thought of either one of them—sort of like Nicholas Cage being Francis Ford Coppola's nephew or Miley Cyrus being the daughter of Billy Ray—but it was a fact nonetheless. I saw an interview with Barbara Walters where Joe said he was proud of Jonah's success and that the two were working out their "differences." Differences? Can you imagine when Joe Baronstein, America's hero, had to tell his wife of twenty years that Christian pop star Jonah Baron was his son from an affair he'd had with a makeup artist seventeen years before? And that she had the paternity tests to prove it.

As I said, I don't go in for the boy bands (or the Jesus sound), but it's believed Jonah is the second coming of Justin Timberlake. They even call his fans "disciples." Scary. At seventeen, he'd already opened for Westlife and Day26, which was impressive. But Joe Baronstein was

Jonah's father, and I think that might have helped just a little, right? And spare me the "I changed my last name and I did it on my own" crap you read about in *People*. I mean, explain Kate Hudson to me, please? Has she made a good movie since *Almost Famous*?

Anyway, in his defense, Jonah Baron wrote all his own music, and he had actually done a lot of missionary work. But, more importantly, he was rumored to be a virgin, complete with a promise ring and everything. I was impressed with his position on the subject. Unlike myself, he certainly wasn't a virgin for lack of opportunity. That was for sure. He was really cute in person. Standing next to his father, the resemblance was uncanny…except Jonah was young, blond, and didn't have the big honker. My crush started shifting a little. Then I noticed that Copilot Ted Montgomery and stewardess Erin were shaking everybody's hands and waving good-bye. Where the hell were they going?

J:

Update:

A) Jonah Baron is here too. You know, THE VIRGIN…like us. He's cute and is flying in the cockpit with Joe. Weird to see them together.

B) This means Erin and the copilot will not be on board. Somebody feels it's safe to let Joe fly us solo the last leg of the trip. Anyway, I smell too bad and am too tired to worry about it.

C) I'll text when we land.

X, F.

I sent the message and turned off my phone. The flying time to Madagascar was two hours and fifty-four minutes. I was asleep before we reached cruising altitude.

PART TWO:
WELCOME TO HELL

"I think celebrities suck."

—Eddie Vedder

I Hate You, Joe Baronstein

I've heard it said that after a trauma, a person's sense of time and perception gets fuzzy. Maybe that's what happened to me. I'm still not sure. I'll just tell you what happened as I remember it. That's the best I can do.

All I know is that by the time we finally got everyone out of the ocean and back onto the landing strip, the plane was almost gone. The only visible sign was the back end, which was slowly disappearing into the sea like a whale's tail. We all stared silently as the water swallowed the whole thing up, and then it was as if there had never been a plane at all.

"You idiot!" Milan shrieked, soaking wet and pulling a long platinum extension right out of her head. "If my iPod is ruined, I'll fucking kill you," she yelled at Joe, frantically searching through her wet Balenciaga bag for undamaged goods.

"Your iPod?" Eve barked incredulously. "I almost drowned! And you pushed me out of the way, you little monster."

"Don't be so dramatic," Milan said, wringing her tank

top out and shivering. "You didn't almost drown. We were three feet from land the whole time." Milan looked comedic standing there in her wet fur vest with pieces of her long hair missing from the ears down. She was like a gorgeous Amazonian rodent looking for cheese as she began scrambling to collect her things. She picked up a travel-size hair gel and threw it at Eve.

"Why don't you have something to eat and chill out!"

"Jesus Christ, Jesus, Jesus Christ" is all Joe said as he stared into the placid ocean at the spot where the plane used to be. His leg was bleeding.

"Where is everybody?" Chaz asked, looking around for paparazzi or a rescue team at the very least. I turned around and took in the scene. It was a good question. Where was everybody? We were standing on some kind of elevated patch of land. The ocean was below us, and the "landing strip," which was behind us, was nothing but an overgrown dirt road. In the distance was a thick mass of what looked like gigantic bonsai trees that sprang from the dry earth unexpectedly. The only sign of human life was an ancient-looking control tower, which was lying on its side, making crackling noises. That must have been the initial crash.

"I thought you knew how to fly a plane!" Milan yelled at Joe. "Is landing on actual land out of your area of expertise?"

"Hey!" Joe barked at Milan. "Back off. I can't think."

"Obviously."

"Where are we?" Eve asked, looking around. "I thought we landed." Her giant head was poking out of the white poncho, which was stretched out like a long dress, making her look like a drowned Q-tip. She couldn't have weighed ninety pounds wet.

"Oh my God, maybe we're dead!" Chaz squealed.

"Oh shut up!" Milan shouted.

"Oh Jesus," Joe moaned again, his head buried in his hands.

Maybe I *was* dead, I thought, as I absorbed the wet and disheveled faces of Milan Amberson, Eve Larkin, Jonah Baron, Joe Baronstein, and Cisco Parker. Or maybe I was dreaming. It was uncanny. I mean, what was I doing here with these people? What had happened?

The plane wheels had touched the ground. Joe announced our arrival from the cockpit and that it was safe to turn on electronic equipment. Everyone turned on their cell phones except Eve, who was shakily applying her last lipstick coat in preparation for the photographers. The runway was so bumpy it felt like riding a road bike over gravel. I honestly thought I might puke so I reached for the barf bag just in case. I tucked my phone inside the barf bag so I'd know where they both were in an emergency. I rolled the bundle into my back pocket. We were still taxiing along when Milan unbuckled her seat belt and got up to use the bathroom. That's when I felt the bump and then watched her (like it was in slow-motion) as the plane suddenly stopped hard and she flew backward toward the cockpit door. And then the whole plane slowly tipped forward and felt like it was sliding. When I opened my eyes, the plane had leveled out again, but it was rocking back and forth like we were on a boat. I definitely got the impression that we were floating. I actually think we landed at one end of the "runway" and then taxied right over the other side and straight into the ocean.

What was weird was that none of it was particularly scary. There was no screaming or anything. It was more disorienting, like when your knees buckle and you're suddenly not standing anymore. It wasn't until I looked out the window and saw all the water that I freaked. The plane was in the water! Everyone was silent except Milan.

"What the hell is going on?" she squeaked from a fetal position, curled up against the cockpit door.

I was waiting for somebody to do something, but nobody moved. They all just sat in their seats like we were in a movie and the director was about to yell, "Cut!" I finally unbuckled my seat belt and ran to the cockpit. Milan rolled aside to let me pass, and I pushed the door open hard.

"Mr. Baronstein!" I yelled, as I took in the scene. There was blood all over the dashboard and on the window. "Oh my God! Are you OK? Oh my God."

"He's fine," Jonah said. "It's just his knee," he said, frowning. "He was trying to block his face from the impact."

"Well, open the freakin' emergency doors!" I yelled. They both stared at me like they were trying to place my face or something.

"Hey, you!" I shrieked at Joe. "Open the doors—the plane is sinking."

"They should open automatically," Joe said, snapping to attention and pushing a few buttons and levers. "It's jammed," he said, examining the lever like a foreign object until Jonah helped him pull it down and I heard the door release pressure. I ran out into the cabin, followed by Jonah. Joe just sat there staring at the dashboard.

"Get out!" I shouted at Joe. Jonah didn't seem to notice or care that his father was semicatatonic.

"I've got to send an ELT," I heard Joe say weakly.

"Dad, just get up. Let's go," Jonah instructed, reluctantly helping his dad out of the cockpit.

Eve, Milan, and Chaz were bickering as they attempted to push the emergency exit door up and open. The plane was still floating, so we had plenty of air and time to all get out. With the help of Joe and Jonah, the door finally released, but not before water started slowly flooding into the plane.

"I've got to get my stuff," Milan said as she started dragging her feet through the water back toward her seat.

"Forget your stuff," I yelled. "Just get out. Everyone, get out." Milan ignored me and went back for her purse, pushing Eve and Chaz against the door in the process. For whatever reason, Cisco still had his seat belt on and was looking out the window.

"Hey, Thor!" Milan said as she passed him on the way back to her bag. "Get up!" He just sat there. America's ten-million-dollar-a-picture action hero just sat there doing absolutely nada. Jonah unbuckled Cisco's belt and managed to get him out of the plane, but not before Eve and I were out and swimming toward the nearby bluff. My shoes nearly slipped off in the water.

The plane was only about eight feet from the base of the island, so it didn't feel like we were in any real danger of drowning. What was odd was that the water was deep and there was no beach the way there always is in the movies. The island sprouted out of the water like a little iceberg. Eve and I hovered at the slimy base waiting for the others. We saw Milan slide out of the plane and start swimming (holding her bag above her head) until she pulled herself up onto the wing of the slowly sinking plane. With her legs straddling the wing like a saddle, she began trying to throw the contents of her purse up and over the steep side of the bluff. Her glitter BlackBerry bounced off the side of the small cliff and landed back in the water, where it promptly sunk.

"Shit!" she cried. "That's my whole life."

Jonah yelled at Milan to get off the wing as her added weight—minimal as it was—was causing the plane to submerge faster, and Cisco was still inside. In retrospect, seeing as the imminent danger was indeed minimal, Milan probably had the right idea. I mean, we easily could have gotten all of our stuff out before the plane went under. But I think we all assumed getting to land safely was more important than saving our electronics and makeup bags. At least, I thought so before I saw fat Chaz doggy paddling to shore, resting his laptop on the plane seat he was using as a floatation device.

As I said, the water around the island was deep. There was no beach. The only way to climb up the side of the landing strip was to hug it and push with your legs like a horny monkey. I know it's nuts, but I was actually lucid enough to want everyone else to go first so that nobody (especially Cisco) could see me in the humiliating posture that Academy Award-winner Eve Larkin was assuming. It was ugly. I saw that Jonah was still making his way to the rock with Cisco on his back. (Can Cisco Parker not swim?) I insisted that Chaz go next so that he might help pull the rest of us up. Why I thought he was equipped for such a job I have no idea. The sight of his fat ass and chubby legs humping the mountainside was hilarious. Milan laughed unabashedly.

"Screw you!" Chaz cried as he clutched the cliff and pushed off with his pink, shoeless feet. I started laughing too. He turned around to give us the finger, and his laptop went crashing into the water. I heard a little cry escape his lips.

Milan managed to scale the side only slightly more gracefully, and I followed her in the hopes that I could get to the top before Cisco could see me. The last one up the bluff was Jonah, who made it quickly. Halfway up he looked back at his guitar, which was floating out to sea. Tears were streaming down his face. I considered going after it but changed my mind. What if there were sharks or something? He could afford to buy a new one.

About an hour later, by the time we were all out of the water, the plane was gone. "Where are we?" I asked.

"I don't know," Joe said, dragging his palms down the sides of his face. "I think we're in the wrong place."

"What do you mean we're in the wrong place?" Jonah asked.

"I mean, I think I landed on the wrong island."

The Injustice Collectors

As my mother would say, I think we were all in a state of shock. We were nowhere near where we were supposed to be. There wasn't even another island in sight. We had been due to land at Andapa Airport at around 9:30 that morning. I think we "landed," albeit in the water, about an hour later than that. It took us a while to get everyone safely out of the plane and onto the runway. By the time any of us were able to even begin to process our situation, it must have been around midday. The sun was blindingly bright, but the air was surprisingly cool and dry.

I reached in my back pocket and was beyond relieved to feel that my phone, rolled in the barf bag, was still there. God bless the barf bag. The keyboard was still working! I tried to call my mom, but there was definitely no reception seeing as we were obviously like five hundred thousand miles out of range. Before I knew what I was doing, I was writing a text to Jordan. It didn't matter that she'd never get the message. It was a habit.

"Is this some kind of a joke?" Cisco asked after he'd

collected his wits. "Is Ashton Kutcher hiding behind a tree with a camera crew?"

"If only there were a tree," Eve said breathlessly, draping her wet poncho around her unkempt black hair like a hat to protect her face from the blazing sun. She reminded me of a carefully wrapped gift that had been savagely opened by a small child.

"Over there," Jonah said, pointing to the thick mass of trees about a hundred yards off. The topography was like a receding hairline, with us gathered on the bald part.

Milan was either too high or too dumb to realize anything was seriously amiss. She was soaking up the sun like she was at a hotel pool in South Beach. Chaz was staring at her round butt like it was something on display at the deli counter. If it weren't so obvious he were gay, I'm sure she would have filed a sexual harassment suit.

Jonah had driven a long stick into the dirt and was staring at it for about twenty minutes. When a shadow slowly appeared, he put down another stick. I was hypnotized watching him.

"What are you doing?" I finally asked.

"Figuring out where we are," he said, placing another stick at the end point of the shadow. "That's east," he said, pointing to the right, "and that's west."

"Really, how can you tell?"

"I'll fill you in later," he said in a beefy tone that made

me want to laugh. He was obviously really impressed with himself. Not that it wasn't impressive.

"East of what?" Chaz asked. "The Beverly Center? I mean, what possible difference does it make which way is east if we don't even know where the hell we are?"

"I'm going to have a look around," Jonah announced, ignoring Chaz. "Stay put."

"Whatever you say, Marco Polo," Chaz sighed, shamelessly inserting a fat finger in his nose.

"Let me know if you find anything good in there," Jonah said as he turned to leave.

"Aye, aye, Captain," Chaz saluted.

Things felt a bit leaderless without Jonah. Joe had been poking around the old control tower. I watched him standing with his hands on his hips walking around it in circles. He looked suspiciously like my dad the time the car broke down last summer and he lifted up the hood and proceeded to stare at the engine blankly, waiting for the transmission to start dictating operating instructions. My guess was that Joe was trying to avoid our group, as there was little question he was responsible for the mess we seemed to be in now. My crush had turned to dust, needless to say. He finally limped back over to us looking less than optimistic.

"You can't fix it, can you?" Chaz asked, looking up at Joe, using his chubby hand to block out the bright sun. I heard a tiny bit of well-timed desperation in his voice.

"Of course he can't fix it," Milan mumbled. "It's older than he is." She was lying on her stomach with her tank top hiked up to avoid tan lines. Her head was resting on her balled-up, drenched fur vest, which looked like a dead porcupine.

"It's true," Joe said. "I don't even know what it is. That thing is from another century."

"What the hell, man?" Cisco asked. "Is this for real? I thought you knew what you were doing!" He was holding his wet T-shirt against the deepening bruise he had on his left cheek.

"So did I," Joe said, hanging his head.

"What happened?" Cisco asked.

"I'm not sure."

"How 'bout a guess then?" Milan asked.

"There was some kind of electrical problem," Joe started. "The radar froze up on me. I didn't want to alarm you by making an announcement. Since I could easily make out the runway and the control tower, I just figured I'd bring her down by instinct." He paused. "And *I did*, you know. *I did* land her safely."

"In the ocean," Milan said flatly.

"I had no way to know how short the runway was," Joe said, staring at Milan with a glazed expression. "There was *no way* to know how short that runway was."

"Or that it was the wrong runway, on the wrong freakin' island," Milan added, snapping her fingers an inch away from Joe's dazed face. He startled before she continued, "You'll excuse us if we don't applaud your *instincts* with lots of hugs and kisses."

Joe rubbed his temples.

"You should stick to acting, friend," Cisco said to Joe. "Do one thing and do it well."

"Blah, blah, blah," Milan said, opening and closing her hand like a puppet. "So now what?"

"I don't know." Joe said. "I guess we wait. I've got such a headache."

"I'd offer you an Advil, but they were in my *suitcase!*" Milan said.

"I can take a look at the tower," I said, desperate to change the subject. "I can sometimes fix stuff."

Milan gave me a dismissive once over.

"It's not fixable," Joe said. "It's dead."

"That's just great, man." Cisco was examining the T-shirt for evidence of blood. There was none.

"Am I bleeding?" he asked the group, ignoring the drying blood caking on Joe's knee.

"No," we all answered.

"We need to channel Sayid," Chaz added theatrically. I could tell that there was a small part of him that was thrilling at being part of this weird charade.

"Yeah," Milan laughed. "He's so hot."

Chaz winked at Milan with a sinister smile.

"Who's Sayid?" Eve asked. Milan turned her head around and looked at Eve like a troll.

"Are you kidding?"

"He was a character on *Lost*. He played a former Iraqi soldier who could fix anything," I explained nicely, grateful to have something to contribute to this absurd conversation.

"I don't own a television." Eve said snottily.

"Boy, things are *that* bad for you, huh?" Milan asked. "Maybe your agent could buy you one? I'm sure he's got free time. You know what? I'll have my publicist send you one. You don't have to pay me back."

Eve smirked, not taking the bait.

"You should Netflix it," I said. "It's was a great show."

"Who are *you?*" Milan asked, as if she were both seeing me for the first time and totally irritated by my constant presence. Her eyes settled on the blank rectangle where my name tag used to be.

"Francesca."

"Not your name. I mean, who are you? What are you doing here? Are you somebody?" she asked in all seriousness. Chaz laughed. Was she kidding? I was really not in the mood for celebrity attitude at the moment. She was a bitch.

"Lay off, Milan," Cisco said. "Who are *you?* Are *you* somebody?"

Eve laughed. "Is that an existential question, Mr.

Roark?" Eve asked with a flirting wink. Cisco smiled at Eve with obvious approval.

"What the hell are you guys talking about? What's a Roark?" Milan asked, looking totally annoyed as she rotated onto her back, revealing a perfectly tan, flat stomach.

"*The Fountainhead*," Eve said triumphantly, taking in every inch of Milan's perfect body. "It's a *book*."

Blank stare.

"By Ayn Rand…" Eve continued, waiting for a glimmer of recognition on Milan's face but knowing happily that she'd get none. "I noticed Cisco was reading it on the plane."

"Whatever," Milan responded. Cisco smiled at Eve, and she giggled to herself. It was obvious she thought she'd really hit it out of the park with the literary knowledge. Like we didn't all read Ayn Rand the summer after ninth grade.

"Well, isn't somebody going to call someone or do something?" Milan asked, looking at Joe. "Radio control or something? I mean, enjoyable as this diversion from civilization has been, I can't stay. I assume they're still going to make us do this stupid charity benefit, and I have to be back in L.A. for my birthday on the fifteenth."

"There is no radio, Milan," Joe said. "That's the problem."

"No, Joe," Milan said, sitting up coolly and pulling her shirt down over her big boobs. "The problem is that you landed our plane on the wrong island, before dumping it in the water, and then made us get off the plane without our stuff. Despite the fact that there was plenty of time to get everything out. If I had my BlackBerry they could find us faster. It has a built-in GPS. It was brand new, man," she said angrily, kicking up some dust with her foot.

"There's no wireless here. This isn't Starbucks, Milan." Cisco said. Eve, Joe, and I all laughed, but for some reason I got the death glare.

"You think I'm funny, Bozo? " Milan shouted, turning her full attention on me and looking at my air-dried hair with disgust. I didn't say anything, but the "Bozo" comment, combined with her asking if I thought she was funny, immediately brought to mind my favorite scene in *Goodfellas*. I burst out laughing.

"Uh-oh," Chaz squealed.

"I'm here to amuse you?" she asked again, totally oblivious to the fact that she was now reciting the scene almost verbatim.

"Well, you are now," I cried with laughter. The *Goodfellas* reference was just too funny. Even Joe started laughing, but he buried his face in his shirt to stifle the sound.

"Sorry," I said. "It's a line from *Goodfellas*."

She gave me a blank stare.

"The mafia movie? You know, 'I amuse you? I'm here to make you laugh?'" I said again, throwing in a slight Italian American accent and hoping she'd see the humor. Nothing.

"Joe Pesci?" Joe said, looking at Milan beseechingly.

"What the hell is a Joe Petchi?" Milan snapped with an uncanny Valley girl twang.

"He's an actor." Joe said. "A great actor."

"Look, if it makes you all feel better to make me feel stupid then go right ahead. But let's face it, I mean, who's the stupid one?" She paused for dramatic effect. "*You*, who can't land a plane…*on land?*" she said, looking at Joe. "*You*, who move your lips when you read *The Fountainpen?*" she said, looking at Cisco. "Or *you*," she said, pointing at Eve, "who set an apartment building on fire with a patchouli incense stick?"

"It was a candle," Eve responded dryly. I prayed to God Milan was done, but no such luck.

"Or you two parasites," she said, waving her long, tan hand at Chaz and me, "who have nothing better to do than follow famous people around so that your own lives don't seem so dull and empty!" She was trembling now.

Did I deserve this? She was starting to get on my nerves.

"Or *you*," I heard myself say, "who can afford a closet full of two-thousand-dollar Balenciaga bags but can't remember to put on underwear when you leave the house."

"Snap!" Cisco roared with laughter, and everyone else started clapping, except Milan, of course. I had just told Milan Amberson off. I suddenly felt great. I was dying to tell Jordan. Bozo my ass, bitch!

Just as she turned to unleash her wrath on me, Jonah came trotting back from the other side of the island.

"There's nothing around," he said breathlessly. "I don't know where you were supposed to have landed, *Dad*, but this ain't it." He emphasized the word *dad* to the point where it sounded like he was being facetious.

"And," Jonah continued, "there's nobody waiting for us except some sand crabs on a small beach on the other side. You really screwed this up." His hostile tone suggested he was almost enjoying humiliating his father.

"Did you cover the whole area already?" Joe asked, wiping sweat off his balding brow.

"Of course not. We can take a better look around tomorrow."

"Tomorrow?" Milan balked.

"Anyway, it's good you sent the ELT," Jonah finished up, looking at Joe with a perverse smile on his face.

"I didn't send it. You know I didn't. You told me to get out of the cockpit before I had a chance."

"What?" we all said, none of us knowing what an ELT was, but it sounded like a really bad thing for Joe not to have done.

"*I* told *you?*" Jonah screeched. "I'm seventeen. And since when have you ever listened to me?"

"Oh, tell it to Jesus, Jonah," Joe shouted. "I can't listen to this shit from you right now."

Jonah smiled smugly—as though he was satisfied he had gotten the reaction he was looking for. Personally, I thought what Joe said was super harsh. And it was so not something that either Squiggy Small or Detective Matt Spacey would say. All actors are frauds and fakers. None of them are nice…except Cisco Parker, maybe.

"Look," Milan said, getting up and pacing frantically around her dead fur pillow, "can you two work out the father/son issues on somebody else's time?"

Jonah looked at Milan and smiled. Joe took a deep breath and reassured us that it didn't matter about the ELT.

"They will be here soon," he said. "The radar track wasn't out that long."

"What radar track?" Jonah asked, having missed our earlier conversation. "How long isn't that long?" he asked. "Five minutes? Ten?"

"It was a little longer than that."

"How much longer? And why didn't you tell me it was out?"

Joe rubbed his temples with his thumb and forefinger. "I didn't want to scare you," he sighed.

"So how long was it out?" Jonah asked again.

"I told you I don't know. I wasn't watching the clock, Jonah. I was preoccupied with landing the plane safely."

"Or *maybe*," Jonah asked in a challenging voice, "you were preoccupied with visions of being a hero?" He nodded at Joe encouragingly. "Is that it? I mean, you lost contact and didn't send a distress signal? What kind of bullshit is that?"

"I told you we weren't in distress. I could see the runway just below us, I just assumed…" Joe trailed off.

"I need a cigarette," Milan announced, pulling a ruined wet stick out of her purse. "You guys are boring me, and I'm cold." The sky was getting darker now.

"And how are you planning on lighting it, Ms. Amberson?" Jonah asked, still glaring at Joe.

Milan then pulled a lighter out of her little wet stash of stuff. She tricked it back with her thumb. It worked. "A little gift from God," Milan said, smiling at full movie star wattage. Jonah looked at the lighter and smiled back. I couldn't help but think they'd make a great-looking, albeit odd, couple.

"Can I have that, please?" he asked, extending his hand.

"No way, Virgin Mobile."

"It's Jonah," he corrected her, still grinning. "We might need it to light a fire later."

"Later?" Milan asked. "How long do you think I'm staying here, Captain Miracle? I mean, the world might not notice that you guys are gone, but they'll be looking for me."

"It's true," Eve said. "What will *In Touch* write about if you don't get arrested Saturday night for drunk driving north on the 101 south?"

"Somebody's been following my press, I see," Milan retorted in a fake British accent that rivaled Eve's.

"Well, you are ubiquitous, Milan," Cisco said.

"Oh, daddy got a dictionary!" Chaz clapped. He obviously remembered the David Letterman thing too. I was stunned that he was calling out Cisco Parker. Ballsy.

"What's that you said?" Cisco asked, really looking at Chaz for the first time. Chaz suddenly looked like a Chihuahua who'd been barking at a pit bull and just realized there was no car window (or computer screen) between them.

"I'm so sorry," he squeaked pathetically.

"Look," Jonah interrupted, "I'm sure a rescue team will be here soon, but considering he forgot to send an SOS, they may not have figured out what's happened yet. And it'll be dark in a few hours, so give me the lighter, please."

Milan handed Jonah the lighter reluctantly, brushing his palm with her fingertips flirtatiously.

"Well, I'm not staying here overnight," she said with the bat of an obscenely long set of eyelashes.

"Whatever you say," Jonah answered, slipping the lighter in his back pocket.

How Do You Spell SOS?

With no cell phones or watches, it was impossible to know what time it was. The only indication that time was even passing was the slow lengthening of the midday shadows. Cisco, Eve, and I were still sitting on the runway waiting for the rescue team. Jonah had gone off to survey the island with an eager Milan trailing him like an enthusiastic apostle. Joe and Chaz had gone looking for fresh water.

I didn't know what to do with myself. Since Eve didn't seem to recognize me as a human being (i.e., anybody famous), she was taking advantage of her alone time with Cisco. I was a third wheel on a deserted island. How perfect. Really, I might as well have been invisible. She was one of *those* girls. And she made that awful model mouth expression to accompany her constant whining.

J:

Eve Larkin sucks. Remember the hair gel diet rumor about her? I can totally see it.

F.

"What are you doing?" Eve suddenly asked me, snatching my phone out of my hand mid-text. "Does your phone work?"

"Hey," I yelled, trying to grab it back. "Give it to me."

"Yvette? Hello? Hello? Yvette?" She cried into the phone after frantically dialing a number and turning away from us.

Cisco and I stared at her.

"It's dead," she snarled, uselessly pressing the send button. Her back was turned to me. "What are you doing with it then?"

"Texting a friend. Give it back."

"An imaginary friend?"

"Whatever, it's a habit." I was relieved that she didn't read what I wrote about her. Though she certainly would have had it coming. She was beastly.

"Sorry," Eve whined as she turned and handed me my phone back. "I thought maybe you were getting reception. I really need to talk to my manager so I can fill her in on the hundred and twelve humiliating ways I'm going to destroy her career for getting me into this mess." Just like that, she turned her attention back on Cisco and emitted a little guinea pig giggle. She reached up to the dark bruise on Cisco's face with a phony look of concern.

"It really hurts," he winced.

"I think it's just bruised." Eve was fingering Cisco's cheek and sitting as close to him as was humanly possible without being swallowed. I wanted to scratch her big fish eyes out. I was staring at my phone but listening to every word.

"Anyway," Eve said in her faux accent, "it can be camouflaged before you start shooting. When I got that nasty case of poison ivy before the '01 Academy Awards, my skin looked absolutely flawless during my acceptance speech." Eve paused, seemingly waiting for some sort of a response from Cisco. He didn't say anything and just continued rubbing his cheek with a worried expression on his face. Eve took this as a cue to keep talking.

"Thank God for Gina. She's a makeup magician. I mean, I almost committed suicide after those pictures of me taking out the trash without makeup showed up all over the tabloids. The press was ruthless." She laughed self-consciously. "But isn't it always."

"You were like twelve when you won the Academy Award, right?" I asked, even though she wasn't talking to me. "You wore foundation when you were twelve?"

"I did when I had poison ivy all over my face! Maybe it sounds superficial to people like *you*," she paused, looking at my hair with horror and searching for my name, "but skin is the essential ingredient for an actor. I just don't feel myself with even a small blemish."

"But this freckle is cute," Cisco said, pointing flirtatiously to an itsy bitsy mole on Eve's upper lip.

"Oh my Gaawd," Eve shrieked, momentarily forgetting she was supposed to be British as she pulled away, buying her face in her hands dramatically. "I tried to have it removed, but all the doctors said it would leave a scar!"

"Chill, it's cute. Freckles are cute," he said.

She looked over at me and winced sympathetically. Freckles are not cute. I was the evidence.

"Freckles are fine for *others*, but I won't permit them."

"Anyway," Cisco continued, "I totally hear you. That's why I'm worried about this," he said, caressing his cheek. "I mean, I don't really care about the way I look, but everyone else does, right? And I can't exactly wear makeup for the World Environmental Conference I'm hosting with Gore on the twentieth." Cisco stroked his face thoughtfully. "Oh man, and I've got the Operation Smile rally with Reese on the twenty-third."

"What's that?" I asked

"It raises money for kids with facial disfigurement. I definitely can't wear makeup there. Right? That would be weird?"

"Um, yeah, that would be weird," I answered.

"Wearing makeup is never weird," Eve pronounced.

Were these two kidding? I was buying that Cisco didn't care about the way he looked about as much as I bought that Jessica Biel was "awkward" in high school and that everyone made fun of her. Please. I hate celebrities. And BTW: I saw those pictures of Eve taking out the trash in *OK!* and it was so not poison ivy. Pimple face. If I had to listen to this conversation for five more seconds I was gonna lose it.

"Do you guys think maybe we should do something useful while we wait?" I asked, hoping to change the subject.

"Like what?" Eve yawned, leaning against Cisco's shoulder. Yuck.

"I don't know, maybe we should write SOS in the dirt really big in case a plane comes by? I saw a documentary on the History Channel where some people were stranded in North Carolina a long time ago, and I think they did something like that." This may have been a totally lame suggestion, but it sounded more productive than listening to these two discuss the fine points of good skin care.

"North Carolina?" Eve squawked.

"That's a good idea, Francesca," Cisco said, clapping his big hands together and standing up. I couldn't tell if he was being sarcastic. He had the arrogance of somebody who was used to being worshipped and could treat the less blessed like used tissue paper. Not that it detracted from his utter gorgeousness in any way. And besides, my plan got Eve off his lap, so that was something.

"Let's do it!" Cisco cried enthusiastically. "Good thinking." He brushed Eve Larkin and the dirt off his jeans.

Although I was trying to stay focused, his body was unreal. I'll never forget the way the sun trickled off the bleached hair on his muscular arms. It was just too much. And his wavy dark hair was so damn shiny it looked like it was still wet. I desperately wanted to touch it. That the wires growing out of my head were also called hair is a testament to the inequality of all things.

"Oh, come on! Please. SOS? Are you serious?" Eve asked us from the ground, shielding her eyes from the sun. "We'll be here another few hours, max."

"How do you know, Eve? We could be here for a week. Jonah Baron seems to think we are here for the night at the very least."

"Jonah Baron is a dramatist," Eve said.

"That's the pot calling the kettle black." Cisco laughed.

"What does that mean?" she whined, sticking out her lower lip like a little girl. I would have liked to kick her back over the cliff. I loathe girly girls.

Cisco didn't answer but turned to me and asked what we should do, like I was the camp counselor or something. Again, I tried not to notice that his tone was a little patronizing. It was almost as if he thought I was suggesting a fun role-playing game. I couldn't tell if his puppy dog enthusiasm was charming or annoying, sort of like Owen Wilson. In any event, I was starting to get that Jonah and I were the only ones taking this whole "our plane landed in the water and nobody seems to be coming for us" thing seriously.

"OK," I said patiently, like I was talking to slow children, e shook his head.

at's when I noticed that Cisco's SOS rock points were
en backward. Well, at least the S's were—the O looked
obviously. Cisco looked really satisfied with his work
e stared down at the markers with his hands on his
He looked at me for approval.

In, it's backwa—" I started to say.

Let's get started," Joe interrupted.

Bu we have to…"

Fray, you and Joe write out the first S, and Chaz will
this. Cisco, you do the O," Eve ordered. Did she
cae Franny?

Bu said, trying to point out that we needed to fix it
ore arted to write, but everyone seemed to be dead
oning me up. Chaz looked at me and mouthed,
e's ic," like Cisco had a life-threatening disease
y want him to know about yet. And that's when
ali totally coddled somebody like Cisco Parker
Sat! I mean, I wasn't willing to sacrifice being
cue nobody had the balls to tell Cisco that he'd
tte2 instead of SOS. Forget it. That wasn't my
e, n't in the ass-kissing business. What had he
de? This wasn't finger painting for your self-
his was serious, even if I was the only one
Plus, this guy got over five million dollars
uld use a dose of reality.

"Why don't you and I go find some sticks to write with," I
said to Eve, "and you start laying out the letter points with
these rocks," I told Cisco, pointing to some stones along
the runway. "The letters will have to be big when we start
working on it, so make sure the points are at least twenty
feet from top to bottom. We'll have to push the sticks into
the dirt so the sign doesn't wash away if it rains."

"Rains?" Eve asked, looking up at the cloudless sky.

"Just in case," I said. Eve rolled her eyes.

"OK?" I asked Cisco, pointing to the stones. He looked
at me like I was speaking a foreign language and then
nodded. I knew if I had suggested that I stay and help
Cisco, Eve would have protested. To my utter surprise,
they both agreed. I made a mental note that actors like and
need a director.

Eve and I left Cisco busy on the landing strip while we
went our way in search of sticks. She sauntered behind me,
dragging her feet and hunching her shoulders like Eeyore.
It was pretty obvious she wasn't going to be putting her
all into this…especially since there were no cameras docu-
menting the momentous occasion when Eve Larkin was
forced to do something other than wait for somebody else
to do it for her.

If I'd actually gone into the jungle, it would have been
easier to find branches, but Eve wouldn't go, and she didn't
want to be left alone. I tried to ease her in slowly, but she

insisted that her tick allergy prevented her from entering grassy, wooded areas. I tried explaining that Lyme disease wasn't an allergy, but she wasn't having it.

"Look, I'll just wait here alone," she moped, plopping down on the dirt.

"Fine," I finally agreed. I was already sick of her. I was fairly certain she'd take advantage of my absence to "regroup" with Cisco ASAP. Whatever. No wonder she hadn't made a good movie in five years.

There was a little transitional wooded area that had a pretty good collection of fallen branches. The shade was an enormous relief. It was also strangely peaceful not listening to everyone snapping at one another for five minutes. I spotted a big piece of wood that I thought I could break apart pretty easily, but my left shoe was now falling apart from the water, so I had to break the wood with my hands while weighing it down with my knees. I got a massive splinter in between my thumb and forefinger. I hadn't had a splinter since the summer my dad made me do Outward Bound after sixth grade. I'd forgotten how much they hurt.

The pain in my hand slowed things down. As I continued snapping twigs off the wood, I convinced myself that a band of starving cannibals was watching me. All kinds of strange noises soon had me absolutely obsessing on cannibals. *Were there still cannibals in Africa,* I asked myself, as sweat started dripping off my nose,

or had they all eaten one another? I couldn't single detail about Africa, but I was having backs from a gory documentary I'd seen Island a few years ago.

Though I was sure the Red Cross would I still couldn't help wondering which of us we first if it actually came down to that. I decide Chaz, as he was both meaty and dispensable ized that with those criteria, I'd be dinner night. I tried not to think about it and ha to breaking the wood into strips when I hea rustling of leaves. Enough jungle time for m

The sun was a blaze of cotton candy pir I was in the clearing. I realized I must have b than I'd thought. Naturally, Eve wasn't the she'd be a little worried and feeling guilt me. Anyway, that's how I justified my fou mad sprint back.

I saw Cisco—and, of course, Eve—a landing strip. Chaz and Joe were back to in the air to announce my return. Like

"I told you she'd get them," I heard "What's her name again?"

"Here," I said, tossing the last t the ground.

"Did you find water?" I asked Jo

"Cisco," I said, looking at him with all the conviction of a school guidance counselor, "we need to turn the S's around because... because..." as he looked at me with his wavy dark hair and his huge, liquid green eyes, I found that I, too, was a big, fat, yellow chicken. "Because when the planes come, they will be getting an aerial view, and it's almost like a mirror effect, so we have to write the letters backward."

I could hear the collective sigh of relief. "Of course," Cisco said. "That totally makes sense. You're really smart, Francesca."

Eve seethed as I sent her my best smile. He didn't like me, but I liked that she thought he did.

The five of us spent the next half hour correcting Cisco's points. Everybody blew off my suggestion about pushing the sticks into the dirt. "Not a cloud in the sky," Chaz hummed as he started directing everyone on how to best engrave the letters into the soft dirt.

When we were done, we had an impressive SOS sign. It would definitely be visible from a plane. Then the pink sky suddenly turned steely, and a rainstorm the likes of which I'd never seen poured down on us. The transition was supernatural. I could almost hear God laughing as our SOS turned to mud. Chaz stopped singing. On the upside, it was raining so hard nobody heard me say "I told you so."

"So now what do we do?" Cisco shouted to be heard,

looking directly at me. I'd opened the barf bag in the hopes of using it to collect some drinkable water. I knew it was important to stay hydrated. In seconds, the force of the rain ripped the bag apart.

"I don't know," I said, crumpling the barf bag and trying to hold back my tears of disappointment. "I guess we sit and wait here." I leaned back and opened my mouth in an attempt to catch a little drink.

"It's pouring!" Eve cried. "You want to squat here like a herd of stupid birds?" She started digging through Milan's bag in search of a specimen collection cup.

"If we move, Jonah and Milan won't be able to find us," I explained, swallowing what little water I could get and using my hands to whisk away the rain like windshield wipers. "Let's just stay put."

Girl Gone Vile

It wasn't long before Milan and Jonah reappeared in the rain. The sight of them was oddly reassuring. At first.

"The beach is about two miles off," Jonah started to explain, shouting in order to be heard above the rain.

"What the hell are you doing?" Milan suddenly asked Eve, who she'd just noticed had taken advantage of her absence by emptying out a prescription pill bottle from her Balenciaga bag and using it as a little cup to collect rain. Everyone looked at Eve nervously.

"I'm sorry. We've been waiting for you guys forever, and I was so thirsty. I needed something to drink from. Besides, there was nothing in the bottles but ocean water."

"Did I say you could go through my stuff?" Milan screeched as she snatched the bottle out of Eve's hand and pushed a mat of wet hair off her face. Milan looked seriously pissed. She reached for one of the sticks I'd found and jumped Eve, holding the twig under her chin like a knife. I kid you not. "You listen to me you washed up, snotty tragedy. You touch my stuff again and I'll kill you. I'll *kill* you!"

I could understand why Milan was less than pleased at having Eve go through her things, but after all, this was an unusual set of circumstances, and Eve hadn't taken her stupid pills. The rain suddenly stopped, and the pink sun reappeared like a painted on smile.

"Dear God! Help me!" Eve peeped as her eyes bulged out of her moon face. "Get this psychopath off me." Eve definitely didn't strike me as the sort of girl who had been in a lot of bar fights. In fact, she sort of seemed like she'd spent most of her life curled up inside a satin jewelry box.

Joe rolled his eyes as he peeled Milan off Eve and calmly motioned for me to see if Eve was OK. I reluctantly sat down next to her. She buried her head in my lap and started weeping and heaving. It was obviously making me super uncomfortable to have Eve Larkin sobbing hot tears of injustice in my crotch. You know how I feel about touching.

"That's the one and only Academy Award–winning performance I've ever seen out of you," Milan hissed as she finally broke free of Joe's grasp and looked down at Eve crying.

"Bravo, bravoow!" she continued in a fake British accent. She clapped demonically as she stared down at Eve. Milan was a terrifying girl. So tough. Probably all those chick bar fights over Jared Leto. Or maybe it was growing up in the back of her mom's station wagon, driving from audition to audition. Either way, Eve was definitely out of her league.

Something told me the girls hadn't gone quite this wild in England. Even the Americans.

"Give it a rest, Milan," Joe ordered.

"Do you not get that I *need* my pills, you asswipe?"

"I didn't take them!" Eve pleaded.

"I think pills might be the last thing you need," Jonah said.

Milan's head snapped around like the girl in *The Exorcist* before she pointedly told Jonah, "Go to hell!"

"Don't say that, Milan. Please." Jonah looked seriously wounded. His reaction was totally weird and disturbing. Nobody said anything for a minute or two.

"Oh no, are you gonna go all Ted Haggard on us?" Chaz asked Jonah, finally breaking the silence.

"Let's just calm down, hold hands, and pray," Jonah said, looking at our six disbelieving faces like we were his fallen disciples.

"Dude," Cisco groaned, holding up both hands in mock protest.

"Please, are you serious?" Eve asked, wiping the tears from her eyes with my pants and leaving gigantic, unapologetic splotches of black mascara all over them. She didn't look like the polished Spanish princess from the airport anymore. She looked like a billboard for one of those horror movies starring demonized children. *Chuckie-etta.*

"I don't pray, you freaking freak," Milan yelled.

Jonah looked all business now. "If you won't pray with me,

129

then plan with me. We need to collect some water and food. The sun is going to set fast. It's going to get dark quickly now."

Jonah glanced down at the remains of our SOS sign. "Nice work," he laughed with a condescending lilt. "Would have worked better if you drove the sticks down."

"I tried to tell them," I started, in what came off as a lame attempt to both impress Jonah and blame everybody else. Chaz rolled his eyes. Jonah looked at me blankly.

"Oh man," Milan cried, still digging through her bag for evidence of theft. "My metabolism pills were in there too. If I gain one pound, you loser, I…"

"Come, pray," Jonah interrupted, holding out his long hands.

"Aren't you enjoying yourself a little too much, Skipper?" Joe asked Jonah. "Are you planning on building a colony and converting us?"

"Look, as I see it, we can sit on the dirt complaining or go get some supplies to make the night pass as smoothly as possible. And we need to build a signal fire. It will be easier to keep it going on the beach."

Everybody paused to absorb Jonah's words, and much as I hated to admit it, he was making sense. And then he ruined it by saying:

"It wasn't raining when Noah built the ark, you know."

"Do you always talk in bumper stickers?" I asked him.

"Extreme times demand extreme faith."

I took that as a yes. He was so self-righteous. That's when I remembered Joe's pilot speech back in New York and decided these two had more in common than they realized. They were both know-it-alls. I hate know-it-alls. Especially know-it-alls who obviously know nothing. Like Captain Water Landing and his baby Jesus.

"If you think God's gonna get me through the next two hours without a Klonopin," Milan said, "you're not just a Jesus freak, you're also an ignoranus."

"Ignoranus," Chaz laughed. "That's rich!"

I held back a laugh. Those two were like fifth graders.

"You are the reason I hate religion!" Milan continued, ignoring Chaz and pointing a finger at Jonah. "And it's just such a waste because you could be pretty hot if you were normal." She paused as she eyeballed his black skinny jeans with a look of outright disdain. "And hired a stylist."

"You don't hate religion, Milan, you're just afraid because you've strayed," Jonah said calmly.

"Shut up, you poser douche!" she snapped. The inability to pop a pill was clearly rattling her nerves.

"Stop it, Jonah! That's enough already," Joe shouted. Jonah looked at his father and delivered a withering smile.

"Look, can we all just work together until they find us? Maybe we can catch some crabs for dinner."

"I do love a crab cake," Chaz cooed, smiling at Jonah lustily.

"I don't eat shellfish," Cisco said.

"Neither do I," Joe agreed. "And besides, maybe we should stay put for the night. Since this is where we landed, it makes sense to stay here in the event that they catch a signal from the black box."

"Why don't *you* stay here?" Jonah suggested antagonistically. "Alone?"

"If you're right, then it wouldn't hurt to have a fire going here too. All you have to do is keep it flaming so the rescue plane sees it. We can use the extra wood Francesca gathered to make it. Can you handle that? You can rest up your leg. It's a good two-mile walk to the beach. It might take an hour in the dark."

Joe's mouth formed into an angry, tight line before he managed a slight nod. He looked furious, and I didn't blame him. But he had gotten us into this mess, so whatever. Frankly, I wasn't sure he'd have enough wood to keep the fire going that long, but I was so psyched Jonah Baron knew my name I didn't really care.

In retrospect, Joe was right about us all waiting at the landing site, but for whatever reason we followed Jonah's instruction. It wasn't so much that we thought Jonah actually knew what he was doing, but his passion was mildly contagious and, like I said, this was a group of people in need of a director. Joe might have been right, but Jonah's "vision" was more convincing.

"Okeydokey," Chaz said as he pushed himself off the

ground and sidled up next to Jonah to gather dry kindling for the fire. "What other snacks will Jesus be offering? I'm famished, and I hope the Lord is in a 'givethy' mood." He paused. "Mmmm, I'd love some Chicken McNuggets with sweet and sour sauce. Does our savior like white meat or dark?" he asked, looking Jonah up and down. "I like white meat myself. Tall, hairless white meat."

After the signal fire was going, Jonah used it to light one of the larger wood sticks to act as a guiding torch. It didn't work the way it does on TV. Ours blew out in about fifteen minutes. I happened to know that it needed to have a wick—courtesy of Mr. Krauss's eighth grade science class—but I was pretty sure nobody had any paraffin, and I didn't want to insult Jonah's masculinity. So, as I privately predicted, we were now walking by nothing but moonlight. It was amazing how quickly it got dark. I was behind Eve and kept getting whacked in the face with the tree branches that Cisco held for her but which she didn't feel necessary to hold for me. Nice. My left foot was red and blistered. I think we'd been walking for about thirty minutes when we heard a welcome sound.

"Do you hear that?" Eve suddenly asked, unleashing a particularly vicious branch right in my face.

"The plane! The plane!" Chaz shouted, jumping up and down.

We all looked into the air and saw two white lights and

a small red one. Without a word we instinctively turned around and started running back to the spot where we'd left Joe with the signal fire. The "path" was a blur of trees and moonshine. I'd never run so fast in my life.

It quickly became obvious that we weren't going in any particular direction. It was too dark, and for some reason we couldn't see the signal fire. All we could do was hope that the plane had seen it.

"I think we're walking in circles," Chaz moaned.

"No we're not," Jonah pronounced. "I'm following Polaris. We're heading north."

"What's a Polaris?" Milan asked.

"It's a star," he said, pointing to the sky. "Just above the Big Dipper. See it? That means we're definitely heading north."

"But we're not in the Northern Hemisphere," I corrected him. "That can't be Polaris."

"For real?" Jonah asked in a tone that belied all sense of authority and leadership.

"I mean, I'm not 100 percent, but I think so. And I'm pretty sure that's not the Big Dipper."

Silence.

"So your whole rock and stick routine was crap too?" Chaz asked Jonah.

"I must be really tired," he said, rubbing his eyes, as if that were some kind of an excuse.

"Look," I suggested, trying to ease Jonah's embarrassment,

"none of us know exactly where we are. I'm just assuming we're in the Southern Hemisphere based on our having flown out of Johannesburg. I could be wrong," I offered, knowing that I wasn't.

"Well, this is just great," Chaz spat. "Astronomy lessons from Beavis and Butthead."

"Who cares?" Cisco said. "We're out of here anyway."

When we finally found Joe, about an hour and a half later, he was asleep.

"Well look at that," Jonah seethed, staring at the orange ashes and sticking his heel in Joe's back to rouse him. "He's sleeping."

"Not. Not asleep," Joe mumbled, waking up and scrambling unsteadily to his feet.

"What's going on? Dear God, what happened to you?" he asked, looking at my scratched-up, bleeding face.

"You let the fire go out?" I asked. "Does that mean the plane didn't see it? That they don't know we're here?" It was all I could do not to burst out into tears.

"What plane? What are you talking about?" he asked, rubbing the sleep from his red, puffy eyes and massaging his head.

"Why don't you just shoot us all?" Milan shrieked, yanking out an extension with her left hand. "What the hell is the matter with you? Do you like it here or something?" She threw the hairpiece on the smoky embers. They sparked enthusiastically. "A plane came looking for me, and now it's gone because you needed a goddamn nap!"

"Not you, Milan, *us*, a plane came looking for *us*," Cisco corrected.

Joe's face suddenly took on an expression of profound sadness. It was as if this second mistake had deepened his uncertainty. And there was no publicist or manager to protect him from the indignity of his failure.

"Whatever. Now we're stuck here all night because this antique necrophiliac can't keep his eyes open," Milan said.

Chaz let out a depressed snort.

"Narcoleptic," Eve corrected.

"Oh shut up, you cow!"

"I'm so sorry. I must have nodded off," Joe apologized.

"Nodded off? You nodded off?" Milan shouted, her face about two inches away from Joe.

"Oh get away from me," he pleaded, giving her a gentle push back on the shoulder. "You exhaust me."

"Well, get used to my face, you dumb ass, since you just blew our ride out of here."

We all made it to the beach in a bleak forty-five minutes. At the risk of offending Jonah's survival skills, I nonetheless suggested tying cotton to a bunch of branches so that we could easily keep a guide light going. Jonah reluctantly agreed to give it a try, and Milan enthusiastically offered her shirt for material. Who needed a shirt with those hooters, right?

In any event, it looked like we were definitely spending the night. Joe trailed behind us like a chastised dog. Pissed off as we all were, we were still confident that it was just a matter of time until the next plane showed up. The key was to get to the beach, build a big fire, and just wait.

After thirty minutes or so, the beach made its abrupt appearance from the knotty jungle.

"Oh," Eve cried, taken by the swift change of scenery. I imagined it was how a bug must feel after being released from a glass jar. It was like taking a deep breath after holding your breath in an overcrowded elevator. The moonlit beach itself was a boomerang-shaped disc of white sand, punctuated with building-sized boulders. The openness was like nothing I'd ever seen. The suddenness of such beauty would have been mesmerizing had we not been so tired and hungry.

After Jonah got a fire going, we banked up against one of the huge rocks for warmth. I started "texting" Jordan in an attempt to not think about food.

"It's super queer that you're texting messages to somebody who isn't getting them. You know that, right?" Milan asked.

"I'm not actually in need of your approval, but I appreciate your thoughts on the subject."

"I'm just saying."

"What *are* you writing?" Chaz asked me.

"None of your business."

"It better not be about me," Milan added.

"Don't worry."

"I wasn't. I'm just saying."

"I'm parched," Eve whined. "I'm so tired. I need a pillow."

"Here, use this," Chaz said, pulling a wig off his head and throwing it at Eve, who swatted the wiglet away like a flying cockroach.

"Oh my God, you're bald!" she cried.

"Oh my Gaaaawd," Chaz responded mockingly, rubbing the perfectly shiny dome where his "hair" had been.

Milan was beaming.

"Ahhhh," Chaz moaned, massaging his head. "That is soooo much better!"

"How did it stay on in the water?" I asked incredulously.

"God, you ask the dumbest questions, Francesca."

"You look way better without that thing," Milan said without a beat. Chaz smiled. I could tell these two were destined to be great friends. Oddly, Chaz did look better without the piece. His face suddenly looked witty and distinguished rather than fat and dope-ish.

"I am *never* going to fall asleep," Milan complained, staring transfixed at Chaz's head while simultaneously fingering her empty prescription bottle. Jonah was on fire patrol, and the rest of us were preparing to bed down on the beach.

"I mean," Milan continued, glaring at Eve, "there's

seriously like no way I'll ever fall asleep." She slapped around spastically at a mosquito.

"For the thousandth time, there were no pills in there," Eve groaned.

"Um, yeah, I wasn't talking to you."

"I won't be able to sleep either," I said, trying to empathize.

"I wasn't talking to you either."

I guess she was still mad about the underwear comment.

She reached out absently to stroke Chaz's head. He leaned in like a loyal cat.

"What were they anyway?" Cisco asked.

"What?"

"The pills?"

"Klonopin," she twitched. "And metabolism pills."

"Drugs are bad news," Cisco announced, "I don't do drugs."

"Um, they weren't *drugs*. My doctor gave them to me."

I noticed Joe stiffen, but he didn't say anything.

"I'm a weed man," Cisco clarified, contradicting his earlier statement that he didn't do drugs. "It's the natural way to fly."

"Pot's great too," Milan nodded at Cisco pleasantly. "I just don't like trashing my lungs."

"But don't you smoke like five packs of cigarettes a day?" I asked.

"Yeah," she said, popping a soggy Froot Loop in her

mouth before offering them exclusively to Chaz. "That's why I need to be extra careful."

"Klonopin is for anxiety," Jonah said, looking at the Loops. "They're not even sleeping pills."

"What do you know about it, Floaty Toes? Isn't your body a holy vessel?"

Jonah laughed. "I was addicted to Xanax. Benzos are killers."

"You were addicted to drugs?" Chaz asked. His head was now in Milan's lap, which she was rubbing like a crystal ball. She was looking at Jonah with a newfound respect.

"Yeah. But I'd appreciate not reading about it on your blog," he said to Chaz.

"My readers don't care about you."

"Well, let's keep it that way."

"That shouldn't be a problem," Chaz sneered, licking the sugar powder off the inside of the Froot Loop bag.

"What's a benzo?" Eve asked

"Benzodiazepines," Jonah answered, looking pleased that the conversation hadn't been abandoned. "It's a class of drugs. Central nervous system depressants." The crackling fire spotlighted his face. His blond hair and pale skin made him look like a tall, white Crayola crayon. The effect was a little spooky.

"I never knew you were a drug addict," I said, stupidly revealing both my interest and my familiarity with tabloid journalism.

"I didn't either," Eve added, tucking her knees under her T-shirt. With a little push, I thought to myself, she'd roll down the beach like a ball.

"It was all before I got famous, so nobody knows."

"Not to be rude, but maybe you're just not famous enough for anyone to bother digging up your past or writing a book about you," Milan suggested with a smile. Chaz nodded in agreement.

"I thought your mother wrote that book about you?" Eve asked Milan.

"For someone who doesn't own a television, you really do know a lot about me," Milan quipped, rolling her eyes. "Are you a lesbian? Are you, like, in love with me or something?"

"Oh yes, my Sapphic sister. I'm in love with you," Eve said.

"I thought so," Milan said dryly.

"Really, though," Eve scowled, "I'd go ballistic if my parents betrayed me like that. Not that they would dare. I'd have them skinned and turned into boots first."

"Classy," Chaz said with a look of disgust.

"You don't know anything about it," Milan snapped. "And why would anybody want to read, let alone write, a book about *you*, anyway?"

"You may have a point, Milan. Professionalism and talent aren't salacious."

Milan looked thrown. "Do you ever just speak English?"

"Um, like totally, yeah," Eve said, slipping into a Valley girl twang. The impression was awkward and a little cringe-y. Chaz made a face. Milan tucked her head into her big shirt (which Chaz had given her after she offered up her own for the torch) and laughed so hard her whole body was shaking.

"Anyway," Eve said, trying to ignore them and turning to Jonah like a schoolmarm, "you were addicted to psychotropic drugs?"

Jonah nodded. "I don't talk about it to the press because it feels exploitative."

Joe let out a loud snicker.

"You mean you were a little junkie until your mother convinced you that being religious was a more effective way to jump-start your career," Joe suddenly said. It was the first time he'd said anything since we left the landing site. "Using Christianity isn't exploitative as long as you lie about your unsavory past? Is that right?"

"I suppose if you didn't understand you could look at it that way."

"Didn't understand what, Jonah?"

"What it was like growing up your bastard son and watching Mom drink herself into oblivion every night to numb the pain of your abandoning us."

I dug my fingers into the sand and prepared myself for another speech from Joe. And boy, did we get one.

"I hate to be the one to burst your cloud of delusion, Jonah," Joe snarled, squashing an enormous mosquito on his forehead, "but Beverly was a drunk the day I met her. The only reason she's sober now is because I refused to give her a dime of child support unless she cleaned up her act." He smeared the bug off his forehead, leaving a rather tribal-looking trail of red blood in its wake.

"And the real reason *she* became a Christian," Joe continued, "is because she saw it as the most vicious way she could think of to drive a wedge between us. And, of course," he added, holding up his finger, "being the perennial stage mother, she saw an opportunity in the born-again business. She's nothing if not a star fucker." Joe laughed to himself. "And all the better if she could prostitute her son out rather than herself! It's time to grow up, Jonah."

"How dare you talk about her like that," Jonah seethed. "She's been there for me, which is more than I can say for you!"

"You know damn well I've tried to have a relationship with you, despite all of my lawyers, managers, agents, and therapists telling me to just let it go. You're the one who rejected me over and over again, Jonah. It's a real sad story the two of you have concocted, but if you're going to talk about our family to the press, you should at least get the facts straight."

"Oh, so now we're a family? You don't know what you're talking about."

"Really? I think maybe it's you who doesn't know what he's talking about, Jonah. All your mother wanted from me was my checkbook. I don't want to offend your virgin sensibilities, but did Bev ever mention that she'd also slept with Mick Jagger and Bill Irwin? My only distinction was that I got her pregnant. Correct me if I'm wrong, but I don't think you were catching a draft in the two-million-dollar house I bought for the two of you to drown your sorrows in after she told me she was pregnant."

"You're blaming me?" Jonah laughed. "I was a fetus."

"I don't blame you, but I take offense at being painted as this monster. Two short weeks your mother and I were together," Joe continued. "Two weeks. I've paid my dues, Jonah. I tried to be there for you, but you were too busy getting high to notice. Who do you think paid for the thirty-thousand-dollar-a-week rehab facilities you were in and out of four times from the age of thirteen to fifteen? God?" he asked. "Really, Jonah, I'm glad you finally made it to step twelve, but couldn't you have found Jesus at step two or three?"

"This actually is kind of blogworthy," Chaz whispered to Milan. She nodded, half-smiling. I was frozen. I couldn't believe Joe and Jonah spoke to each other with such hatred.

Joe paused and then continued berating his son.

"And when your wise old mother did convince you that your singing career wasn't gonna happen until you found a niche market, isn't that when you *really* saw the light, Jonah? Hallelujah!" Joe raised his hands in mock enlightenment.

"Praise the Lord!" Chaz chirped, applauding as he absorbed the show. Everybody ignored him.

"And the irony," Joe continued, getting into Jonah's face, "is how quickly Beverly herself found Jesus when that first check came in. Little Beverly Frumovitz, a born-again! What a joke! That's all very religious, Jonah, but why don't you just can it? Nobody's shopping for your brand of bullshit here. We've got enough problems."

I was definitely texting Jordan on this one. Somebody had to record this conversation, right? Joe was shaking, he was so angry.

"Anyway, Milan," Jonah said calmly, looking at my phone suspiciously and picking up where he left off, "benzos are the devil's candy. It took me almost a year to get clean of that junk. But I did have help."

"From the Lord, no doubt?' Milan asked facetiously.

"And my mom," Jonah said, looking at Joe.

"Do you ever stop talking?" Joe asked, rubbing his head still. "Some people benefit from drug therapy, Jonah. Just because you misused them doesn't mean they aren't helpful to people who take them responsibly."

"Do you ever stop judging me…and Mom?" Jonah asked Joe, his shrill tone betraying a hurt he'd obviously been trying to hide.

"And Jesus? Do you ever stop judging Jesus?" Chaz asked Joe mischievously.

"I'm not judging Jesus, for Christ's sake, I'm Jewish."

"Well, so am I, but I don't get my panties in a ruffle over a little Jesus banter."

"You're about as Jewish as a ham and cheese sandwich on Wonder Bread," I said. I didn't like Chaz much, but he did seem to have a gift for lightening a mood.

"I am Jewish!" Chaz insisted. "Born-again. Like Jonah, only I was addicted to the pork dumplings at Szechwan Palace until Abraham at Katz's Deli showed me the way." Chaz rubbed his fat stomach, "I'm already 110 pounds lighter since I started my all–gefilte fish diet. It's *delicious!*" he shouted, smacking his lips together.

"I thought you loved crab cakes?" I said, laughing despite myself. "Not a kosher foodstuff."

"No?" Chaz asked, feigning concern. "Well," he said, wiping his hand over his bald head, "I'm not a Hasid, for God's sake! I'm a dabbler."

"Jesus was a Jew," Jonah added humorlessly.

"If you say the word 'Jesus' one more time, I'll never speak to you again," Joe said.

"Jesus," Jonah said.

Without a word, Joe got up and moved away from the fire. We all settled down uncomfortably in the sand for the night. And I thought my relationship with my father was bad.

Little Homer and the Odyssey Back Home

The morning sun, reflecting off the white beach, was almost blinding. I squinted as my tired eyes adjusted to the light. The dreamlike quality of the night before was vanquished by the bright sunshine. This was no dream. All of it was real. Where was the rescue plane? Why were we still here? Where were we going to get water and food? How were we going to get home? Why was Cisco Parker's face buried in my armpit?

His hands were nestled into my enormously puffy hair. I stared down at his long, dark eyelashes and tried to stop the loud and juicy sneeze I felt tickling my nose. No luck. He untangled himself with no trace of embarrassment and a few casual apologies. He was obviously a guy accustomed to waking up with strangers in unfamiliar places.

J:

Cisco's morning breath stinks of raw herring, but I'd cut off a finger for a kiss. I swear J., he's prettier than Rachel Bilson.

.F.

I hit send out of habit just as Jonah came running on to the beach screaming.

"I found fresh water! Hey, wake up, wake up!"

His enthusiasm stirred everyone. I could see that Joe was down by the shore rinsing out his clothes. At Jonah's arrival, Joe reluctantly headed back to the group. That's when I noticed Milan, curled up in a ball, twitching. She was wearing Chaz's oversized purple shirt and her hair was in rough sections with odd chunks dangling precariously around her ears. She was sitting next to a pile of extensions she'd obviously spent all night plucking. Yipes.

"Well, where is it?" Cisco asked, perching himself up on his perfectly shaped elbows. His cheek was now green, black and blue, but I sensed there was no reason to bring it up.

"Yeah," Eve said, "I'm parched."

"It's about a mile from here. There's a fresh stream. We just need to find a way to collect it so we don't have to keep going back and forth."

Milan was rocking. She clearly hadn't slept at all.

"What about food?" Cisco asked, rubbing his eyes. "I'm so hungry, dude."

"Me too," Eve said, spitting sand out of her mouth.

"If you'd like a Frappucino or scrambled eggs, you'll have to wait until Rachael Ray or the Coast Guard show up," Jonah snapped.

"Relax, dude, I just said I was hungry."

"All you guys do is sleep and complain. Ever heard of an attitude of gratitude?" I could totally relate to Jonah. Looking after this bunch was as gratifying as looking after my mom and Em. It was always about what you didn't do. Still, the rhyming was obnoxious.

Jonah tossed a baby turtle down on the sand in front of us.

The turtle was so little and deeply cute. I had a sudden urge to pop him in my pocket. When I was nine, my dad and I tried to start breeding spotted turtles. For whatever reason, turtles were the only animals my mother would allow us to have in the house. I named them all Homer after Homer Simpson. They all died, as is the fate of the childhood pet reptile.

"What's that for?" I asked, reaching down to stroke his little head.

"Breakfast and a cup. We eat the meat and use his shell for water." He looked really pleased with himself.

"Yuck. You have got to be kidding. I'll pass," Eve said, pulling her shirt around her mini body in defense.

Cisco eyeballed the turtle suspiciously. I could almost see the civil war raging between his inner carnivore and his outer vegetarian.

"No offense, Jonah," I said, snatching the turtle up and tucking him under my arm. "But that's a terrible idea.

Homer's just a baby. And there's not enough meat to satisfy any one of our appetites, let alone all of ours."

"Who the hell is Homer?" Milan jerked to attention. "Another imaginary friend?"

I looked down at the turtle. Joe and Jonah rolled their eyes.

"I'll do it," Milan said, reaching for Homer.

"Do what?" I asked. "I thought you were busy withdrawing."

"Kill it. You're a bunch of pussies. I'm hungry."

"No," I said with authority. "You can't be *that* hungry yet. And he's not going to fill you up. Besides, if he's surviving here," I said, stroking Homer's head, "that means there are worms or crickets or at least tadpoles."

"You eat tadpoles, fish-face," Milan said. "I'll stick with turtle. They're on the Zone," she laughed.

"Forget it," I said, backing away from her.

"Francesca," Joe reasoned, "we are going to have to kill something bigger than a worm. And eat it today. It's that simple."

"I'm fine to kill something, just not a turtle. Plus, what if they show up in a few hours? Do you want Homer's blood on your hands?"

"What is the matter with you?" Jonah asked. "It's a stupid turtle. Who cares?"

"I do! This is one of God's creatures! I'd expect you of all people to understand." I knew I sounded insane, but

I wasn't about to justify my childhood attachment to the turtle to Jonah Baron.

"That's ridiculous. It's natural. Do you not eat meat?"

"I do, but this is differ—"

"Because it's not sliced and diced and sold between cellophane at Safeway? You should be more connected to what you put into your body."

"I just don't like to think of my food as having such a sweet disposition."

"Well, that's a good reason to eat you instead," Milan piped in, rather wittily, she obviously thought. Chaz laughed. My hair was so huge I could see it out of my peripheral vision. I'd have killed for a rubber band. I felt like a freak standing there in front of them with my clown hair and turtle friend.

"Look, I'll figure out something else," I said. "Let's look for clam shells or coconuts. Doesn't that make more sense?"

"Give it to me, Francesca," Cisco said seductively as he reached for Homer.

"Hey!" I said. "I thought you were a vegetarian."

"Really," Eve looked at Cisco with disdain. "Aren't you a PETA spokesman?"

"This is different," he told us in a firm voice. There hadn't been a lot of range in Cisco's expression so far, but here, at last was something interesting. It was hunger.

"And besides," Eve continued, "you wouldn't have a clue how to kill it."

"Is that so?" Cisco asked, inflating with manhood. He lunged back at me, and I turned on my heel and ran to the beach, cradling Homer to my chest, fast as I could go in one shoe. Cisco started chasing me but tripped. I looked back and saw him, facedown, with a mouthful of sand. He really was cute, but he wasn't the most coordinated guy. I started to laugh, thinking about telling Jordan. This guy needed a stuntman just to take a leak. Suddenly I saw Milan heading toward me. Now that crazy bitch was fast.

Everyone else started screaming and cheering as I made for the water. I turned back once I reached the shore and saw Milan, running, grinning like a serial killer, blotchy spray tan, pieces of patchy, disconnected blond hair circling her face like a vision from *The Blair Witch Project*. I liked her better medicated. I kissed Homer on the back and tossed him as far as I could back into the ocean. It's possible he didn't survive the landing, but I figured any fate was better than being eaten alive by the Brat Pack.

"You crazy, delusional bitch!" Milan started shrieking. "What is the matter with you? If you don't get me something to eat, I'll, I'll…"

"You'll what? What will you do?"

Milan was shaking and practically foaming at the mouth. Chaz came up behind her and put his hands on her shoulders.

"Don't touch me, you fat fuck," she shrilled, shaking him loose. "I have got to get out of here! If I don't have a cigarette, I'm seriously going to kill her," she said pointing to me. "Her body will keep us going for a good year."

Was that another comment on my weight? I wondered incredulously, looking down at my thighs, which even from that angle didn't seem *that* much bigger than hers.

Chaz smiled at Milan, trying to soothe her. "Honey, she's a piece of lint on your Dolce and Gabbana. Just ignore her and maybe she'll go away...like a pimple."

God, he was rude. He led a quivering Milan back to the beach. I found myself standing alone on the shore. Nobody was even looking at me anymore. I realized I had better figure out a way to feed these people or I was going to be on a *Survivor* team of one. Not that solitude might not be preferable to this group. I slunk down in the sand and tried to think of something until I heard Jonah call my name. I turned around and headed back to the group.

"Let's just put this crazy episode behind us and focus on getting food and collecting water, all right?" he asked, looking directly at me. I nodded.

"We have to assume nobody is coming for a few days," Jonah said in a feeble attempt to restore sanity. "And we have to plan accordingly."

"Of course they're coming," Milan said. "Why are you so negative?"

"Not negative. I'm just realistic. I don't know where the search team is, but I do know we need to gather as many amenities as we can before we get dehydrated and hungrier. So, Eve and Francesca, you guys go look in the woods for berries, nuts, anything that looks edible. But do *not* eat anything. Bring it all back here and we'll do a test."

Why did I keep getting stuck with ineffectual Eve Larkin? I could see it already: Eve sitting in my shade while I risked my life climbing nut trees.

"Milan and Cisco," Jonah continued, "you guys go try and find some sort of vessels or shells to transport water." Milan smiled while Eve and Cisco exchanged sympathetic looks.

"Chaz and I will go see if we can find any animal tracks. Maybe we can kill something for lunch."

"Um," Chaz interrupted, "I'd rather go with Milan and Cisco. I'm more gatherer than hunter, but thanks for thinking of me."

"You're coming with me," Jonah clipped, military style. "I need someone strong."

"But I'm not strong," he whined. "I know it's deceptive, but trust me, there is no muscle under all this fat. There's just layer upon layer of fluffy nougat. Imagine a human 3 Musketeers bar if you will."

"Let's go," he said to Chaz, ignoring his protest.

"Who elected you Boy Scout leader anyway?" Chaz asked, pouting.

"You want the job, be my guest," Jonah responded.

Chaz shuffled the sand around with his chubby toes. He

looked a bit like Fred Flintstone with his big, bare chest and tan shorts.

"And what's he doing?" Milan asked, glaring at Joe.

"Whatever he wants. Bird watching. Who cares."

Joe ignored Jonah.

Eve cleared her throat, "Um, I can't really be out too long in the midday sun without sunscreen."

Everybody turned to look at her. She didn't seem to be kidding.

"Whaaat?" she asked, already trying to creep into my shadow. "I'm very fair," she said, looking at my freckled arms again in horror.

Eve seriously didn't get it. It was as if she thought Yvette was going to pull up in a limo any minute with some SPF 45 and a macrobiotic sushi platter. Personally, I would have done anything to team up with Cisco and Milan, or even Jonah and Chaz, but after the Homer incident I decided I should just keep my mouth shut.

All About Eve

It was going on an hour, and Eve and I were still sitting on a white patch of sand that separated the flats from the jungle. She was afraid to go inside, and nothing I said was persuading her otherwise. She just sat there like a troubled anime character with her big head and blinking eyes.

I started texting Jordan out of boredom. Occasionally, Eve shaded her eyes with her hands and glanced up at the sky in anticipation of the next Boeing 747. She looked lost from the inside out.

I had to remind myself who she was because frankly she was pretty unimpressive. There was something profoundly blank about her. She reminded me of a kid's book my dad used to read to us about a chameleon that was depressed because he would never have a color of his own. She was just like that chameleon, casting about at the end of a stick, instinctively looking for something or someone colorful to get hold of and climb on to. She was gray. She was sad. She was nobody without an audience.

"I think we might have to go farther in," I suggested, after I finished texting.

"Why did Jonah send Cisco off with Milan?" Eve asked, absently scratching at a colossal mosquito bite on her neck. She was covered in bites.

"Is that what you've been thinking about this whole time?"

"It's not fair. I just don't see why I couldn't have gone with Cisco."

"I wouldn't worry about it. He doesn't like her. Nobody does."

Eve's face lit up. "Really?"

"Really."

"Do you think she's pretty?" Eve asked me.

"Who?"

"Milan!"

"I guess, if you like that sort of look."

"What sort of look?"

"You know, tan, tall, blond, and muscular."

"As opposed to what?" she deflated, "Pale, short, and flabby?"

"I'm just saying. I think you have a more unique quality."

"You do?" she asked, suddenly taking great interest in what I had to say.

I could tell she wanted me to elaborate on how good looking I thought she was, and, loathe as I was to kiss Eve Larkin's ass, I needed an ally around here, and Eve was obviously going to have to do. I was also beginning to realize that the way to this girl's heart was through her ego.

"Yeah, I mean, you're beautiful. Milan is just pretty. You're interesting, she's pedestrian." It was beginning to scare me how easily the lies were flying out of my mouth.

She smiled up at me, flattered. I was fairly certain her "team" blew this sort of smoke up her ass on a regular basis, but from them it probably didn't count. A compliment, to matter, had to come from a stranger.

"You're really pretty too," she said lamely. "I could never carry off that hair and those freckles."

Thanks a lot, I thought, pressing my hair down. This is what Jordan and I like to call poison candy. It seems good at first, and then it gets stuck in your throat and you choke on it. I would have liked to tell her that I didn't need that kind of affirmation, but let's face it, a) I did, and b) it was the only language this girl spoke.

"I'm not, but thanks," I said, smiling. "So, what do you say we venture in a ways?"

"One more question. Please don't tell anyone I asked you this, OK?"

"OK."

"I know it sounds really superficial, but how bad do I look?" She straightened up again and looked up at me with those far-set eyes embedded in that pasty white moon face framed with a mat of lank, black hair. Her pale lips were pursed in anticipation, and I could see the slight shadow of a moustache. There were two giant mosquito bites on her left cheek and her neck. Her head was moving around a little in what I can only describe as a sort of Parkinsonian jerk. It was obvious the question was close to her heart. Eve is the sort of girl who'd sacrifice two more days without food for one reassuring glance in a mirror. I mean, there was no denying that Eve was attractive, but unlike Milan, her beauty was more an observation than an announcement.

That said, she definitely made the most of what she had with the tools of civilization. And a blow dryer, hot wax, loads of makeup, and eight hours of sleep seemed to be essential to her beauty regimen. At the moment, she was more Cousin It on crack than Oscar-winning actress.

"You look good. Natural," I lied again.

"Really? Because I feel like crap."

I would have liked to kick Eve in the ass. Here we were looking for food, and she was fishing for compliments and obsessing on her appearance. I mean, was she for real? Did she not get how bad she'd look dead? That said, I knew if I wanted her to focus and be motivated, I needed to give her the food she needed. So I did. I took a good long look at her and paused thoughtfully for a minute before speaking. I did this for effect.

"I sort of like the way you look better this way. It's less

'done,' you know? It's kind of a totally fresh look for you."
Lie, lie, lie.

She ruminated over this for a good forty-five seconds
before running her fingers through her hair and roughing
it up for effect. Then she smiled and looked at me for
approval…like I was taking her goddamn picture or something. I nodded stupidly, marveling at how completely
lame she was.

"You're sweet, Francesca. I'm glad you're here." Despite
myself, my heart skipped a tiny beat. Were Eve Larkin and
I becoming friends?

"So," I said, "what do you say we venture in a bit?"

"I'd really rather not," she said Britishly. "They'll figure
something out for us to eat." She settled back onto her rock.

"Who will? Milan and Cisco or Chaz and Joe? C'mon,
don't count on it. The only shot we have is Jonah, and he
needs help."

"This whole thing is just crazy. I keep thinking it's a
dream. A bad one. I feel like I could pass out, I'm so thirsty.
And my feet are killing me. I never should have come back.
I could fucking kill Yvette."

"Come back?"

"To the States," she squirmed, fingering a huge, red blister
on the top of her perfectly pedicured toe. "We would have
worked through it. I overreacted." She looked wistful as she
examined her foot.

"Who? What are you talking about?"

Eve's eyes filled up with water. "My boyfriend. Ex-boyfriend." She was far away.

"We had a fight a few months ago," she continued. "I overreacted probably. Yvette's been trying to get me back in L.A. for years, so she really jumped on it. But she's always hated him. Four years of having to justify him to my manager. How twisted is that?"

"Pretty twisted." I said. "Who is he?" I asked, curious why I didn't know she'd even had a boyfriend, let alone a boyfriend of four years. You'd think I would have read about it *somewhere*.

I must have sounded too eager, as she suddenly looked up from her foot and eyed me suspiciously.

"Anyway," she continued, slipping back into celeb mode by evading my question, "Yvette thought this little African goodwill tour would be good for my image. Idiot. Ouch!" she cried, popping the water blister. "Nice bloody image."

"Well, think how great the PR will be now—once they find us."

"*If* they find us, you mean," she said, grimacing as she squeezed the water out of the blister.

"They'll find us eventually."

"But will we be alive?" Eve asked, voice rising.

"Not if we don't figure out the food and water problem. And once we do that, think of this experience as a good opportunity to get to know Cisco better. That'll drive your ex crazy. Plus, if we are stuck a couple more days, we'll get to see what happens to Milan's figure without her metabolism pills. Whatever those are. That's something to look forward to in and of itself."

"And once all of her fake hair falls out," Eve said, really cracking herself up over the prospect of a bald Milan.

An abrupt snort aborted her laughter as she suddenly turned to me with a sense of urgency.

"I don't like him, like him," she announced, referring to Cisco and sounding like a defensive seventh grader.

"I know, I'm just saying."

Eve paused.

"OK," she said, looking into the jungle, "but you go in first. I'll follow you."

The woods were very thick and green. The trees made such a dense canopy that the sun barely peeked through. It was hard to make out what was two feet in front or behind. I whacked the leaves with my stick the way they do in the movies, but they just whacked me right back. Eve was so busy protecting her precious face that I found I was spending more time making sure the trees were parted for her than I did looking for anything edible. Suddenly I heard a chattering sound above.

"I think I hear monkeys!"

"Omigawd," Eve said.

"What?"

"I hate monkeys!"

"Why? Who hates monkeys?"

"Monkeys eat people."

"They do not."

"They do!" Eve assured me.

"No, they don't." I said, suddenly questioning myself. "But they do eat fruits, so that's a good sign. There must be food around."

"Didn't you hear about that monkey that bit off that woman's finger and her husband's penis?"

"No, I can't say that I did, Eve. No."

"It was all over the news."

"What news?" I obviously wasn't above reading the *National Enquirer*, but the monkey story certainly hadn't made the cover of the *New York Times*.

"Monkeys are dangerous animals. Don't be fooled by the cute exterior," Eve said like she was imparting some sage wisdom.

"Look," I explained, "I'm sure those monkeys were just mad about something like being trapped in a cage or being forced to wear velvet vests and dance to accordion music."

"I can't deal with monkeys!" she yelled up into the trees. We heard a scurrying sound and some rustling of leaves.

"Oh, bloody hell!"

"C'mon, Eve."

"My feet really, really hurt," she complained, staring up at the trees anxiously.

"So do mine, Eve," I said, pulling a pebble out of my shoeless heel.

"I have to stop and process," she whined, ignoring me and plopping herself against a big tree. "I'm not like you. I don't have the constitution for this. I hate monkeys. I hate the outdoors. I loathe the beach. I hate the mountains. I don't even like convertibles. I hate picnics."

"Then wait here while I look around," I said. She was exhausting.

"Alone?" she asked, grabbing my hand.

"You're not alone. The monkeys will keep you company."

"Ha-ha."

"Look, Eve," I said, shaking my hand loose, "I get that being uncomfortable isn't your thing, and I get that you've been famous for so long that you don't know how to breathe without a staff of six and a chilled Pellegrino, but you have to help me out. You're the only one here who seems mildly normal," that was me lying again, "and I need you to make an effort. I know eating isn't your thing, but starving to death seems like an extreme diet…even for you."

She paused in order to consider.

I kept talking, as she wasn't interrupting me.

"Seriously, if we don't get food, then we don't eat, get it? What if you pretend this is research for a movie or something?"

"That's stupid." She paused. "What kind of movie?"

For an actress, she certainly didn't have a lot of imagination. I was really beginning to feel like a preschool teacher. I was trying to come up with a compelling improv proposition when she interrupted me.

"I can cry on cue," she announced proudly.

"Wow."

"Want to see?"

"Um..."

Suddenly she was bawling, rolled up in her weird little animal ball and convulsing with sobs. I settled in for what looked like another useless hour or so. And that's when it happened.

"Ouch!" Eve whined, covering her head. A huge, coconut-looking fruit had fallen from the tree above and landed right on her big head.

"Look!" I shouted. "It's food! You did it!" I looked up and saw about four animals that didn't actually look like monkeys, but close enough. They had big, bat-like ears, and their faces looked almost bear-like. They sounded like they were laughing.

"Oh my God, look at the baby monkey-things," I said, pointing up to the tree. Three little gray and white monkeys were staring down at us playfully swishing their long, striped tails. Lemurs? Bush babies? I had no idea. "God, they are awesome!" I cried. "They're incredible."

"Run!" Eve shouted, taking off before I had a chance to stop her. If the girl really thought monkeys were akin to lions, she certainly didn't seem that concerned with my welfare. Though why I should have found this surprising, I have no idea.

I considered how I was going to scale the tree for more coconuts when another one fell down. I think the monkeys were making a gift. I felt very Jane Goodall.

"Thanks!" I shouted up into the tree.

I stood there for another few minutes waiting for either another coconut or the first civilized conversation I'd had in two days, but nothing happened. I was able to climb pretty high up onto one of the trees and knock about four more coconuts down. They were huge and heavy. I could only carry a couple so I hid the rest under some branches and leaves. We could come back for them later. I picked up two coconuts and headed off to find Eve.

When I finally exited the woods I saw her waiting for me and smiling. She was wearing her pants and a bra. The contrast between her tired face and her doll-like torso was almost freakish. Her skin was white as snow, and her body, unlike Milan's, looked like it belonged to a twelve-year-old girl. Her breasts were smaller than mine. So much for the implants rumor.

"Where's your shirt?" I asked, unconsciously holding the coconuts to my chest like two big, fake boobs.

"Sorry I took off," she said sheepishly.

"That's all right. Look what I got."

"Look what *I* got," she countered enthusiastically. She offered me her T-shirt out of which she'd fashioned a sort of makeshift basket filled with what looked like cranberries. She looked deeply satisfied with herself.

"Ohhh!" I cried and we both started jumping up and down and hugging each other like two fools. The berries were flying around everywhere.

"I wonder if they're any good. Let's get back to the beach and find out."

"They are," Eve said, smiling. That's when I noticed that her lips were stained red.

"Did you eat them?" I asked, horrified.

"I couldn't resist. Just a few. They are really juicy and sweet. Here," she said, offering me a berry.

"But Jonah said we should wait," I protested.

"Jonah? What does he know? Trust me, they are sublime."

I knew better, but I was so thirsty that I cautiously ate one berry. It exploded in my mouth like a sweet, ripe grape. Heaven. I felt instantly revived. My instinct was to inhale them all, but I resisted. Instead, I managed to convince Eve that we should take them back to the shore for the others. We could collect more with the coconut shells after we'd figured out a way to crack them open. Her mood was manic and giddy, and she greedily shoved about ten more berries in her mouth before she gave me a juicy kiss on the cheek and started singing "What a Difference a Day Makes." Side by side, we triumphantly trotted back to the beach with the coconuts and the remainder of the berries.

That's One Hell of a Rash

I told you not to eat anything," Jonah yelled at me.

"She wouldn't listen to me," I cried. "I told her to wait."

"What is it with you that you can't just follow simple instructions?"

"What am I, her nanny?"

"You're useless!"

"I am?" I shrieked, remembering the Polaris episode but holding my tongue. I'd been accused of a lot of things in my life, but being useless wasn't one of them. And besides, I'd found the coconuts. How about that attitude of gratitude, buddy?

"Don't yell at her, man," Cisco shouted.

"Was it too much to ask that they wait before eating anything? You couldn't sacrifice your short-term discomfort for your long-term safety?"

"Nobody elected you our leader, Jonah," Cisco continued in my defense. "Like Ayn Rand says, 'The man who speaks to you of sacrifice is speaking of slaves and masters and intends to be the master.' We don't need any masters here."

"Really, Cisco? Can I tell you what we don't need here?"

"What's that?"

"Literary quotes."

"I'm just saying, man," Cisco said, saying nothing at all.

"Would you look at Eve?" Jonah motioned to her. "Look at her!"

We did. Eve's white skin was now the color of marinara sauce. Little yellow blisters were forming circular colonies all over her face and neck. The mosquito bites weren't even visible anymore. And it looked like the rash was spreading. I prayed my only having eaten one berry would spare me this ghastly fate. And it was ghastly. I started to feel itchy.

"How bad is it?" Eve asked, looking at me.

"Not too bad," I lied.

"Get me Milan's compact. I need to see," she ordered to the group.

Milan nodded, motioning for Chaz to grab her bag, which was behind him. He slung it over his shoulder.

"No!" Jonah snapped, as Chaz reached for the purse.

"Listen, you fairy," Jonah went on, "you get that mirror and I'll knock your head off. It will just upset her."

"Jonah!" Joe said, shocked.

"What did you call me?" Chaz asked, hand pressed to his chest dramatically. "Did you hear what he called me?" He looked around at all of our astonished faces. It was pretty shameful, but we were too busy with Eve to address it.

"Am I going to die?" Eve asked Cisco, who was sitting vigil on the sand next to Eve. She opened her eyes as she spoke.

"No way, babe, it's just an allergic reaction."

"Compact!" she ordered, squinting her eyes at me. I looked at Milan.

"It's gone," Milan lied, making a pretense of digging through her purse. "I can't find it."

Jonah sent Milan an appreciative glance.

"Here it is!" Chaz announced, triumphantly retrieving it from Milan's bag and smiling at Jonah. I thought I saw Joe smile a little.

In one swift motion, Jonah snatched the compact out of Chaz's hand and threw it angrily into the ocean.

"Oh that's just *great!*" shouted Milan, white with rage. Her teeth were clenched. Chaz was momentarily silenced by the violence of Jonah's action.

"Please, Francesca," Eve softly begged, reaching for my hand. "Take a picture and show it to me. Use your phone. I want to see. I really do." She sounded so desperate.

"I can't," I said, looking at Jonah with uncertainty.

"You look fine, Eve," Joe consoled her.

"I'll do it," Chaz volunteered, glaring at Jonah while swiping my phone out of my grasp. He positioned himself above Eve. "Say cheese!"

"Chaz!" Jonah yelled, grabbing the phone out of his

hand—but not before I heard it click. "Put it away or I'll toss it too!" he threatened, handing the phone back to me with a grave expression.

"Sorry," I whispered to Eve, taking my phone and quickly putting it in my back pocket for safety.

She looked defeated.

"Are you sure you should sit so close?" Chaz asked Cisco. "I mean, it could be contagious."

"Shut up, man," Cisco said as he casually let go of Eve's hand. "I've worked with poor people in New Delhi, Thailand, and New Orleans. I've been exposed to way worse than this."

"Um, poverty isn't contagious." Chaz said. "I, for one, would rather die alone on the other side of the island than be discovered looking like that," Chaz added looking down at Eve.

"Oh my God," Eve moaned.

"You're dying alone one way or the other," Joe said to Chaz. "Don't be such a prick."

"Really," I said, "you'd think going bald in your teens would make you empathic."

"Pardon me, Pippi," Chaz said and moved back a few steps. "I didn't realize you and Eve Larkin were BFFs."

"We're not!"

Eve burst out crying, but the tears stung her face, so she stopped and just whinnied like a dying pony. I wanted to be alone. I didn't want to cry in front of this group. I banked up against a rock and took out my phone.

> J:
> Eve looks like a hot pizza.
> F.

"I'm not sure now's the time to be sending imaginary letters to your friends back home," Jonah said, frowning up at me.

He was being mean.

"Well, I'm not sure it's the time for praying either."

"Give me one of those coconuts," he snapped, standing up. Why was everyone ordering me around in this group? It was getting on my nerves. So what if they were famous? They weren't my chaperones. Most of them weren't even that much older than me.

"Hey, I don't work for you!" I shouted, holding back my own tears.

"Not now, Francesca. Just give it to me," he demanded. God, it was so obvious nobody took me seriously. I handed over my hard-won coconuts as a sort of peace offering. He snatched them away and studied it for a minute.

"I hid more under a tree," I said sulkily. "So we'll have more later."

"Good." Jonah looked at me for a minute and then nodded. "Thanks."

"Where did you find them anyway?" Chaz asked. "Did you climb up a tree or something?"

"Yes."

"Where'd you learn to do that?" he asked. "Astronomy school?"

"Piss off."

"Uh-oh," Chaz said, mocking me in a little boy's voice, "Big Red's weally, weally mad!"

"Just ignore him," Jonah said. I wasn't sure, but I think he felt badly about calling me useless.

He tossed the other coconut to Cisco. "We have to open it. Maybe if Eve has some food and liquid it will slow the process down." Cisco looked at Jonah like he'd just asked him for some antibiotics and an iced tea with a slice of lemon.

"What are you waiting for?" Jonah looked at Cisco impatiently.

"I don't know how to get this thing open. Do you have a knife?"

"Of course I don't have a knife, Cisco! Figure something out," he shouted. "Maybe Ayn Rand has some ideas?"

Cisco looked at Jonah like a scolded five-year-old boy. He was cradling the coconut like a teddy bear. I didn't get the sense he got yelled at too often.

"Let me have it," Joe said kindly. Cisco threw him the coconut like it was on fire.

I went back to my phone because everyone seemed to sort of let me alone when I was typing. I knew they thought I was a freak, but I needed to check out. It was pretty obvious none of these people ever needed or wanted alone time. In fact, I think they were afraid of it.

J:

1) Joe is trying to crack a coconut open with a rock.

2) Now he's banging said coconut against a tree.

3) Now he's banging his head against the tree.

F.

"If I had a video camera, I'd be a rich, rich man," Chaz sighed ruefully as he watched Joe sobbing and slobbering all over the pristine coconut.

"It's all my fault, it's all my fault, it's all my fault," Joe was saying repeatedly as he now hit his head with the coconut repeatedly. When we saw blood, Milan pushed Jonah over to Joe.

"Make him stop!" she pleaded.

"It's good for him to take responsibility for his actions."

"Get over yourself, Jesus Jr., he's hurting himself!"

"Joe," Jonah said, halfheartedly trying to stop him. Joe shrugged him off and continued his Bellevue audition.

"She's going to die, and it's all my fault," Joe shouted before collapsing on the sand, hugging the coconut like a baby and weeping. "She played my daughter in *Afternoon Rain*. She was just a baby. She's still a baby. Look at her. This is my fault."

"You're not helping," Eve whispered, eyes bulging out of her head in panic. Jonah had a perverted look of self-satisfaction on his face.

Cisco got up and tried to pry the coconut away from Joe while simultaneously pulling him in for a hug. Sweet.

"It's not your fault, dude. It's not your fault."

"It's kind of his fault," Milan said.

I retreated to the nearest rock.

> J:
> Remember when your dad cried at the end of that Vanessa Hudgens movie we saw in sixth grade and you couldn't look at him for a week? This is worse.
> Cisco is man-spooning Joe. I am so uncomfortable.
> F.

"Stop doing that, you freak!" Milan shouted at me. "This is totally out of control. Is Eve going to die?"

I laid the phone down in the sand.

"I can hear you," Eve whispered from behind us. We all turned and saw that the rash was now all over her body. Her face was swollen to the size of a soccer ball. She'd go ballistic. It was good Jonah tossed the mirror.

"Holy shit!" Chaz screamed.

"Oh my God," Eve cried, touching to feel her face. "What? Fuck, Jonah. Where the hell is that camera, Francesca? Jesus Christ!"

"There's no need to take the Lord's name in vain," Jonah said, kneeling over Eve and stroking her hair. "Or mine. You're going to be OK. Just relax."

Eve adopted her gentle "I'm talking to a cute guy" tone and pleadingly asked Jonah for a "dribble" of water. Everyone was gathered around Eve, and our collective fear smelled like bad breath.

"Close your eyes, Eve," Jonah said soothingly. "We'll get you water."

"Oh, Jonah," she cried, clutching his leg with one hand and Cisco's arm with the other. "Please."

Jonah motioned for us to walk a few feet away from where Eve was splayed out in the sand.

"We have to carry her to the water," Jonah whispered. "Until we can figure out how to transport water here, we have to move her there."

"But what about the rescue team?" Chaz asked on the verge of hysteria. "What if somebody comes and they don't see us in the jungle?"

"I'll wait here," Joe said. "Just bring me water as soon as you can."

"Yeah, right." Jonah snapped. "You think any of us trust

you to keep the fire going after what happened?" We all glared at Joe.

"It won't happen again. Just go," Joe pleaded. "I can't bear the sight of you all anymore."

It was obvious Jonah thought leaving his deranged father alone on the beach was a smashing idea. I wasn't so sure, but I didn't say anything.

Joe's eyes were bloodshot, and his posture was bent. He looked like he'd been beaten. He looked depleted. He looked like my dad after another failed "date night" with my mom.

I Can Do Anything
You Can Do Better

Do you even know where you're going, Jonah?" Cisco asked again. "'Cause it doesn't seem like you do. And while I get that you're doing your Christopher Columbus routine, we're the ones carrying an extra 120 pounds back here."

"One hundred six," Eve gasped. It was the first thing she'd said in hours. I took this as a good sign.

"I can't even see straight, I'm so tired," Milan complained. "My eyes are all blurry."

It was getting late. The sun pierced the treetops like orange laser beams. We'd been walking for what felt like miles, carrying Eve's red, blistered body along for the ride. The jungle was without scenic variety. It was just a lot of trees. Jonah had said the fresh water was only a couple of miles from the beach, so I think we were all beginning to wonder if he was lost. What was taking so long? The tension between Cisco and Jonah had been mounting since we began to suspect that Jonah didn't know where he was going. We all had foot blisters and were thirsty and hungry in ways none of us could have ever imagined. There hadn't been a lot of conversation. Mostly just quiet resignation. The burden of Milan's exhaustion was dampening her spirits. Cisco was holding Eve's feet, Milan and I had her middle, and Chaz had her head.

"Why do I have to carry her head?" Chaz whined for the hundredth time. "It's sooooo heavy."

"My thighs are totally chafing," Milan said. "How is it possible that I am getting fat on a starvation diet? Does sleep deprivation make you retain water?"

"You look scrumptious," Chaz said.

"Oh my God," Milan moaned. "What if I'm getting my period? Do you have tampons, Francesca?"

"No," I whispered, mortified. This was just not a conversation I could have in the presence of Cisco Parker.

"Well, what am I supposed to use if I get my period? Tree bark? God, I hate my period," she continued on her menstruation monologue. "And don't you love the way they never gave away any *useful* information on *Lost*? I know exactly what to do should we happen upon a polar bear or a locked hatch, but what the hell did Kate and Juliet do when it was Tammy time?"

"Open the hatch, cork the snatch," Chaz laughed.

"But with *what*?" Milan asked in all seriousness. Chaz shook his head.

The fact that Milan spoke of her period with such

candor, aloud, in front of cute boys, spoke volumes about the emotional distance between us. I'd have been horrified to even utter the word *tampon* in front of anybody but Jordan. Even my mother and I didn't discuss such things.

"Well, look at that, girls," Jonah said quietly to all of us, pointing to what looked like a striped hyena bred with an aardvark standing under a tree and eating bunches of small, pumpkin-shaped fruit.

"Oh my God, that is so cool," Milan whispered, dropping her end of Eve and nearly knocking me over with the surprise of Eve's full body weight.

"Hey, watch it!" Eve said.

The animal looked up at us momentarily before continuing with its feast.

"Oh God. Sorry." She reclaimed her half of Eve. "What should we do?"

"Get the fruit," Jonah said. "If he can eat it, it's probably not poisonous."

"This is awesome," Cisco said, motioning for us to gently lay Eve down. "I killed a walrus with my bare hands in *White Death*. I played Sir John Franklin's son."

"Yeah, *played* is the operative word in that sentence," Jonah laughed as he began toward the animal.

Cisco stopped him with a firm grip on the shoulder. "I'll do it," he said, pushing Jonah back a bit. "This is what I do."

"Do where? In Malibu?" Milan asked.

"This should be entertaining if nothing else," Jonah said, making way for Cisco. "You don't have to kill it, Polar Boy, just scare it away so we can get the fruit."

Cisco nodded before running to the tree, doing the very best imitation of Bugs Bunny's Tasmanian Devil I'd ever seen. He was screaming, shaking his body, kicking his legs, waving his arms, and baring his teeth. Absolutely ridiculous looking.

The animal stopped eating and looked up at Cisco before letting out a long, loud, guttural snort. I think it was his version of a laugh. Then it started digging a narrow trench with alternate strokes of its forepaws, crouched close to the ground, and deposited the biggest piece of poop I'd ever seen. Seriously, it was like half the size of Eve.

"Oh duuude!" Cisco shrieked. "No way dude. Do you smell that?" Cisco ran back and hid behind Chaz.

"That's right, Sir John. *She'll* protect you!" Jonah laughed.

"You're lucky I find your shameless homophobia titillating," Chaz said. "Insulting, yet oddly refreshing."

Jonah chortled as he patted Cisco on the back and walked right up to the hyena/aardvark. As he got close, the animal puffed up like a scared cat before it casually disappeared into the wilderness. Jonah bowed. We applauded.

"Jonah's got bigger yam bags than Cisco!" Milan sang.

Cisco shrugged and smiled. His ego was made of Kevlar.

Despite the ghastly poop stench, we all ran to grab

some of the fruit. Watermelon it wasn't. It had a tough purplish skin and a layer of bitter green fruit surrounding a large seed.

"This is disguhhsting," Chaz garbled, mouth half open and stuffed full of fruit.

"Slow down, man" Jonah said. Chaz was frantically popping them in his mouth like kernels of popcorn.

"Holy shit," I said, dropping my fruit as I looked up at Chaz, who had a fleet of black insects marching out of his open mouth. "There are freakin' bugs coming out of your freakin' mouth."

"Omagawd, omagawd, omagawd!" he crowed, looking down at his share of fruit, which was riddled with insects. He started doing a crazy Jimmy dance: slapping his face, spitting out the fruit, and then running behind a tree to retch.

We were laughing our heads off. It sounds mean, but it was funny as hell.

We took care to make sure the remaining fruit was bug-free before we continued eating. We didn't exactly have a lot of options. Jonah tried to squeeze some of the bitter juice into Eve's mouth, but she turned her head away. He begged her to take a little, but she refused.

"Good for me, bad for you," Chaz said to Eve, snatching the fruit from Jonah's hand and popping it in his mouth. He wasn't one to get hung up on a bad experience. We collected the remaining fruit before standing up.

"Can we please switch positions?" Chaz asked us, looking down at Eve in preparation to start moving again. "I'm telling you, her head is like a seventy-five pound bowling ball."

"I think this end is even heavier," Cisco countered. Eve squirmed.

"You're really some kind of pussy," Milan snapped at Cisco. "Weren't you like Spider-Man or something?"

"Captain Marvel," Cisco said, readjusting Eve's feet over his shoulders. He didn't seem embarrassed at all.

"Well, that's even worse," Chaz laughed. "But let's do a switcheroo, 'cause I think watching you walk from behind may give me the strength to carry on."

Cisco laughed, and they switched places. I guessed the bitter plum juice had everyone feeling better.

"Now, make it worth my while," Chaz told Cisco. "Do a li'l swishing."

Cisco complied with a little jig, and the effect was comic. So he wasn't a real superhero. What a stupid expectation anyway. At least he could laugh at himself. I sort of loved that he didn't take himself so seriously. I mean, he was just an actor, right? Why should we expect him to be a real superhero, for God's sake? How stupid.

"Look at that ass," Chaz whispered to himself. "He must be gay. Nobody straight looks like that. It's painful to look at him, he's so gorgeous."

"Keep it to yourself," Jonah said. "You're making me sick."

"*Ja, ja*, Adolf."

"How you doin'?" Cisco asked Eve tenderly, as he cradled her head in his hands. Eve opened her eyes and looked up at Cisco and tried to smile. The effect was grotesque. Cisco winced and smiled back.

"You OK?" he asked again.

Eve shook her head and closed her eyes again. She really did not look good.

"The water! I hear it! I found it!" Jonah announced a half hour or so later. He sounded suspiciously surprised, considering he'd been acting like he knew exactly where he was going all along. The stream ran through a little clearing of trees. It was almost dark now, but I sensed we'd have some sunshine here in the morning.

"Praise the Lord!" Chaz chimed facetiously.

"Amen," Jonah replied.

J:

We found water! I love water! I went swimming with them! I know this is weird, but Jonah looked so awesome all wet you would have died. He's so tall, and I have to say his ability to get shit done is kind of sexy. If he weren't a gay-bashing Christian he'd be almost as cute as Cisco. Almost.

Milan's boobs are different sizes. She's ogling Jonah. She actually looks like she's gaining weight, which is odd considering we haven't really eaten. What's up with that?

On the downside, Eve won't drink. I think she's in some sort
of a coma.

F.

"Maybe we should Purell her?" Chaz suggested, staring
down at Eve and eyeballing my Droid. "I think she needs
disinfecting."

"That's a shit idea," I said.

"Why's that, Professor Freckle?"

"The rash is just a sign of something going on inside
her body. All Purell will do is sting the hell out of
her. If anything, she needs some kind of soothing oil
or aloe."

"Mmmm, unfortunately my Crème-de-la-Mer is back in
L.A. with my cigarettes," Chaz rejoined.

"Hey, do you still have that tapioca pudding in your
bag?" I asked Milan.

She nodded.

"Tapioca?" Chaz lit up. "You've been hoarding tapioca?"

"I forgot about it," Milan shrugged.

"Forgot about it?"

"It's not to eat," I interrupted, taking the pudding pack
Milan unearthed from the bowels of her bag.

I drooled as I slowly unpeeled the top off the little plastic
cup.

"Can I at least lick the lid?" Chaz begged. I gave him

the foil top and dumped the tapioca all over Eve's lumpy, crusty face and chest. Then I massaged it around, trying not to make a face. Not a good sensation.

"Now she *really* looks hot," Chaz laughed.

"What does it do?" Jonah asked.

"It's an anti-inflammatory. My dad used to put it on us when we got poison ivy. Not pudding, but a tapioca starch. It's homeopathic."

"Tree climber, star navigator, Dr. Quinn: Medicine Woman. You're like our own little Daniel Boone," Chaz said, chewing on the foil.

I could feel Jonah cast an appreciative eye on me, but I pretended not to notice.

"Who's Daniel Boone?" Milan asked innocently.

"You got to love Hollywood," Jonah said. "Where else does a preschool education pay the bills?"

"Yeah, like the music business is so ripe with intellectuals," Chaz said.

"My point," Milan continued, "is at least I don't pretend to be anyone I'm not."

"What does *that* mean?" Jonah asked in a clipped, shrill voice. His face was all wound up.

"All your bullshit 'boy of the wilderness' crap. Francesca knows more than you do."

I couldn't help but smile. Jonah shrugged, looking oddly relieved.

"She's beyond depressing," Milan moaned, standing over Eve, soaking wet.

"I think you're dripping on her," I said.

She stepped back a bit.

"I think my thighs are touching. Do I look fat?"

• • •

I carefully arranged some tinder and kindling in the shape of a cone. When I was done, I asked Jonah for the lighter and lit the center. It was a good fire. I was feeling more confident now, and building a good fire was another skill my dad had forced me to learn *before* shipping me off to Outward Bound. He believed going into every situation with an advantage over others was good for one's self-esteem. He was right. My fire was manly. It *was* way better than Jonah's. "Useless," my ass.

We all decided we should try to get some sleep. Jonah insisted we take shifts sitting with Eve. Chaz was assigned the first two hours.

When I woke up about four hours later, he was sound asleep. Lucky for him, Eve was still breathing. I was staring at her big face in the darkness when I realized Jonah was behind me.

"She's OK," I said, as if he'd asked.

"Yes," Jonah said, clapping dirt off his hands.

"What are you doing? Why's Chaz sleeping?"

"I guess *she's* tired. *She* can't do anything for Eve anyway," Jonah snickered. "It's in God's hands now."

I couldn't help but notice that Jonah's tone was a little cool.

"You know," I said, tiring of Jonah's brand of humor, "All that *he/she* pronoun stuff is really insulting. I know Chaz acts like he doesn't care, but I can't imagine it makes him feel very good. And honestly, it's not funny, and it doesn't seem very Christian."

Jonah turned away from me and resumed stacking branches into a big pile.

"What are you doing?" I asked him again, changing the subject.

There were about thirty long branches assembled. He must have been up all night.

"I'm building a debris shelter. It's crude, but I can't think of anything else. As soon as Chaz and Cisco wake up, they can help me prop it up."

"Why don't we build dugout shelters instead?" I asked.

Jonah turned to look at me.

"You know," I added nervously, "like sniper holes."

"I know what a dugout shelter is, Francesca. It's too wet here. It won't work."

"You just cover them," I said, "with branches and dirt and debris. You make a kind of sandwich roof," I explained, remembering the way we did it on Outward Bound.

"Please, Francesca, just trust me."

This from the guy who was traipsing after the North Star

in the Southern Hemisphere. Anyway, I decided to let it go. Maybe he was right about it being too wet.

"All right. Why can't Milan and I help you?" I asked, looking over at Milan who was flat on her belly with her head turned to the left and her eyes wide open. "She's always awake. Might as well make use of her. We can help too."

"The guys can do it."

"Sexist much?"

"You girls should look after Eve."

"But you just said there's nothing anybody can do."

"Maybe you can fetch some more coconuts, Francesca. Or why not write in your diary. I don't care," he snapped, suddenly sounding really irritated with me as he returned to his branch gathering.

"What's your problem?"

"There's no problem."

"It sure sounds like there is."

He abruptly turned around to face me.

"Well?" I stood up straight and put my hands on my hips in a posture that I hoped suggested strength and indifference.

"You want to know what my problem is?" he asked violently, moving in really close and bending his head down so he could look me in the eyes.

Ummm, not really, I thought, suddenly feeling anything but strong and indifferent. I felt the blood rush to my face. I was grateful it was dark out.

"The turtle rescue was bad enough," he started, "but I specifically asked you not to eat the berries or let Eve eat them. And then making me look like an idiot in front of everyone with that Big Dipper crap. I may have been wrong, but do you think it helps us work together if they have no faith in me? And now you're giving me shelter tips? How are we going to dig seven trenches, Francesca? With our stainless steel shovels? Do you have any idea how long it would take to dig by hand, and how hard it would be? Does it ever occur to you that you're not always right? It's like you're sabotaging my efforts here. It's pissing me off."

"What?" I was really very surprised by his accusation, but I could sort of see how Jonah could see things that way, too. That said, what was I supposed to have done? Should I have pretended he was right about Polaris when I knew he wasn't? That wasn't my style.

"I'm not one of your fans, Jonah. I'm not just going to blindly follow your lead…especially if you're wrong."

"And I'm not asking you to," he interrupted. "I just don't understand you," he continued. "It's like you're more interested in proving how smart you are than in helping me deal with this situation. And it's not like I can count on *them*. My dad's an idiot, Chaz is lazy, Cisco's useless, and Milan is…" he stammered, looking for the right word, "I don't even know what Milan is. Detoxing, I guess." He paused for a second. "You're obviously smart, but it's about more than that. It's about working together for the greater good. I thought you understood that. Obviously I misjudged you."

Ouch. Now I got why kids look up to Jonah. His approval suddenly felt important to me. His sense of moral superiority was convincing and just a little bit sexy. That said, I wasn't letting him know that. Judgmental drug addict! Who put him in charge anyway? I knew as much about survival as he did. His fires sucked.

"I see you're a real forgiving Christian. First Joe, now me. Very charitable. You think I don't feel bad about what happened?"

Jonah ignored me and began arranging the branches into piles according to size.

"Whatever," I said.

"Yeah, Francesca. Whatever. It's so cool not to care."

Careful, Your Roots
Are Showing

It was afternoon on day three, and we still hadn't been found. What if we were trapped here forever? What if we were left for dead? Nobody talked about it, but we were definitely getting worried. It was nice to have potable water, but I hated the darkness of our "camp." Even on this sunny day, the canopy of trees made it a damp shadow-land. It was depressing. I envied Joe on the beach.

On the upside, at least we had a little food. I'd spent a few hours that morning gathering more coconuts, and we had a decent collection now. Milan, to her credit, had come up with an ingenious way of opening them. By twisting the clip of one of her extensions through the tops of each shell, we were able to make a hole big enough to drink from. Once the juice was gone, we shaved away at the hole until it was big enough to fit two thumbs inside. At that point, Jonah was able to pry them apart with his hands so we could eat the meat. By about two o'clock, after we'd all had our fill, Milan and I had prepared about five coconuts for Jonah to carry over to Joe at the beach.

We'd even fashioned a usable canteen to carry water back and forth.

It was getting dark by the time Jonah returned. The air was getting chilly, and the lowering sun was bleeding through the awning of trees with a popsicle-orange light. All day, while Milan and I had been sitting vigil with Eve and working on the coconuts, the men—and I use that term loosely—had been attempting to build Jonah's survival shelter out of branches, mud, and leaves. Chaz looked like he was going to drop dead of a heart attack at any moment. The whole project was comic at best, but it's not like there was anything else for them to do, and Jonah did have a way of getting even the most reluctant people to follow his lead.

Milan and I were pouring small amounts of water into Eve's still grotesquely swollen mouth. She hadn't said a word in over twelve hours. Between the coconut assembly and our nursing duties, Milan and I had found a sort of rhythm. We got along surprisingly well. I actually kind of liked her. She was funny and smarter than I would have ever given her credit for.

And she was so pretty. I watched her tend to Eve with secret fascination. I was smitten by her beauty. It was entertainment in and of itself. The short distance between her flared nostrils and full upper lip was almost cartoon-like in its feminine perfection. The curve of her eyelids reminded me of an Egyptian statue. Her skin was so glowy it looked like she did nothing but exfoliate from the moment she woke up in the morning until the second before bed. I looked at my freckled hands and winced. I couldn't imagine what it must be like to look like that.

Her hair was half gone by this point. The shorter pieces were brown, and the longer bits were platinum. When she wasn't working on a coconut, she was yanking out the longer strands and tying them around her fingers until the tips went dark purple. I watched her do this for hours on end. If she weren't a smoker, she'd assuredly be bald. This was a girl who needed to keep her hands in motion. And yet, despite the patchy hair, the red mosquito bites, and the dark under-eye circles, she was still a beauty. In fact, her flaws only accentuated the fact that this girl simply could not look ugly.

The twitching had eased up, and with the exception of the insomnia, it seemed the worst of her withdrawal symptoms were over. Her sleep deprivation had made her vulnerable. It was hard to be a bitch on no sleep. It depleted what little energy she had left. She was too tired to be defensive.

"How come you go out to clubs without panties on?" I asked, knowing she might actually give me an honest answer. I was confused why somebody so inherently "able" under primitive circumstances would behave like such an idiot in the civilized world.

"I don't know," she said, without missing a beat. "Attention, I guess."

"Who wants that kind of attention? Isn't it humiliating to see your hoo-ha on the cover of a magazine?"

"I think it's funny that people are interested. What do I care?"

"C'mon," I pushed.

"People want a spectacle," she explained, scratching her scalp furiously. "You kind of end up playing the part you get, you know?" She paused for a minute. I thought I heard clucking.

"Anyway," she continued, massaging her scalp with a look of ecstasy on her face, "since I'm not even considered for good roles anymore, I'm sort of an employee of the tabloids. If I don't keep it interesting, I might lose the last good job I've got."

"But why don't you get it together? You're really a good actress."

"It's not that simple, Francesca."

"Why not?" I asked. It seemed to me like she had every opportunity in the world and was doing everything in her power to make sure she ended up a *Whatever Happened to Milan Amberson? E! True Hollywood Story*. I didn't get it.

"Maybe you're afraid of asking to be taken seriously. Maybe you're afraid of failing," I suggested.

"Maybe so, Dr. Phil-ys."

"Nicole Richie got her act together," I pointed out.

"Oh please! Her day consists of crafting the right outfit to push Evergreen and Delilah down the slide in."

"Harlow and Sparrow," I corrected her.

"Sweet Christ," she sneered, "there's nothing at stake for her except a possible scolding from the Fashion Police."

"That's true." I hadn't thought about it before. Milan's tabloid sisters weren't even actresses or models. Most of them were nothing but the privileged daughters of parents who were famous way back when my mom was young. I looked over at Jonah, who was driving a stake into the dirt, and wondered if he fell into this category. I didn't think so.

"Yeah, who *are* those girls anyway?" I asked, happy we were getting along so well.

"Tragedies with stylists."

"Do they even have jobs? What do they live on?" I asked.

Milan laughed. "They get paid to go places, Francesca. They, *we*, get paid to show up."

"Really? How much?"

"It varies. Once I got offered three hundred thousand dollars to go to some kid's bar mitzvah in New Jersey."

"Jesus. Did you go?"

"I was going to," she said, yanking out about six hairs in one angry fistful, "until I found out they offered Kim Kar-douche-ian five hundred thousand dollars."

"You turned down three hundred thousand dollars to go

to a bar mitzvah?" I gasped. "Because they offered some-body else more?"

"I've got my pride," she said. "I'm an actress. I should be worth more. Right?"

I nodded. That the conventions and customs of Milan Amberson's world were beginning to make sense to me was a little frightening.

"At least Nicole Richie's a mother," I said. "That's something."

"It is? I've got a uterus too. It's not like getting pregnant requires some special talent."

"No, but she seems like a good mom."

"So what?" Milan rolled her eyes. "The whole 'fash-ionable stars with their creepy, spoiled babies' movement makes me want to barf. All anybody wants is attention. Good, bad, it doesn't even matter. You think I check into to rehab biannually because I'm a drug addict?"

I gathered "yes" wasn't the right answer, but it was certainly the obvious one. I mean, the girl did like herself a pill.

"I'm a recreational pill-popper, not a drug addict," she clarified with some annoyance. "Rehab gets play when all else fails. I'm addicted to attention. Who isn't?"

I wondered if maybe Milan was right. Maybe we were all addicted to attention. Maybe we were all insatiable narcissists. It certainly explained Facebook. Maybe civil-ians just didn't act out so dramatically because there wasn't a receptive audience. It explained the inanity of my friends tweeting about their boring whereabouts.

"I really should just pop out a baby," she mused, snorting like a pig. "I'll name it Lollipop and let the press take pictures of me buying sparkly diapers and Louboutin booties at Kitson."

"Kitson?" I asked, knowing full well what it was but not wanting to betray the depth of my tabloidism.

"It's a shop where *those* girls parade around for the paparazzi under the guise of shopping," she sighed. "Man," she spat, "I can't wait until we get back home. Not being dead is gonna be so good for me and so bad for them."

"It really is," I said, trying to fathom all the media coverage.

"Boring people suck."

"Don't you hear that?" I asked, holding up my hand and straining to hear the distant clucking noise again.

"No," she said, squishing a little bug that had popped out of her hair and landed on her tan thigh.

"Anyway," she went on, "I'm a singer now too. I'm working on an album."

"Oh yeah?" I cringed, hoping she wasn't going to start singing. That kind of thing made me really uncomfortable. What if she was bad? What would I say? I enjoyed being part of an anonymous and judgmental public group. I had no interest in being an audience of one. She immediately launched into the yet-to-be-released single off her debut album, artfully entitled *Let's Drink and Get Nasty*. She sounded like Elmo being de-furred.

I didn't say anything.

"It'll sound better in the studio," she explained, "It's all in the mix."

Unless "the mix" included another singer, I wasn't convinced. I nodded, smiling awkwardly. I really was speechless. I just couldn't wrap my head around the fact that she seemed to act like an idiot on purpose. It was counterintuitive. Then again, she was gracing the covers of the magazines that I was shelling out my allowance to buy. So maybe I was the idiot.

"I wrote it myself," she said, ignoring my discomfort and continuing to hum the catastrophic chorus.

"Listen," I interrupted, holding up my hand.

"To what? I don't hear anything."

"Stop singing. Listen!"

For a second I could hear clucking again. Then it stopped.

"That's just Chaz hyperventilating," she said. We looked over at fat Chaz, shirtless, who was gracelessly propping up branches like an unsteady parade float.

"Jonah's hot, don't you think?" Milan asked me, staring at Jonah and canvassing her scalp for the best patch of hair to attack. Despite what appeared to be his total lack of interest in her, I could tell she was hatching her plan to seduce him. She had a satisfied smile on her face like the victory was already hers. I was pretty sure she was used to success in this arena. Bald or not.

"No," I answered.

"That's because he calls you on your prissy bullshit."

"Um, no. That's because he pretends to be a good Christian and he doesn't even know what the word means. He's so self-righteous. I can't stand people like that."

"Or maybe it's because you're so obsessed with Cisco you can't see straight?"

"Oh my God, that is so not true," I protested. "As if he'd ever even look at me anyway."

Milan nodded in agreement. Rude.

"Can you light a fire?" Milan asked. "I'm getting cold."

"Listen, there it is again. Don't you hear it?"

She paused.

"No," Milan finally said, straining to hear, "but my ears are kinda blown out from listening to music."

"Me too," I smiled.

"What do you listen to?" she asked, looking at me. I knew this was a test of some kind, and loath as I was to admit it, I didn't want her to think I was a loser. I like old country music but sensed Loretta Lynn wasn't the right answer.

"I like Radiohead," I said. Everything else went clear out of my head the way it always does when anybody asks me what my favorite anything is. Saying "Radiohead" is the equivalent of saying your favorite food is pizza. Safe, but really boring.

Milan nodded and smiled, looking really bored.

"What about you?" I asked.

"Wanda Jackson, Patsy Cline, Dolly Parton, Hank Williams, and Willie Nelson." Then she started singing.

These shabby shoes I'm wearing all the time
Are full of holes and nails,
And brother if I stepped on a worn out dime
I bet a nickel I could tell you it was heads or tails.

To her astonishment, I joined her for the last chorus.

I ain't gonna worry wrinkles in my brow
Cause nothin's never gonna be all right nohow
No matter how I struggle and strive
I'll never get out of this world alive.

"That's so cool you know Hank Williams!" she said, laughing.

"I *love* country music."

"Old country."

"Yeah, just the old stuff. I can't believe you know Hank Williams! Hey, why don't you do a cover of one of his songs?" I asked, by way of broaching the fact that *Let's*

Drink and Get Nasty sucked. I knew she wasn't going to abandon her musical aspirations, but I could at least steer her in the right direction.

"You think?" she asked. I could tell she liked the idea.

"I don't think most people would get it," she said.

"You gotta make it your own, dawg. It'd be hot!"

"You totally watch *American Idol*!" she howled at my Randy Jackson imitation.

"I do," I admitted. "And I kinda love it."

"Holy shit!" she yelled.

"You don't like *Idol*?"

"There's a chicken in my Balenciaga!"

I turned around and saw a perfectly huge, full-grown chicken with its head rooting around Milan's bag.

"Don't move," she ordered, as she slowly stood up.

"Shouldn't we call Jonah?" I asked.

"Why, so he can preach to it?"

"C'mon, he does know what he's doing. What about Cisco then?'

"What about Cisco then, what?" Cisco said, suddenly standing behind me. A shiver ran down my spine as I felt his warm breath on my shoulder. I thought I might faint at his proximity. I focused on looking ahead, as I knew if I looked at his face my knees would buckle. I pointed to the chicken. Why I hadn't yet absorbed that Cisco was just an actor and not a hunter or an action hero is beyond me.

Without a word Cisco went clumsily lunging after the chicken. He looked really short and silly in his squatting hunter mode. His clumsiness made me like him even more. It was sweet.

"Don't scare it!" I yelled, clapping my hands like a cheerleader at the big football game.

Instead of running away, the chicken just stood there staring at him. Cisco skidded to a halt and put his hand in front of the bird's mouth so it could smell him like a dog. It was fairly obvious Cisco thought this was his redemption moment after the aardvark episode. The chicken pecked his hand, hard.

"Ouch!" he yelled. "You asshole," he shouted, rubbing his hand.

"Did you just call the chicken an asshole?" Milan laughed.

Cisco reached down to grab the chicken by the neck, and it pecked him again and again. Before he knew what was happening, the chicken was forcing Cisco to back away.

"Cock fight!" Milan cheered.

"Round one to the chicken!" I laughed.

"You really are a douche," Milan said to Cisco. "I can't believe you got your ass kicked by a chicken."

"You think you can do any better? It's got no fear. It's a psycho chicken."

Milan walked over to the chicken and swooped it upside down by the feet before getting a hold under its belly.

It struggled a little and then relaxed. She wandered back over to us triumphantly.

"OK, twist its neck," she commanded, eyes darting back and forth between Cisco and me.

"Are you out of your mind?" he asked her.

"C'mon you guys, we need to eat. I've had it with the animal rights love-in. Have your PETA party back in L.A. where somebody gives a shit."

I had to agree with Milan, but I still didn't think I could kill the nice chicken.

"Here, then," she said, handing the bird to me to hold. It was squirming around a lot now, and I was squeezing it hard. I could feel its little heart beating fast. Without a word Milan patted the bird on the head and broke its neck. I dropped the dead bird on the ground, horrified.

"Where did you learn to do that?" Cisco asked, in awe. We both stared at Milan with newfound respect and fear.

"When you grow up taking care of everyone, you learn how to get shit done."

"Like killing farm animals?" I asked. I mean, I felt like I took care of shit too, but this was different.

"Did you grow up on a farm?" Cisco asked, captivated. I think it was the first time he had really looked at Milan. I felt a stab of jealousy.

"No, mostly in the back of a car driving across the country with my family to auditions. But sometimes we had no

money, and when you have to eat, you have to poach food."
Milan paused. "I haven't done that in years. It felt good."

"Is that a chicken?" Chaz asked, clapping dirt off his
hands and running over with Jonah to the scene of the
crime. I'd never seen him move so fast.

"Why would there be a chicken on a deserted island?"
Jonah asked. "It doesn't make sense."

"Who cares?' Chaz returned flippantly.

"Yeah, don't people have to breed chickens?" I asked,
trying for the thousandth time to make things up with
Jonah and failing.

He ignored me, of course.

"I agree with Chaz. Who cares?" Cisco said. "Let's cook."

"I've never met such a carnivorous vegetarian," I said,
smiling.

Cisco looked right at me and grinned. His dimples were
working overtime. Gorgeous. Screw the provenance of the
chicken, it was chow time.

The prospect of a chicken dinner had us all feeling perky.

"But how did it get *here?*" Jonah asked aloud again.
"Maybe it's left over from when the landing strip and
control tower were working?" He wasn't one to lose focus.

"I don't care if it rollerbladed from Times Square," Chaz
sung. "Let's Shake 'n Bake."

The Dinner Club

Oh my God, that's disgusting! I can't believe you ate that," Milan squealed, laughing.

Chaz was crunching on the bones of what was left of our coconut chicken feast. I marinated the chicken in coconut juice and cooked it whole, kebab style. It tasted ridiculously delicious. Yes, we were starving, but my culinary skills didn't go unnoticed. Even Chaz was being nice to me. By the time we were done eating there was nothing left but a pile of bones. On a dare from Milan, Chaz ate the head, eyeballs and all. The crunching sounds were so revolting and hilarious. Chaz kept rolling his eyes back as if he were in culinary ecstasy, but it was obvious he was about to barf.

"I'd do anything for your amusement, dahlink. You know that."

"You guys should date," Cisco said, laughing. "You sure you're gay, Chaz?"

"Oh yeeeah," Chaz said, pulling a bone out of his mouth, "and I'm saving all my love for you," he beamed.

Cisco laughed, and Jonah got up and walked away. Chaz called after him, "Jonah, honey! Don't be offended. I just prefer brunettes. But you know I'm available for you too."

"We're cool, Chazzy," Jonah replied, grabbing more wood for the fire.

"I really do find his homophobia oddly provocative," Chaz whispered to Milan, rubbing his belly. "Is that wrong?"

"I just can't believe he's so shameless about it," she said. "It's so un-PC."

"Christians are dicks," Cisco added.

"Totally," I nodded and smiled. Milan looked at me and chuckled.

"Whatever you say, Cisco!" Milan mocked me playfully. She seemed to think I agreed with everything Cisco said.

"I just don't understand straight men," Chaz ruminated, picking at a piece of chicken wedged between his back teeth. "I mean, why would anyone want to deal with all that," he said, pointing at my crotch area, "when they can enjoy all this," he said, gesturing to his package.

"Hey! Why are you pointing to me?" I asked, mortified. I looked at Cisco, who was looking at my groin area along with everyone else. Jesus Christ.

"I don't know. All those freckles and red hair. It just looks like it would be really unappetizing."

Milan laughed hysterically, covering her mouth with her hand in mock coyness. So much for our "friendship."

"Like peeling through your layers of fat and body hair is a sexy proposition?" I asked Chaz.

Milan laughed even harder. She had no loyalty.

"Well, I have zero interest in what you're packin', Chaz," Cisco said, "But Francesca's hot. Sexiest head of curls I've ever seen."

Milan stopped laughing.

"Maybe on a desert island," Chaz scowled with disdain. Cisco and I locked eyes, and I looked away fast. I knew Cisco Parker didn't actually think I was "hot," but I had never been so appreciative or grateful for a compliment. Then again, I don't think I'd ever been called "hot" in my life. He was a good guy. And did I mention his eyelashes?

"Well," Chaz asked, as Jonah returned, "why not take a walk on the wild side? How 'bout a little sample o' heaven here on earth?"

"I'll pass, Chazzy girl, but thanks for the offer."

"Do you people even have sex?" Chaz asked Jonah.

"What people?"

"You know, praying, wafer-eating, rosary-wearing people?"

"Don't be stupid," I said.

"Sure," Jonah laughed. "But I don't," he added, much to everyone's surprise.

"So you're really a virgin?" Milan said in disbelief.

"Yes," he answered without apology.

I took out my phone immediately. This was a group conversation I didn't want to have. My "journaling" had become a sort of way of hiding. They seemed to think my habit just freakish enough to leave me to it. And as I, unlike the others, actually needed to be alone sometimes, it was beginning to function as a sort of Do Not Disturb sign.

"I'm waiting until I get married," Jonah answered Milan. "Abstinence makes the heart grow fonder."

"Are you serious, man? I thought all that promise ring crap was just PR." Cisco's expression looked as if he'd just heard that Angelina Jolie had chest hair.

"Oh my God. A real virgin! I have to have you now," Chaz said as he jumped up and tackled Jonah from behind. Jonah tried to run, but Chaz pinned him down and was dry humping him. Funny.

"Me too!" Milan squealed, jumping on top of Chaz until all three of them were rolling around on the ground and laughing. It was the first time I'd seen Jonah relaxed. I wanted to tell him I was a virgin too so the two of us could roll around together. Frankly, I was just sick of being a virgin. It was embarrassing.

All of a sudden, Jonah pushed Chaz off him. "Get off me, you faggot!" he yelled.

We were all stunned into an uncomfortable silence. Nobody moved for a few seconds. I took back my sentiments about Jonah. He was an asshole. It was the first time Jonah's homophobia seemed to bother Chaz because it felt really hostile and personal. I mean, how could it not?

Jonah stood up, wiping the dirt off his jeans as if they were contaminated. What was weird was that Chaz, who was never at a loss for words, didn't say anything in his defense. He just snickered. Maybe he was too shocked to speak. All I knew was that Jonah really had it coming. His born-again-ism was like a gigantic zit on an otherwise pleasant personality. I'd never met anyone so wedded to his religion and all its stupid ideas about sexuality. I didn't even think people still used the word *faggot*.

"Call him that again and I'll tell everyone from Perez Hilton to Barbara Walters the many ways you screwed me left, right, and center, each and every day we were stranded here," Milan said calmly, shooting Jonah her best death glare. "And don't think they won't believe it. Then you can take your 'abstinence makes the heart grow fonder' slogan and shove it up your tight ass."

Nobody spoke for what felt like a very long time.

"All right," Jonah finally said, holding up his hands in surrender. "I'm sorry, Chaz. I shouldn't have said that. I just don't get why you would choose to do something so disgusting."

"First of all, I didn't choose anything," Chaz balked. "And second, there ain't nothing disgusting about my fondness for the male member. I don't comment on your wish for fish. Talk about disgusting."

Jonah sat back down but didn't say anything more.

"So Milan, when did you lose your virginity?" Cisco asked, awkwardly attempting to pierce the uncomfortable tension and get the attention back on to him.

"When I was twelve," she said flatly, shaking the dirt out of her hair remains while still glaring at Jonah.

"Jesus!" we all said in unison. I put down the phone.

"To who?" I asked.

"None of your business," she snapped. "I thought you were journaling in space?"

"Lighten up, Milan," Cisco came to my defense. "We're all sharing."

Milan paused. It was obvious she wanted to talk, but she'd been backstabbed so many times, it was probably hard for her to trust anybody. I mean, her own mother wrote an exposé about her, right? That said, we were all so bored there was nothing left to do but talk.

I looked over at Chaz. He was done licking whatever wounds Jonah might have inflicted. Now he was practically drooling out the side of his mouth waiting for Milan's answer. Much as he liked Milan, I'm pretty sure he was making mental notes for his website. How could he not be? Even I thought about my essay for *Seventeen* and laughed to myself. *Seventeen*! I could sell this story to *People* for millions. I'd be the new Dicole Richie for young girls.

"So," Chaz said, prodding Milan, "who'd you lose it to?"

"An executive at Accordian," she answered, pulling out a strand of hair and splitting it into two pieces.

"Your dad prostituted you out?" I asked

"It wasn't like that. I really liked the guy. My dad didn't know what was going on. He doesn't think that way."

"You were twelve. Do you not get how wrong that is?"

Milan shrugged.

"How old was he?"

"I don't know, thirtyish."

"God, that is just gross."

"Did he help your career at least?" Chaz asked her.

"Kind of. But when he insisted on getting a cut, my dad threatened to call the police, and he got fired. Now he's a manager at Wendy's."

"Ewwwww," we all chimed.

"Your dad sounds like a real prize," Cisco said.

"Fuck you. He was doing the best he could for us. Anyway, it doesn't matter." Milan looked sad. "Obviously it all worked out for the best."

"Yeah," Cisco said, "you're a model of healthy American adolescence, Milan. Every mother's dream."

Chaz jumped to Milan's defense. "You're not exactly Jonah Baron, Cisco."

Chaz was referring to Cisco's first girlfriend, Sundance Olivier, a famous pop star, who wrote a top-forty song about Cisco dumping her two days after they lost their virginity to each other. I wondered if that really happened or if it was all a press spin. I would have liked to have asked Cisco, but it really wasn't my business. But apparently it was Chaz's.

"Did you pop Sundance Olivier's cherry?" Chaz asked bluntly. "I mean, did that whole thing really happen?"

"Oh, it happened." Cisco smiled wistfully. "We were fifteen and doing *Beach Party Bongo* together. It was awesome. I loved her. I'll always love her."

Milan rolled her eyes behind Cisco.

"And you treated her so well," Chaz added facetiously. "Too bad you destroyed her by leaving no actress un-humped in her wake.

Cisco chuckled as if nodding to his old, bad boy days. "Anyway, what can I say?" he offered up by way of an excuse. Chaz looked at him with mock disgust.

"That you're a whore. I mean, how many women have you slept with since your public deflowering?"

"Who's counting?"

"Nobody can get that high."

"Whatever man, that was all before."

"Before you discovered how sexually satisfying it is to recycle?"

"Something like that," Cisco smiled, scratching his head. "Besides, she wasn't my first. That part was for the press."

"Who was?" Milan asked.

"Dana Worchofsky."

"Worchofsky?" Chaz laughed. "She sounds hot. Does she have a snout and tail?"

"She was really hot. She was my mom's best friend."

"You're a pig," Milan sneered.

"Was a pig," Cisco said, holding up his hand to correct her.

"Ahhh, so now you're a pig masquerading as a humanitarian."

I laughed. Milan was pretty quick with the one-liners.

"Well," Chaz said, clearing his throat, "the first time I had sex was with my cousin, and it scared me unstraight. God, it was awful."

"Yeah, sex with family relations usually is," I said. I forgot I was supposed to be hiding.

"Not that part," Chaz corrected me. "Just the whole vagina business in general. Not for me. Sin or not," he said, looking at Jonah, "now I stick to people who share the same equipment. It's amazing how good the ride is when you're with somebody who drives the same car!"

I was still staring at my phone, both hoping and praying that somebody would and wouldn't ask me about my virginity. Nobody did.

After a while, Jonah started to sing "Amazing Grace,"

and we all fell into a kind of trance. It was the first time I'd ever heard him sing. He might have been a narrow-minded jerk, but his voice was otherworldly. Totally and completely off-the-charts magical. I don't know why this was so surprising, considering he was a famous singer, but it was really easy to forget that these people were actually talented and not just lucky assholes. Even though he obviously hated me, I was officially crushing on him. Even Cisco looked moony.

"He's awesome," Milan whispered to me, digging into her hair.

I hoped bearing witness to real talent might make her reconsider a singing career. I waited silently for her epiphany.

"Is your head like totally fucking itchy?" is all she said.

Between a Rock and Hard Place

Eve's breathing was uneven by the time any of us remembered to go check on her. In all the excitement over the chicken and virginity, we hadn't given her a thought. Nobody even thought of asking her if she wanted to eat. I realized I was as self-involved as everyone else here. I felt guilty.

"We should have saved some chicken for Eve," I said to Jonah, scratching my head. It really was itchy.

"She can't eat," he said, assuaging my guilt a little. "She just needs to drink. Assuming she wakes up."

Eve's face was now purple, as if all the blisters had joined together into an unsightly map of hives.

"Proof is in the pudding," Chaz laughed, unable to resist a dig at me.

"It's getting better," I said. "Rashes always look worse before they get better."

"Maybe we should just put her out of her misery," Chaz said, licking remains of chicken juice off the webbing between his fingers.

"I can't handle this," Milan cried. "I'm not good with dead people."

"She's not dead," I hissed. "And stop talking about her like that. She might be able to hear you."

"I'd shag a midget for a cig," Milan said, still twitching a little.

"Maybe," Cisco paused thoughtfully, "this whole thing is like a hidden blessing for you, Milan. Like an opportunity to cleanse your body of all toxins. Make a fresh start."

"A fresh start as what, Cisco? A chunky, high-strung baldy with a raging case of head lice and an associate degree from AA?"

"I've helped a lot of people in more trouble than you," he said, swatting at a mosquito.

"Um, thanks, Mr. Saving the World One Organic T-Shirt at a Time. I'll pass." She belched loudly. "You know what you need?"

"Enlighten me," he smiled.

"Polyester Birkenstocks. Or a hearty moisturizer made from organic whale semen."

"Hilarious."

"I bet your house is made out of tofu."

"Actually, it is eco-friendly. Solar powered, totally green."

"God, I am sooooo sick of that expression. When will this fad pass already?"

"It's not a fashion trend, Milan. Do you not get what's happening to our planet?"

"Can you even name the others?"

"Can you?" he asked. She shrugged. I had a feeling neither one of them could if pressed.

"You're amazingly unevolved, Milan."

"And you're about as spiritual as a maxi-pad with wings." She bit the very last piece of excess nail off her right hand and spit it out. "My head is so itchy I'm losing my mind," she said, scraping her fingernails through her scalp violently. "Even my eyes itch. I'm so over this place."

"Well, if you're done, then I guess we should go," Cisco mocked her angrily. "It's too bad you want to go, because the rest of us are really having such a blast. Isn't that right? Hey, Eve? You having fun?"

"Screw you, Cisco," Milan cried, looking around desperately for a place to sleep. She looked very fragile. Her heavy, teary eyes settled on Chaz. "Can I crash on your stomach?"

"Come to daddy," he smiled, patting his copious belly. Milan smiled gratefully.

Within ten minutes, both Milan and Chaz were out. Chaz looked like the Cheshire cat. Seeing Milan sleeping actually made me happy. Good for her, right?

Cisco and I sat vigil by Eve while Jonah stoked the fire. He was in one of his moods, and it didn't seem like he wanted to be part of the conversation. He was glaring at us. I tried to think what I might have done to piss him off in the last hour, but I couldn't think of anything. He suddenly stood up and announced that he was going back to the beach to bring Joe some water in the shell of one of the coconuts.

"I guess it's just us," Cisco said, looking at me as he laid his water soaked T-shirt over Eve's forehead to help bring down her fever. His shirtless torso was enough to make me forget all about Eve. Again.

"Do you think she'll be OK?" I asked, knowing he had no idea but looking for conversation. I was so dumb around Cisco.

"Yeah," he said sweetly. "I do. I don't think the world has seen the end of her yet."

I laughed. I laughed at everything Cisco said even though none of it was particularly funny.

"You're good with her," I said stupidly.

"My mom was sick a lot when I was a kid."

"I hope she's OK now," I said, knowing full well that she died when Cisco was ten.

"She died when I was ten."

"God, I'm so sorry," I cried, acting surprised, but of course I already knew this from my PhD in tabloid journalism.

"Yeah, she was awesome," Cisco shrugged and looked down at Eve.

"My dad died recently," I added, hearing the lie slip out before it had even formed in my head.

"Really?" Cisco looked at me. "What happened?"

"A car accident," I eked out before bursting into tears. Why was I crying, for God's sake? My dad wasn't dead. I don't know if it was the exhaustion, the hunger, the desire to bond with Cisco Parker, or the guilt about the original essay, but before I knew it, I was retelling the tragic story of my beloved father and the bereft family he had left behind. And, worst of all, I totally believed it! By the time I was done, Cisco was crying too! I am going to burn in hell!

"Come here," Cisco said, opening those gorgeous brown arms for me. He was the resident hugger.

I worked my way around Eve's battered and blistered body and nestled into the wondrous crook of Cisco Parker's manly embrace. He stroked my hair and told me repeatedly that he "knows" and that "it would be OK." And I cried and cried over my thriving "dead" father. I was aware that I was a big asshole for lying, but it just happened. And I felt better than I had in days.

"Look at me," he said, as he lifted my chin with his finger. I did, and despite the fact that Academy Award–winning actress Eve Larkin may have been going into rigor mortis not two feet away, and despite the fact that a molting Milan Amberson was passed out on the belly of the body that hosted the loudest mouth in Hollywood, I saw Cisco's candied face coming toward my mouth, and the only thing around us was the warm fire, the beautiful stars, and the soft wind. I knew he was a player, but he was so cute. I really didn't give a crap about his reputation. No doubt this sort of thinking is responsible for 90 percent of unwanted teenage pregnancies.

I hate to go into details, but I will. Let me start by saying I've only kissed about three boys in my sixteen years, and I'm not certain any of them were actually of the same species as Cisco Parker. They were fumbling, awkward boys groping their way around the gymnasium they perceived to be my body. But this—this was totally different. I was doing my best not to geek out.

Cisco's warm, soft mouth melted over my lips, and when I felt his tongue slide into my mouth, I thought I might pee. If this was a pity kiss, he was an even better actor than I'd given him credit for. As his large hand cradled the back of my neck, I decided that we had in fact died on that plane and I was in fact in heaven. I suppose that would have placed Eve firmly in hell, but it just was not my problem at the moment.

"I love the way your gorgeous red hair feels," he whispered into my ear, kissing the outer rim softly.

"It's so soft, so *thick!*" he annunciated as he took two heaping fistfuls of my crunchy hair into his hands. I was so swept away by the feelings I was having that I was almost believing what he was saying, despite the well-known fact that my hair feels like a cat's tongue, and I couldn't help but wonder if it didn't perhaps stink a bit after three days without being washed. All that, and I was fairly certain a family of head lice had decided it was just the sort of real-estate they'd spent a lifetime looking for.

"And you smell like fresh hay. I always thought redheads smelled, but you smell awesome, baby."

I laughed again, wading in his pool of compliments. I felt small and delicate, like Natalie Portman. I loved it.

"I like you, Francesca," Cisco purred. "You're so pretty, so real," he whispered, bringing his hand across my neck and down over my flat chest. I swear to God, I knew I shouldn't be doing this, (that Eve would slaughter me, that Milan and Chaz would laugh, and that Cisco was a noto-rious womanizer), but none of it even mattered. I mean, if I was going to die here on the island, or even if we got rescued tomorrow, what, I ask you, would be the down side to losing my virginity to Cisco Parker? Nobody would ever believe me, but Jordan and I would know.

Cisco stood up and stretched out his hand. I took it, and we walked a short distance behind some rocks. Before I had time to think about what was about to happen, he pulled me gently down on to the wet ground, and we started kissing again. His hand was under my shirt, and I felt him expertly unsnap my bra. I allowed my right hand to travel up to his silky, dark hair while my left stayed firmly pitched against his slightly prickly chest.

"Talk to me," he whispered. "I like to hear you talk."

"I don't know what to say," I giggled stupidly, suddenly crushing under the weight of my inexperience. I racked my brain trying to think of something original. I mean, this guy must have heard it all. I wanted to get it over with. I wanted to not be a virgin anymore, and I wanted to lose my virginity to Cisco Parker. I couldn't have dreamed it better.

"You're perfect," I finally whispered, wrapping my hands around his slim waist.

"That's good. What else?" he moaned. "Keep talking."

"About what?" I stuttered. I felt pressured, and his need for conversation was distracting.

"Tell me how I taste, what I smell like, how badly you want me. How good I am."

Ummm. Ewww. Was he kidding? I didn't know how "good" he was, but I knew if this continued, I was so not going to find out.

"I want to kiss every freckle," he continued, as his gorgeous face found my breast and he unsnapped the button on my jeans. I could feel his excitement almost as pointedly as the little rock burrowing into my left butt cheek. His hand traced the elastic of the underwear I'd put on two days ago. Then I thought of something to say.

"I'm a virgin."

Cisco suddenly stopped. He looked up at me.

"For real?"

"Yeah, for real." I didn't know what else to say.

His hand stopped moving, and he flopped his head down on my stomach in defeat. He exhaled deeply and rolled over onto his back.

"What?" I asked. "Is that bad?"

"Jesus, Francesca, why didn't you say anything?"

"I just did." I felt like I might start to cry again.

"I mean, why didn't you say something sooner?"

"Like when, on the plane?" I asked, dumbfounded.

"How about when we were talking about it earlier?"

He had a point.

"Nobody asked me."

I felt about eight years old. I mean, even though I was scared and he was freaking me out and I kind of wanted to stop, I couldn't help but feel that I'd just blown a once in a lifetime opportunity with my stupid confession. I should have stuck to lying. It was serving me better. My body felt cold and lonely now.

"It's OK," I said, in what I thought was a seductive tone. "It's not a big deal. I still want to."

"I like you, Francesca," Cisco said coolly, crossing his arms under the back of his head and staring at the stars, "but you must know I have a girlfriend."

"What? Where was your girlfriend five minutes ago?" I barked, sounding more like my mother than I ever thought possible. But really, was this guy for real?

"I just thought we could use the release. I don't want to be your first. It's too much responsibility. And I don't love you."

"Love me? Do you think I love you? Could you be any more ridiculous?" I struggled to stand up while pulling down my shirt and hiking up my jeans.

"Francesca!" Cisco yell-whispered, pulling me back down to my knees. "Shhh. Stop it. Let's just forget it, OK? I'm trying to do the right thing."

I could sort of understand that in his twisted world Cisco did think he was doing the right thing, but I was just so mortified and confused I wanted to disappear.

"Fine," I said, snapping my jeans. "Let's just forget it."

I walked back to the fire and was relieved to see Milan still fast asleep on Chaz's heaving stomach. Cisco came out about five minutes later and patted my head condescendingly before laying down opposite Eve.

"You OK?" he asked.

"I'm fine." Ugh. "Go away."

Cisco rolled over, and I heard the even sound of his breathing about two minutes later. He was already asleep! I obsessed for what felt like another two hours before finally drifting off on the mossy, wet earth.

Your Secret's Safe with TMZ

Jonah still wasn't back when I woke up. The sun was streaking through the trees, creating a beautiful dappled effect on the forest floor. The day felt warm. It must have been late. I was surprised to see Milan awake and working on opening another coconut. She and Chaz were talking about whether or not Milan looked fat (she said she did, he swore she didn't) and taking turns drilling the hairpin into the shell. I looked over at Eve, who was breathing steadily. I didn't remember sleeping so close to her. I reached over and touched her forehead. Her fever had broken. The swelling and redness were way down. She wasn't dying, not that I ever really thought she was. The events of last night came back to me like a car alarm. Instant headache.

"Good morning, Cesca!" Milan sang cheerfully as she waved. My head was throbbing.

"Cesca? What's she so happy about?" Cisco absently asked me, rubbing the sleep out of his eyes and shaking the dirt out of his hair.

I sent him a "how dare you speak to me" look, which passed over him like an ocean breeze.

"How'd you sleep, Fran?" Milan chirped, still smiling.

I ignored her. I'd never felt so lousy in my life. Cisco Parker. What an asshole. And whatever Milan and Chaz were selling, I wasn't interested. Good God, had we really been here only three days? It was like *Groundhog Day* in hell. I couldn't take another day with these people. Cisco got up to pee, and then I heard a splash as he jumped into the moving water.

"Ahhh!" he cried out, "it's freakin' cold!" His voice was like a needle being driven into my frontal lobe.

"What is he doing?" I asked Milan, covering my ears as I sat up.

"Taking a bath. Maybe you should do the same."

"Thanks for the suggestion," I mumbled, knowing what she was getting at but not liking it. I picked up my phone and started writing in the hopes that they would all just leave me alone. It was hard to record what had happened. It was so humiliating. And as if things weren't bad enough, my battery was starting to die. The screen was getting dim. How depressing. I turned it off to save whatever juice was left.

Milan smiled and brought the coconut over to Eve. She poured the juice into Eve's parched mouth. Miraculously, Eve swallowed a bit.

"She's drinking!" Milan sang. "She's drinking!"

Chaz came running over, and we all leaned over Eve to witness her swallowing the coconut juice.

"Thank God," Chaz said, looking at Eve with a scowl. "Maybe you should pour some on that rash. It's unsightly."

"God, you're a heartless son of a bitch," I shouted, whipping around and hitting Chaz in the face with my hair. He grabbed a fist of it angrily and took a mocking whiff.

"Mmmmm, Francesca, your hair smells like pig shit." Chaz and Milan erupted into peals of uncontrollable laughter.

I was stunned. OMG.

"Well, honey," Chaz squeaked, "at least your cherry's intact. Wouldn't want to lose *that* on a desert island."

Had they been listening? God, they knew everything. I hated Chaz Richards. He was just jealous because he could never get a guy like Cisco Parker. Even on an island. Even if it was just for twenty minutes.

"What are you guys talking about?" Cisco said, standing in front of us in nothing but his underwear. His body was stunning. For once, Chaz was speechless. We all were, frankly.

"We're talking about your little tête-à-tête," Chaz finally said.

"What's a tit to tit?"

My God, was he cute, but my God, was he dumb.

"You know, Ciscy, your rendezvous with Francesca."

"You need that fat ass kicked," Cisco said, walking toward Chaz.

"Look little man, if you come near me in nothing but those panties, I swear I'll be forced to rape you. And don't think I can't do it. Did you see how I took Jonah down? And you're half his size."

This stopped Cisco cold. He looked over at me and shrugged helplessly. What a good-for-nothing.

"Did you lick every freckle?" Milan asked Cisco, bursting into laughter again. I saw Cisco smile a little. He thought it was funny? I realized then that Cisco's worldly pretensions were nothing but a mask to disguise his simple, relentlessly friendly character. He took the world lightly. Nothing mattered to him. I felt my heart splitting in two. The pain forced me to acknowledge that I liked him way more than I'd cared to admit to myself. I really felt betrayed.

"What are they talking about, Francesca?" I heard Eve say, as I felt the clutch of her clammy hand clamp around my wrist.

Eve spoke? I mean, yeah, I was thrilled she was awake, but my joy was eclipsed by my desire to send her back into her coma until this conversation was over. I considered telling her she was hallucinating. She was going to freak out when she heard what had happened, and it didn't look like I was going to be able to keep it a secret. I hated everyone. The only thing I was grateful for at that moment was that Jonah was absent.

"Eve," Cisco said, running over to her like she was the Juliet to his Romeo. "You're awake."

She squeezed his hand and smiled, her blistered lips oozing with white pus. He cringed but smiled back.

"You look so much better," he said, stroking her hair. The sight of his perfect, tan body hunched over the monster that Eve had become was something out of a perverted *Beauty and the Beast*. I gave Chaz and Milan my best death glare, silently willing them not to say anything more about last night in front of Eve. I figured not even they could be that cruel.

"Did you sleep with Francesca?" Eve asked Cisco.

"No, God, no," he protested.

"What do you mean 'God no'?" I asked, my ego getting the better of me.

"I just mean, you know, no. Not at all. We just hung out and talked."

"About how good Cisco smells and tastes," Chaz piped in.

Cisco turned to Chaz, and Chaz backed away, making a mock gesture of zipping his lips and tossing away the imaginary key. He mouthed the word "sorry."

"You did," Eve whined. "You slept with *her*," she said, looking at me through her swollen eyelids like I was the hideous, untouchable one. "How could you?"

"Relax," Milan said, "they didn't sleep together. Francesca's a virgin, and even Cisco's not that desperate…yet."

"Hilarious, Milan Amberson," Cisco crooned. Was it my imagination, or were they flirting a little?

I felt stupid and powerless. Why was it I was never in control of anything? It was bad enough being a bystander in my own family, but now I was being held emotional hostage by these ogres?

My impulse was to take off, but where would I have gone? And besides, I couldn't give Milan and Chaz the satisfaction of letting them know that I cared what they thought of me. I hated them. I hated Cisco too. I hated them all. They didn't care about anything but themselves and their own amusement. It was like other people's feelings were a game to them.

"I thought you were my friend," Eve whispered to me, letting go of my wrist. And that's when I realized I was no better than them. I just had a conscience, which, if anything, was a handicap.

"I'm so sorry, Eve," I mouthed back to her. "Nothing happened."

Eve's eyes filled up with tears, and she turned away from me.

• • •

Nobody spoke much after that. Nothing I could say was going to change Eve's opinion of me, and part of me couldn't blame her. There was a general sense of unease as we all worked halfheartedly on Jonah's shelter, gathering supplies and privately collecting our various injustices. Since Eve hadn't been a really lively member of our group the last two days, it was easy enough not to notice her absence. That said, we all felt guilty that it was dark before anyone even missed her.

"When was the last time you saw her?" Jonah asked me.

"Why are you asking me?"

"I just thought you might know. It seemed like you guys had a falling out about something."

It was so obvious that Jonah knew what had happened between Cisco and me. I couldn't be sure who had told him, but I was pretty sure it was Chaz. If there was one thing Chaz loved, it was a good story. I wanted to disappear. I was suddenly aching for the privacy of my own room. I missed my mom and dad. I even missed Emily. I forced back my tears.

"Why don't you ask them?" I said, pointing to Milan and Chaz. "They're the ones who felt humiliating Eve and me was a good way to pass an otherwise uneventful few hours."

Neither one of them said anything. They just looked guilty. Well, at least Milan did.

"We better find her," Cisco said to Jonah.

"Yeah, Cisco, we better do that," Jonah seethed, collecting his things. "Is there anyone else you'd like to screw before we leave?"

"What?" Cisco looked shocked. I honestly don't think he felt he had done anything wrong. Flirting with Eve, making out with me. It was all in a day's work.

"Don't you get that there are consequences for screwing anyone who happens to be standing in front of you?" Jonah asked.

"Like herpes?" Cisco asked, panicked.

"No, Cisco, not like herpes," Jonah sighed. "Like hurting people."

"Sure, but I didn't touch Eve. And nothing happened with Francesca either, right Francesca?"

I mean, I appreciated Jonah's defending me, but I really would have been happy to not have another group conversation about my virginity and subsequent rejection. If I could have jumped into my phone and died, I would have been thrilled. I just ignored him.

"So what do we do?" Cisco asked.

"Go find her," Jonah groaned, gathering up some wood to use as torches.

"I don't want to," Chaz said. "I'm sick of looking out for her sorry self. I'm not her mother."

"We have to, Chaz," Milan said. "She's sick."

"Sick, shmick," he said, "It's like a bad episode of *Gilligan's-Island*-meets-*Survivor*. She's a joy suck. I'm either carrying her big head around, fetching her water, or searching for her skinny rash ass in the middle of the night."

"Maybe she was abducted," Cisco offered up as an alternative to him being at fault for Eve's disappearance.

"She didn't get abducted, Cisco," Jonah sighed. "She went off to lick her wounds. And she probably got lost."

"If she's hurt, I'll never forgive myself," I said.

"Then we better get going," Jonah said angrily. "Just wait here until I get Joe. He's gotta come with us if we're moving. I don't want to lose him too."

"But what about the signal fire?" Chaz whined.

"What about it? It's pretty obvious nobody knows where we are. Or more likely that they think we're dead. It's time to stop swapping rescue fantasies and start accepting reality. There's no reason to keep the fire going now."

"Nothin' like a good dose of Christian optimism to rally the troops," Chaz said. He was pouting.

"I'll be back in a half hour with Joe. Then we'll go find her. She can't have wandered off too far."

Bitch in a Box

"What the hell?" Cisco stopped short, wiping his eyes as if to wake himself out of a dream. We were standing in front of a house. Well, more of a large box or a lean-to, really, but it might as well have been the Taj Mahal.

We all stopped to absorb the vision before us. Maybe it was a mirage? Maybe we were losing our minds? After all, we'd been looking for Eve for over seven hours. It was early in the morning now. None of us had had a proper night's sleep in four days. And aside from the chicken and some coconuts, we hadn't eaten much either. Maybe we were going collectively nuts.

The little house had a simple wooden fence, a crude vegetable garden, and a chicken coop about a hundred yards from the porch. There were a few random chickens wandering about. The paint was a bright and cheerful blue, and the path leading to the front door was dressed with spiffy white stones. It looked like one of those model houses you see on toy railway layouts…only with the face torn off. Since the front of the house was glass, we could all see inside as if it were a dollhouse. And there was somebody asleep, in a bed, under a blanket!

"You guys are seeing this, too, right?" Joe asked.

Joe was happy to be back with the group. He seemed really freaked out that Eve was missing. I could tell he cared about her. He was still heavy into blaming himself for her downward spiral even though Milan had clarified that he was, in fact, only responsible for getting us here and failing to get us rescued, not for Eve's rash and subsequent disappearance. That was my fault.

"Yeah," we said in unison. We were all seeing the same thing. A house, a bed, bookshelves, a table, a sleeping body, and what looked like a real bathroom and a kitchen.

"Should we go in?" Chaz asked. "There's probably food."

"Hell, yeah," Milan answered, hoisting her tattered Balenciaga over her shoulder and heading toward the house.

"Wait!" Joe ordered. "What if it's not safe?"

"This isn't an episode of *Lost*. There are no hostiles, for Christ's sake."

"Joe could be right, Milan," Cisco said. "How do you know?"

"Look, Yogi and Boo Boo," Milan started, "you do what you want, but I see a shower stall, and I suspect that means there's soap and a razor in there. I'd rather get eaten by the natives than start braiding the hair under my arms."

I had to agree with Milan, but instinctively I waited for Jonah.

"What do you think?" I asked him. He always seemed to know what to do.

"I think I'll go check it out. You guys stay here until I call you."

Nobody objected.

We heard a girl screaming a few minutes later. We all ran into the house.

"Calm down, Eve, it's me, Jonah. It's us. Cisco and Jonah."

She was disoriented and ranting. What was Eve doing there?

"Cisco?" she whinnied, catching her breath and grabbing for his hand.

"What are you doing here? How did you find this place?" he asked, stroking her forehead with his free hand.

Eve turned swiftly when she saw the rest of us. I could almost see her mind go blank as she decided what position she should assume. As we stood there staring at her, her expression suddenly changed from darkness to innocent joviality.

She popped out of the bed, knocking over a half-empty bottle of tequila and grasping for the sheets to cover her naked body. The rash looked much, much better. Thank you, tapioca. Her clean hair was tied back with a rubber band, and all traces of the smeared eye makeup were gone. She looked pale but quite well rested. Almost recognizable, in fact.

"Thank God you guys found me!" she cried. "I was so scared." She stumbled a little.

"You were?" Chaz asked. "You didn't look scared. You looked pretty comfortable sleeping there."

"I found this place yesterday. Isn't it weird? And look," she said, tying a knot in the sheet and stepping into the kitchenette. "There's lots of canned food and bottled water."

"And laundry detergent," I said, pointing to her clothes, which were hang drying on a line out the back door. "And shampoo."

Eve reached up self-consciously to touch her clean hair. Her armpits were hairless.

"And a razor," Milan yelled. "You bitch! We've been trekking our tired, hungry asses around thinking you were dead in a ditch somewhere, and you've been washing your clothes and exfoliating? You really suck, you know that?" Milan sounded hurt.

"I'm sorry," Eve said. "Let me explain."

We waited.

"OK, this is really embarrassing, but it's the truth."

She started crying before continuing. I remembered our berry hunt and her showing me how she could cry on cue, so I wasn't totally feeling it.

"I was so hurt that Cisco chose *her* over me," she cried, her gaze sharpening in my direction, "that I just needed to find some still water so I could see what I looked like. How bad it really was. I knew nobody was telling me the truth. I had to know."

She burst into choking tears.

"That is like the rudest thing I've ever heard," I said.

"I know," she cried, "but it's true."

"I didn't choose anybody," Cisco said, obviously flattered. He smiled at Eve. I still hadn't recovered from the episode with Cisco, but his hypocrisy was facilitating the healing process.

"So you let us all worry ourselves sick over you while you went off to find your reflection? That is just tragic," Chaz said. "Tragic."

Eve nodded.

"Anyway, I never found water, but by the time I tried to turn around I was so tired I just fell asleep under a tree. And when I woke up, it was getting light out and I was in front of this, this house. I was sure I'd died and found heaven. I mean, I literally thought I had died. I just crawled into the bed and fell asleep."

"After you showered, did laundry, and made dinner and cocktails?" Chaz shrieked, pointing to the seven empty soup cans and the spilled bottle of tequila. The tequila and soup labels were written in English, but the brand names were foreign to me. "I'm not buying your sob story, Eve. You should have come for us." Chaz picked up a worn copy of *Pride and Prejudice* that Eve had obviously been reading and threw it across the floor. "You're disgusting."

"I can understand," Cisco said.

"You stop defending her already!" Milan yelled.

"I'm just saying," he stammered, diminishing under Milan's gaze.

"How do you live with yourself, Eve?" Milan asked. "You're so selfish. It's all about you, isn't it? Do you ever stop to think about other people?"

It was obvious Eve wasn't going to get away with her crap excuse and needed to switch gears. We were pissed. I'd grown accustomed to her oily maneuvers, but what followed next even surprised me. I realized in that moment that Eve was truly deceptive. People didn't matter to her. Whatever partnerships she formed were premeditated. It was all about gaining an advantage.

"Me?" Eve shrieked, eyes bugging out of her head. "It's never about me!" Eve shot me a withering look. Was this all about my hooking up with Cisco? It couldn't be.

She turned bright purple before she continued.

"You think Peter ever made it about me? Even once? It was never about me. I was always an afterthought," she said, as if discussing a familiar situation with a close group of friends such as she had never had.

"Who's Peter?" Cisco asked, looking confused and a little annoyed at the mention of another guy's name. "What are you talking about?"

"I'm talking about the fact that he never thought about the way that I felt. I'm always the demanding one, but it's funny how I *never* get what I want. Maybe I didn't want to wait until his withered old wife died. Maybe I didn't want to be somebody's filthy secret for four years. I didn't do it on purpose. I was just so pissed off. I didn't know the whole flat would burn down. I was just trying to punish him. I, I…" She was ranting.

"What the eff is she talking about?" Milan asked. "Are you on something?"

Eve nodded dramatically, pointing to a little baggie with a bunch of blue pills inside. Jonah scrambled to pick it up.

"How many of these did you take?" he asked in a panic. "Where did you find them?"

"Two," she sobbed, going with whatever angle she could find. "They were in the bathroom."

"Two?" What a drama queen. We all breathed a sigh of relief as Eve continued to cry.

"What are they? Milan asked.

"H-a-l-c-i-o-n?" Jonah squinted, trying to read the tiny writing.

"Oooooh." Milan reached for the bag, but Jonah snatched it away.

"Dick," she mumbled under her breath.

"Calm down, Eve," Joe said, ignoring Milan and rubbing Eve's back as she heaved on the floor. "Just calmly tell me what you are talking about. Who is Peter? Is this Peter's house?"

"Peter's house?" she asked, wiping her tears and bursting into peals of laughter. "Is this Peter's house? What do you think, Joe? Does this look like Peter McArthy's house?"

I was beginning to think she'd taken more than two pills.

"Peter McArthy?" Joe asked, as his brows knit together in confusion. "What does Peter McArthy have to do with anything?"

You know Peter McArthy from the famous 1970s boy band the Penguins. He's Britain's national treasure. He must be like 108 years old by now. He's got lots of grown children with a famous model he's been married to since forever. They're cool, but they're old people. I didn't understand what they had to do with Eve Larkin.

"I did it on purpose. I burned it down because I couldn't stand the thought of him bringing somebody else there."

"Who?"

"Peter!"

"You were having an affair with Peter McArthy?" Jonah asked.

Eve nodded. We all did a silent but collective "Ewwwwwww." I mean, she could easily be his great-granddaughter.

"I loved him. I still love him."

"You know," Chaz said, interrupting her performance, "while this is most definitely blogworthy, I'm still not really sure what your torching McFarty's house has to do with the fact that you screwed us out of a night of food and shelter. I mean, you obviously know your way around a match. How 'bout lighting a signal fire for us?" he asked, holding up one of three lighters that were resting on the kitchen sink. "We could have been here in a half hour. Sorry old money bags dumped your tired ass, but that doesn't give you an excuse to throw us under a bus, does it, Eve? I mean, if the trail of shit I left behind me in L.A. earned me some kind of honorary victims award, I'd have a purple fuckin' heart."

Eve looked humiliated and ashamed. Chaz was right. Not only had she blown her little secret, it wasn't buying her a get-out-of-jail pass.

Milan farted.

"Dude," Cisco said, recoiling a little.

"Sorry," she said, waving her hand in front of her nose and smiling coyly. Cisco and Milan started laughing hard, which made Eve start crying all over again. Their easy friendliness upset her. It was something she could never understand.

"He took advantage of you, Eve," Joe said tenderly, ignoring Milan's flatulence and wiping away Eve's tears. "That's all there is to it."

She nodded, catching her breath and sobbing into Joe's chest. He stroked her head lovingly. He was relieved that she was better, and she was using his relief to gain some sort of benefit.

I noticed that Eve kept scratching her head. She obviously had lice too. She deserved worse, but it was something.

• • •

We spent the next few hours trying to ignore Eve's sniveling as we got ourselves cleaned up and traded theories that might explain the existence of this miracle cabin. Joe thought it was a vestige of the Second World War, when American armies had had an interest in French North Africa. Jonah thought it was a pirate hut. Cisco's theory was based on a script he'd once read about three guys who escaped a POW camp to climb Mount Kenya. I raised the possibility that it could have been Jimmy Hoffa's home away from home. Of course nobody laughed.

Anyway, none of our theories explained the clear signs of semi-recent habitation, the fresh-ish paint job, the chickens, or the fact that among the copious reading material was a *Time* magazine from 1998 and a *Bitch Girl* novel that I was thrilled and surprised to discover I'd never read. I grabbed that and a dusty copy of *Anna Karenina* off a large wooden bookshelf. Honestly, I was almost as happy to find books as I was to find food and water.

Are You Going to Kiss Me Now?

Drunk. Eve and I were drunk. We sat on one side of the campfire watching Cisco massage Milan's long, tan feet. Now that we had all eaten, showered, and washed our clothes, there was really nothing left to do but wait for our stuff to dry and get plastered. So we did. We probably started drinking at around two in the afternoon, so we were well juiced by the time the sun was setting. Even Jonah was shellacked. I'd never seen him so jovial. As soon as it started getting dark, he and Chaz went looking for extra blankets and pillows, giggling like two old women. We were all exhausted, but none of us were going to bed yet. We were wrapped in nothing but towels, as all of our clean clothes were drying out on the line behind the house. I felt ridiculous and giddy. I felt hopeful.

"Sorry, Fran," Eve mumbled under her breath as we watched Cisco work his way up Milan's leg. Milan was giggling obnoxiously. Eve downed another shot before refilling her glass.

"For what?" I asked, passing my glass under the bottle

for a top-off. As I saw it, she had a lot of things to be sorry about. I just wanted to be clear on what she felt warranted an apology.

"Accusing you of trying to be with Cisco. Obviously he never liked me…or you. He's just a pig."

"Yeah," I blithely agreed, "though seeing him with Milan somehow seems just right. Like why wouldn't the two beautiful people be together, right? I'm just surprised it's taken this long."

"I suppose," Eve huffed bitterly, clearly irritated that I was no longer invested in her or Cisco Parker. She continued staring at them as I stretched out beside her to look at the flamingo pink sky. It was really beautiful.

"Friends?" Eve asked, laying down next to me and smiling.

"Friends," I said, lying down by my dead Droid. Not on your life, I thought.

"He is cute, though, isn't he?" she asked, looking back over at Cisco and Milan.

"He is."

"Was he a good kisser?" She turned her head to me, relaxing her tight mouth.

"God, Eve!"

"Well, was he?"

I didn't say anything for a minute. "Crazy good."

"What's crazy good?" Joe asked, walking over and sitting

down next to Eve and me. "This?" he asked, picking up the copy of *Bitch Girl* and reading aloud in an actorish voice.

"'Simone always noticed how the energy in a room changed the moment she entered. Women absorbed her perfection in an instant and waited and watched as she glided past their respective dates with a careless breeziness. She enjoyed being admired. She loved being envied.'"

"High literature, Fran," Joe laughed, tossing the book down.

"Here's Tolstoy," I said, anxiously defending my superficial choice with a more substantial one.

"You're funny, Fran," Joe laughed. "Full of contradictions."

I wasn't exactly sure to what Joe was referring, but I laughed anyway. I was starting to think maybe Jonah was right about me. Maybe I was obsessed with proving I was smart. That said, Tolstoy really is my favorite writer, but after four days in hell, Kirsten Von Wohdke's *Bitch Girl* series was about all I could absorb.

"What are these doing here anyway?" Joe said absently as he flipped through *Anna Karenina*. "It's all so odd."

"Read some *Anna Karenina* to us, Joe," Eve said, as she made herself comfortable.

He stretched out next to Eve and started to read.

"'All happy families are alike,'" Joe began reading. "'Every unhappy family is unhappy in its own way.'"

It was fun listening to Joe's expert narration of *Anna*

Karenina. His voice was commanding, full of rhythm and power. I could see where Jonah inherited his talent. I thought of suggesting a career in voice-overs if *Hoggalicious Two* was as bad as it promised to be, but decided to keep it to myself. As I sat there, listening to Joe and staring at the emerging Milky Way overhead, I made a mental note to never, ever forget this moment. I knew it would never come again.

After a half hour or so, I left Joe reading to Eve while I went out back with Jonah to take the clean clothes off the line. It was probably only seven o'clock or so, but I was starting to feel like a kid high on NyQuil: hyper and exhausted. I wanted to get dressed and go to sleep. That said, trying to unclip the clothes with one hand, while holding my phone with the other, all without having my towel fall off, wasn't easy.

"Why don't you do the reaching part and I'll fold," I finally suggested.

"But it's so much more interesting this way," Jonah laughed.

I blushed. He was much friendlier with a little tequila flowing through his holy temple.

"Look how well we get along when you're not trying to upstage me," he smiled as we traded positions.

"Ahhh, I didn't realize the great Jonah Baron wasn't to be upstaged," I snorted. "By a girl no less, eh?"

He shrugged.

"You had us in the wrong *hemisphere*," I joked. "I mean, sometimes you gotta step aside, guy."

"OK, that was bad," he laughed.

"Polaris!" I mocked, enjoying the rare opportunity which he was amenable to being teased.

"Fair enough," he smiled, pulling his shirt off the line. "Fair enough."

"Do you think we'll get out of here soon?" I asked, feeling less tired all of a sudden.

"I don't know," he mumbled, poking his head through the neck of his T-shirt. "But I'm sort of liking it." He stumbled a little before regaining his balance.

"Me too!" I admitted, relieved that I wasn't alone. "We must be crazy, right?"

"Maybe," he sighed, tugging Chaz and Milan's clothes off the line and tossing them to me to fold. We worked together quietly for a few minutes.

"The sky here is just so incredible. It's a whole other sky. It's like the *real* sky," he breathed, slowly sliding down and motioning for me to sit next to him and have a look. "Sometimes, when I look at it, I wonder what the point of my life is. All those stars and planets up there. They make me feel insignificant. In a good way, like we're all just here for a minute and we better make the most of it. It's like when you see the Colosseum or the Pyramids for the first time, you know what I mean?"

I'd obviously never seen the Colosseum or the Pyramids, but I did know what he meant. I liked Jonah's take on the world, and he always presented his thoughts in an interesting way. He was good company when he wasn't being an asshole.

"It's like," Jonah frowned slightly, "back home everything is always so urgent all the time. As if any of our shit matters. We're just another band, man. Who cares?" he said in an angry, loud voice. "But between my mom and my manager and the guys in the band and the photographers and all the crazy girls…there's just so much noise. Everyone is always on my case about something. I can't even think straight." He looked at me and checked his anger with an embarrassed smile. "It's just that it's like impossible not to lose perspective. I look up at this sky and I know none of that matters. This is what's real," he said, pointing at the stars. "I feel alive and inspired. Less artifice, more beauty."

I nodded but didn't say anything for fear that my voice would crack. I really did know what Jonah meant.

"Are you OK?" he asked, suddenly turning toward me.

"Just tired," I said rubbing my eyes in an attempt to hide the tears his little speech inspired. I was obviously an emotional basket case.

Jonah reached for my hand and squeezed it. Neither one of us said anything for a few minutes.

"I'm grateful to have met you, Fran. You're not like anyone I've ever met," he said. "You're cool. You're smart. You're pretty amazing."

"You're drunk," I said, pulling my hand away.

"A little," he laughed, bowing his head coyly from under his long eyelashes. There were these little expression lines on both sides of his smile that I'd never noticed before. They were like parentheses on both sides of his playful grin.

"Fran?" he said, recomposing his face into a mask of seriousness.

"What?"

"Your towel is falling off."

"Oh shi…" I started, before realizing he was joking.

"Jerk," I laughed, pushing him a little.

"I wish I knew girls like you," he said. "I hope we always stay friends."

"Me too," I said, feeling oddly touched. I started to stand up to get my clothes. He grabbed my hand back and pulled me down again. I thought my heart would blow through my chest it was beating so fast. He leaned in. I clutched the towel and held my breath.

"Do you still like Cisco?" he whispered.

I shook my head no because I wasn't sure what else to do.

Was it really possible that Jonah Baron (homophobic, born again, Republican) was about to kiss *me?* And was it possible that I was feeling a little tingle at the notion? It was weird. And while I knew it was insanely fickle to be even considering kissing Jonah after my devotion to Cisco, my lack of sobriety was helping facilitate my mounting crush without too much trouble. And besides, I was completely flattered. I mean, who wouldn't be?

"Are you going to kiss me now or what?" I finally blurted out.

"No," he said.

"Then why is your face like two inches away from mine?" I asked.

"I just like to look at you," he said seriously. "I want to look at you." His expression was almost pained.

"Come off it, Jonah," I giggled nervously.

Jonah let go of my hand and started rambling again. He was definitely tipsy too.

"Everyone asks me why I haven't had a girlfriend in so long," he sighed, leaning back and relieving the tension. "The truth is I haven't found anyone good enough."

"Good enough?" I laughed.

"I don't mean it like that. I mean, you know, anybody who held my interest. All these beautiful girls I meet are so nuts. You're different."

"Because I'm not beautiful?" I asked, hating myself for sounding like Eve but unable to resist.

"No, not that," he said, staring at me. "You look great. I mean, those chicks are like sex-starved psychopaths.

They totally freak me out. I can't even tell you how many pairs of underwear I get in the mail every day."

"Ewww. Who would do that?"

He shook his head, looking disturbed. "You're just cool. You don't act like a dumb-ass. I'm just so impressed with you."

Impressed? He was impressed with me. Such a weird thing to say.

"It's like every day you've surprised me in some small way. All the little things you know how to do."

"Well, I do watch a lot of educational TV," I laughed.

"Stop diminishing yourself. You're really an incredible person, Francesca."

I didn't say anything because I thought my voice might come out all wonky and emotional again. I was beginning to think I didn't hold my liquor so well.

"And it's not just what you know but how you think and what you say." He paused. "You make me want to be better. I like myself better around you. I don't know if that makes sense."

"You said I was useless," I said, laughing to clear the sob stuck in my throat.

"I'm sorry," he said. "I didn't mean it."

"I know."

"Woman," he started singing with a sly smile, "I can hardly express my mixed emotions at my thoughtlessness…"

"Oh, I love that song," I cooed, overwhelmed at how

moved I was by the sexiness of his voice. Those "crazy girls" suddenly seemed a little less crazy.

He reached for a piece of my hair and spun it around his forefinger.

"I'm a Jewish virgin," I blurted out in a ludicrous, tequila-driven non sequitur.

"I know," he said excitedly, letting go of my hair and looking up at the sky smiling.

"That doesn't bother you?"

"On the contrary."

I couldn't help picturing Jonah and me having sex together for the first time. I decided not to share with him the fact that my virginity wasn't like some great gift I was protecting but rather more like a pimple that I couldn't get rid of.

I turned my head toward him. Short of a soundtrack and a light dimmer, it was make-out time. Jonah looked at me with a rapt determination and then kissed me. If you could call it a kiss. It was more like a peck really. The sort of peck you'd give a puppy. On the head.

"Good then," he said, standing up and stumbling a little. I was stunned. Maybe that's how Christians kissed? It seemed my virginity was in no immediate danger of getting lost.

"Get dressed, Fran," he ordered, pulling my clothes off the line and turning his head to give me privacy. I was a little confused as I slipped out of the towel and put my clothes back on. I slipped my phone in my pocket. Bad kiss aside, this was gonna blow Jordan's mind.

"Are you all right?" I asked him. "You seem kind of bummed. Do you feel dirty and used? Like we sinned?" I joked, hoping to get a smile out of him.

"Nah, I'm good," he laughed, reaching for my hand.

"I should help Chaz with the food," I said trying to play it cool.

"I'll do it," he said, squeezing my hand again and looking directly into my eyes. I melted a little.

"Are you and Chaz friends now?"

"I'm trying," he said. "I've been an ass. I want to make amends."

"Is that what you're doing with me? Making amends?" I was suddenly paranoid that maybe he didn't really like me that much after all.

"No," he laughed, wrapping his arm around my waist and pulling me close. His breath smelled like the bottom of my mom's wine glass.

"I feel stupid about treating Chaz badly, that's all. You were right. My behavior's been anything but Christian."

"I can't believe you actually care what I think."

Jonah looked at me in surprise.

"Of course I care what you think."

"I'll help him," I said, wiping my hair out of my face

and thrilling at the idea that Jonah might not be as narrow-minded as he initially seemed.

"I'll help Chaz," he insisted. "You go lay out some blankets for us to sleep on. I'll be there in a minute."

When I stumbled out front, Cisco and Milan were gone. All but one of the blankets were gone too. They left the big, itchy one behind. Obviously, things were working out with them. God bless. I had a Christian rocker in my pocket. I really wanted to talk to Jordan. I didn't ever want to forget how good I felt at that moment. And it would be interesting to compare it to how badly I felt two days ago after the Cisco episode. It wasn't so much that I was mad for Jonah, per se, but I really liked the feeling of being chosen. It was amazing. And while I knew Cisco wouldn't care, I liked the idea of showing him that I'd moved on. I hated the idea of him thinking I was some doofus, freckled fan with an undying crush on him.

As nobody else seemed to be around, I took this as a golden opportunity to use the bathroom…and actual toilet paper instead of leaves. I sneaked into the cabin and had just sat down on the toilet when I heard Joe's voice on the other side of the door.

"Don't be ridiculous. Why are you doing this?"

"Just one kiss?" I heard Eve say.

I panicked. Should I let them know I was there? Were they going to hook up? No!

"You're drunk, Eve," Joe said gently.

"*Qu'est-ce que je ferais sans toi?*" she cajoled.

"Where on earth is *this* coming from?"

"You're cute," she cooed.

"Good God, Eve, you smell like a brewery."

"I prefer experienced men," she giggled hideously. "Why not?"

"Let's see," Joe ticked off. "I'm married. You're young enough to be my daughter. And you're three sheets to the wind."

"You'll be gentle with me, *oui?*"

"You're embarrassing yourself."

"You don't like to hear me speak French?" she giggled.

"Jesus Christ, Eve." His voice was suddenly firm.

"C'mon, Joe, you know you want to. It's not a big deal. I won't tell anyone."

"Knock it off, Eve, it's not funny."

"I'm not trying to be funny."

"You're being stupid."

"So?"

I heard her laugh again, and then something slammed up against the bathroom door. Hard. I froze in fear.

"Get off, for Christ's sake! What the hell is the matter with you anyway? That's enough!"

"You pushed me!" she yelled.

"You pushed me!" Joe yelled back. "What's wrong with you? Are you insane or something?"

"Why does everybody hate me?"

"I don't hate you, Eve. There's more to life than who wants to sleep with you. I'm married, for God's sake. I don't cheat on my wife. I don't screw young girls!"

"Well, aren't you the virtuous one," she sneered, her voice betraying her humiliation.

"Look, Eve, this isn't about me. It's about you," he said, sounding more like the movie star he was than the glob of human disappointment he'd become in the last four days.

"Why do you sound like you're mad if you don't hate me?"

"Because I am mad. It's like you want to be a bimbo and you resent not being treated that way," Joe snorted to himself in disbelief. "You're smart, you're talented. Why are you wasting your life acting like a twit? Where the hell is your self-esteem?"

She didn't say anything. At least she didn't say anything I could hear through the bathroom door. I was getting sweaty in the small stall.

I heard Eve make a little whimpering sound. I wondered if this would be a bad time to flush.

"What do I have to do to get through that head of yours?" Joe continued. "You have everything in front of you. You're young and beautiful and talented, Eve."

"I don't feel young…or talented…or beautiful."

"That's because you have no self-respect. You treat yourself as badly as you treat others. Talking to your manager like she's an insect, mooning over Cisco when you know full well he's a player, hitting on *me*," he chuckled, "punishing all of us by running away like a spoiled little brat. Your behavior is incomprehensible. Where are your parents, for God's sake?"

It was a good question. Other than her comment about having them skinned and turned into boots, Eve had never mentioned a mother or father. It was impossible to imagine her as somebody's daughter.

"My parents?" she laughed stiffly. "I don't speak to them. They're provincial. They understand nothing."

"I see," Joe mumbled. "How 'bout friends? Got any of those, Eve?"

"I don't need anyone!" she shrieked. There was something savage in Eve's tone. She was a cultivated little monster.

"You do, Eve," Joe said gently. "You do need people."

"Well, excuse me. What do you know about me, Joe?"

"I know you're unhappy. I know if we ever get out of here I'm telling my daughter she has to wait until she finishes high school before making movies. I don't want this for my daughter."

"Yes, God forbid your precious daughter turn out like me."

"I don't want her growing up under a microscope like you. When I got my first job, I was well into my twenties. I was an adult playing a kid. The studios protected kids back then. At least they tried. It's different today. It's no way to grow up. I can't imagine how hard it's been for you, Eve."

I was loving Joe. He was much better as a parental figure than a decaying action hero.

"Thanks, Joe. That really means a lot," she said sarcastically.

"You know something else, Eve?" he sighed. "That attitude of yours isn't doing you any favors. Look at yourself. You've squandered your youth on a filthy old vampire. Do you feel empowered? Does the knowledge that Peter McArthy wanted you once make you feel less lonely? Does it?"

Silence.

"Old men should be with old women," he finished. Despite myself, I almost started to clap. Take that, Dad!

"What's age got to do with it?" Eve asked. "We had a profound connection. I've never even been with anyone else. You could never understand."

"What I understand is that his behavior was not only inappropriate, it was illegal."

"Oh, please," she moaned. "You're as unsophisticated as my father."

Joe let out a loud guffaw.

"You think what you had with Peter McArthy was sophisticated?" he asked.

"You don't understand."

"I understand that not only did he cheat on his wife,

he cheated you out of your youth. Peter McArthy sucked you dry. And the worst part is that you blame yourself. He crossed a line that he should never have even considered. It makes me sick to even think about it. You're worth so much more than that. I'll kill that lecherous motherfucker if we ever get out of here."

"Screw you, Joe!" she cried, bursting into what actually sounded like real tears. "You were messing around on your wife with Jonah's mom. You're so much better than the rest of us?"

"That was a long time ago. And it was different. We were peers, Eve. And I never claimed to love Beverly. She knew I loved my wife. I wasn't taking advantage of anybody."

"Peter didn't take advantage of me. I wanted to."

"You were fourteen years old! Of course he took advantage. You were a child. You're still a child. We all do regrettable things when we're young, Eve. It's par for the course. And it's OK."

"I'm not a child anymore. I feel ancient. I hate myself," she sobbed. "Do you have any idea how exhausting it is to be so concerned with what everybody thinks of you all the time? Do you? Do you?" I nodded to myself in the bathroom. I could relate to that, sistah.

"Yes, Eve," Joe said. "That's fame."

"No, no," she pleaded. "It's worse. It's so much worse than that, Joe. I notice every facial expression on peoples' faces when they see me. People are nothing to me but mirrors. If they squint, they're jealous. If they smile too much, I look fat. It's like I'm going crazy. People are objects of indifference to me, Joe. All I care about is the way they respond to me. That's all that matters. Isn't that sick? I'm so paranoid. Sometimes I think I'm losing my mind."

"You're an actor. It's in the genes. You'll grow out of it a bit as you get older," Joe said. "I hope."

"I won't," she cried. "I'm a horrible person. I tell you, the only person who cares about me is my agent…and she takes thirty percent."

"I care about you," Joe said. He sounded like he meant it too. I was getting choked up. I was also wondering if I didn't have more in common with Eve than I thought.

"You do?" she cried.

"I do."

"Then stop yelling at me, OK?" she laughed through her tears.

"OK," he said sweetly.

"And don't tell anyone I, you know, made a pass at you?"

"Never."

"You promise?"

"You don't even have to ask," he said. I noticed I was dripping in sweat. I suddenly, desperately missed my dad. My pre-Chandra dad.

"God, I'm a loser," Eve sighed.

"You're not a loser. I'll help you, Eve. I promise. "*Se prendre d'amitié?*" Joe rattled off in a near-perfect French accent. Impressive.

"OK," she gushed, bursting into what sounded like a real slop fest of tears and snot.

After about thirty minutes of listening to Eve cry on Joe's shoulder, I couldn't stand it anymore. I was done. The moment had been lovely, but now that I'd taken care of business, I had to get out. Let them move their therapy session outdoors. I flushed the toilet.

"*Pardonez-moi,*" I said, as I opened the bathroom door and slid past their astonished faces.

Who Put the "Us" in Narcissus?

At least he didn't take her up on it," Jonah whispered as we huddled together under an itchy green blanket. It was the only one Cisco and Milan had left. Jonah's arms were wrapped around my shoulders as we both stared into the licking flames. It was late by now, and I was fighting the waves of sleepiness that kept crashing over me.

"I know," I yawned.

We both looked up at Joe and Eve, who had come out of the house and were talking to each other out of earshot.

"He looks so paternal all of a sudden," I said, noticing their body language.

Jonah didn't say anything, and I got nervous that maybe I'd done something wrong.

"I mean, I know he didn't treat your mom very well," I stammered, snapping myself awake, "and there's no excuse for that, but at least he's been faithful to his wife since, right? And he's a good dad to his other kids. I mean, that's something. Most of these old guys would jump on the opportunity to be with a nineteen-year-old girl…even Eve."

"I guess," he said. "It's just different being the casualty. It's hard to be the one left."

"But you weren't left. It sounds like he was never even there."

"That's some comfort, Francesca."

"I don't mean it like that. I just get the sense you blame yourself, and it obviously had nothing to do with you."

As I said this, I couldn't help but think of my own dad. It was so easy to say the words and so hard to believe them.

Nonetheless, by this time I knew Joe was a decent man. I knew this to be true. Listening to him talk to Eve helped me understand something. My own dad left because he wanted to leave—not because he was driven out by my mom. He made the choice. If he still loved my mother, he would have gone back to her, like Joe went back to his wife after he had his affair. But my dad was never going back to my mom. And maybe that was OK. I knew now that I had been wrong to blame my mother. It wasn't her fault at all that my dad left. She was who she was. And in some ways, it wasn't my dad's fault either. Could I blame him for falling in love with somebody who made him happy if my mother didn't anymore? It wasn't a crime. It was just the state of the union.

It then struck me that my mom wasn't actually in love with my dad either. She was angry, not heartbroken. Her ego was hurt that my dad was the one who ended things.

But most of all, I think my mom was sort of sad that he had found somebody else. Somebody who made him happy. After so many years of marriage, she was suddenly alone. I never thought about how scary that must be for her. My dad was gone, Emily was leaving for college, and I wasn't exactly a grand comfort. I felt a sharp pang of remorse at how terribly I'd treated my mother. I'd really been a monster bitch. I felt grateful to Emily for her kindness. At least my mother had one nice daughter. I'd been so busy collecting injustices and feeling under-appreciated that I never even considered how my mom or Emily must have felt. I mean, it's not like I was the only one who had been left. Was it possible that it wasn't about me at all?

It was ironic. I'd spent the last few days secretly feeling morally superior to Milan, Cisco, Chaz, Joe, and Eve. I wasn't any better than them. It's not like I had such a magnanimous disposition. The only difference between us was that I got grounded for bad behavior, whereas they ended up on the cover of *Star*.

"What are you thinking about?" Jonah asked, inter-rupting my train of thought.

"You," I lied. If nothing else, I wanted to help Jonah understand about Joe. It seemed important, and it felt like something I could actually do to help repair their tattered relationship.

"It's just that I wasn't even a factor," Jonah continued. "That blows my mind. He just didn't care."

"But, Jonah, he wasn't in love with your mom. He loved his wife. He messed up and panicked, I'm sure. It wasn't about you. It was about saving his own ass." I paused. "You know the story of Narcissus?" I asked.

"Sort of."

"He was a Greek hero who hated everyone who loved him. He disdained them. He fell in love with his reflection, and when he realized he couldn't have himself, he killed himself."

"I'm not following you. You think I'm like that guy?"

"It's just that I think we're all a little married to our reflections. To the way we see the world. Sometimes, it's not about us, you know?"

"I guess, but when Joe looks at me, I can see that he hates me. That he wishes I was never born."

"That's not true," I protested, disappointed that Jonah was too big a narcissist to heed the story of Narcissus. I decided on a different approach. "You know what I think, Jonah? I actually think Joe's in awe of you. Like, the first time he heard you sing, that second night we were here, I saw his eyes fill up with tears. I think he's proud of you. And I think he's ashamed of himself."

"There's a thought," Jonah said, disguising his obvious emotion with sarcasm. "It doesn't really matter one way

269

or the other. The world just sees my mom and me as the rejected ones. No matter what I do, or how much success I have, I will always be Joe Baronstein's bastard."

"You're nuts. I don't even think people make the connection any more. It's like Billy Ray Cyrus and Miley. I mean, do you automatically think of Billy Ray when you see Miley Cyrus?"

"Nooooo." Jonah smiled as though he thought Miley Cyrus was hot…which was weird. I elbowed him in the rib.

"Well, there you go. You need to get over it," I said. "Maybe you should give your relationship another try?" I felt his body tense around me and then relax. I was feeling like a fixer, and I liked it.

"I do try," he sighed, looking up at the stars. "It's just the bitterness that sticks around like a bad aftertaste. And everyone acts like it's something I should just get over and move on with. But every time my mom comes home in a rage about some premiere he went to with his *real* family or a vacation he took with his *real* kids, it starts again. It's hard to explain without sounding self-indulgent. It's just this idea that I was an accident and an embarrassment. That's hard. I pray on it a lot. More than I'd like to admit."

"My dad left too."

"Yeah, I know," he said, tightening his grip again. "I'm sorry," he said earnestly. "I'm so, so, so sorry."

"It's OK. Really. I'm fine," I said, puzzled by his tremendous empathy.

He sighed deeply.

"Here I am going on about my dad and my problems, and your dad is dead. I mean, that is…"

"Who told you that?" I interrupted him, horrified.

"Cisco."

"Oh." I felt a cold sweat collecting around my temples.

"I hope you're not sorry he told me."

"It's fine," I said, hoping to put an end to the conversation. He tucked a stray hair behind my ear gently.

OK, I swear I really did consider telling him the truth, but c'mon, the moment wasn't right. Everything was going so well, and I couldn't help but remember how telling Cisco the truth about my virginity had gone so splendidly awry. I just didn't want to deal with it. I wanted it to go away. Maybe I wasn't so evolved after all.

Jonah squeezed me tighter, and I was beginning to hope we'd never get rescued. If I could just freeze time, I could bury my lie.

"I don't want to talk about it, OK?"

"Whatever you want, Fran. I'm here if you need me. Just know that."

"I do," I nodded. I wasn't totally sold on the idea of Jonah and me, but I was enjoying the feeling of having somebody on my side for a change.

Just as I turned my head for a kiss, Chaz plopped down next to us with an open bottle of vodka.

"Who wants to play Would You Rather?"

Not now, I thought to myself. Can't you see I'm cuddling with my potential boyfriend?

"I wanna play!" Milan shouted, walking toward us swinging Cisco's hand. "Hey, are you guys together now?" Milan smiled, taking in the sight of me leaning up against Jonah.

"Yes," Jonah announced before I could say anything. Cisco looked at me, and I immediately looked away.

"That's cool," she laughed. Her tone was patronizing, but I decided to let it go.

Milan pulled Cisco down next to us, and they immediately began an annoying game of footsie.

"Okaaaay," Chaz began, savoring his question like a late night doughnut. "Would you rather be on the cover of *US* looking like you do right now," he asked, pointing to Milan's hair, which had really taken on a life force all its own, "or never, ever get out of this place?"

"Are you kidding? I've already been on the cover of *US* looking worse than this. What do I care?"

We all laughed. It was true. There was the cover of her passed out and drooling in her car, the one of her on steroids after she'd mistakenly inhaled Morton's salt, and the one of her puking on a float in the pool at the Viceroy

Hotel. She really didn't care. On some level she cared less than anyone I'd ever known what other people thought of her. It was a good quality in anyone and quite extraordinary in an actress.

"What about you, Eve?" Chaz asked.

We cackled again. I think we all knew the answer to that.

"With the rash or without?" she asked. It was the first time I'd heard Eve make an attempt at humor.

"With!" we said in unison.

"I'd rather stay," Eve snorted, burying her face in her hands. She actually looked quite beautiful just then. It wasn't just that the rash was going away. She looked relaxed and unaffected. She looked happy. I wondered if maybe Joe had gotten through to her. We played Would You Rather until midnight. It was fun. I was really beginning to enjoy myself.

PART THREE:
LORD OF THE FLEAS

"The curious consequence is that I have become a minor celebrity."

—Edward Tufte

What Are You Doing in a Place Like This?

"Wake up," I heard a strange voice say.

I was soaking wet, staring up into the barrel of a glaring, white flashlight. It must have been raining. I was alone.

"Put it down," I begged, shielding my eyes from the blinding assault. My head was throbbing. "I can't see you."

The light shifted, and I saw the silhouette of a tall, slightly stooped male figure staring down at me. He had on a rain slicker, was carrying a radio and a duffel bag, and had a large pair of earphones resting around his neck.

"Who are you?" I asked, frightened. Where was Jonah? Had they all just left me asleep in the rain?

He directed the flashlight on his face so I could make him out. He was wrinkled, with a long, black moustache, cropped gray hair, and little dark-rimmed glasses. He looked oddly familiar.

"Who am I? Who are you?" he said in a thick British accent.

"Francesca."

"How old are you, Francesca?"

"Sixteen."

"Sixteen? What are you doing here? You're American?"

"Are you part of the rescue team?" I asked, wiping the water off my face.

"Rescue team?"

"Our plane crashed a few days ago."

"Plane?"

"It sank."

"Sank?" he said, worrying the word like a dog bone. "It sank? Are you hurt?"

I shook my head.

"Where did you come from?" I asked, not entirely sure I wasn't dreaming.

"I flew in on a sea plane," he answered, kneeling down so he could get a better look at me. That would explain why I hadn't heard a jet engine. The tequila hangover might explain it too.

"You smell a little boozy."

I nodded. Tears started leaking from my eyes. I don't know why. Relief or exhaustion maybe.

"What time is it?" I asked. He pushed up his sleeve without taking his eyes off me.

"It's two twenty," he answered. "You're here all by yourself?"

"I'm not alone, mister."

"Where are the others? Is everyone alive?" He suddenly sounded panicked.

"Yes."

"Is the pilot alive?"

I nodded.

"Where?"

I had no idea, but I assumed they were in the house. I pointed. He helped me stumble to my feet before following me into the house. I was focusing on walking in a straight line.

He lit the indoor lamp with a familiar ease. They were all inside, dry and asleep. Thanks a lot, Jonah! I was pissed.

"Is this everybody?" he asked loudly. I counted six bodies to be sure.

"Yes."

Milan poked her head out of the sheet she was wrapped up in with Cisco.

"Can you shut up, Francesca, we're trying to sleep," she muttered. "And turn off the light, for Christ's sake, my head is pounding," she moaned, plopping back down.

"Bloody hell," the man next to me gasped. He took a small step back. "Is that…is that…that horrible girl?" he asked.

I nodded.

"The dead one? The starlet?" His face was white as Wonder Bread.

"Milan Amberson," I added, trying to be helpful. "She's not dead."

"Oh, God. And the others?"

"Alive."

"Who?" he asked, voice trembling.

"Cisco Parker, Eve Larkin, Joe Baro…." But before I could finish he'd cut me off.

"Jesus fucking Christ!" he screamed. "Wake up you filthy pigs!" he yelled so loudly I almost peed my pants.

Everyone did. Their astonished faces traveled between the guy and me.

"Oh, this is just fucking perfect!" the stranger yelled, scanning the sea of famous faces in disbelief. "This has got to be a bad joke, folks." He threw his duffel halfway across the room.

Needless to say, he didn't sound so happy to find us alive.

Although this is humiliating to admit, I was so busy obsessing on the fact that Jonah had left me in the rain that I was hardly registering the hugeness of the occasion at hand.

"What's going on?" Cisco asked, a sleepy, dumb look draped all over him.

"We're being rescued," I said flatly, suddenly annoyed with this whole group, but especially Jonah. How could my "boyfriend" leave me in the rain?

"It took you long enough," Chaz said, untangling himself from a mess of sheets. "You people can find a senile grandma wandering around the San Fernando Valley, but you can't manage to trace five celebrities and a lost plane?" At least he hadn't counted himself as a celebrity.

Joe, who was lying next to Chaz and between Jonah and Eve, only managed to stand up with some assistance from Eve. He looked seriously hungover.

"Ned?" he asked in disbelief, squinting his eyes to adjust to the light.

What the? Did Joe actually know this guy, or was he still drunk?

"'Allo, Joe," he said, spraying a ferocious wad of spit halfway across the room. He then rammed his palms into his eye sockets.

I'd spent many hours over the last few days imagining our rescue, and this was most certainly not the reception I'd envisioned.

"Ned," Joe explained, as if perhaps Ned weren't getting it. "It's me, Joe. And look," he said, waving his hand with a wizardly gesture. "Cisco Parker, Jonah Baron, Milan Amberson, Eve Larkin, Chaz Ric—"

"I know who you bloody well are. You're supposed to be dead somewhere off the coast of Madagascar, eh? But you're not dead. You people never go away. You've never made a graceful exit in your life. You're right here, going through my things…on my fucking island."

"Your island?" Milan asked incredulously. "Who would want to live in this little shithole?"

"This 'little shithole' is my writing retreat, miss."

"This is your island?" Joe asked in astonishment. He

started laughing like a maniac. "What are the odds, Ned? It's like a miracle."

"That's one way of looking at it," Ned seethed. "How did you find this place?"

"Find it?" Joe laughed. "It found us."

"Don't you get it? This is mine." He looked like he might start to cry. "Nobody can be here, ever. It's mine!"

"Nobody wants your stupid island, guy," Milan said.

"And, you," Ned shrank in horror. "Of all people, you, here."

Milan shrugged as Ned clutched his chest.

"This has to stop. You have to just go away now."

"Go away?" Joe laughed, jumping off the floor and running over to Ned to give him a hug. He obviously was a little rusty on reading social cues. Joe had a huge smile on his face. "You're a hero, Ned. Forget everything else."

Ned stiffened in his arms. "I don't want to be a hero. I want to be *alone*."

"This, my friends," Joe announced to us, "is Ned Harrison." He wrapped his arm around Ned's rigid shoulder.

"No way," I said, eyes stretching. I didn't think I was capable of being starstruck anymore, but apparently I was.

"Who?" Milan asked.

"You mean Blood Thunder?" Cisco asked, his stupidity outpacing his usual ignorance.

"Oh, for the love of God," Ned said, shaking off Joe and

pinching the bridge of his nose. "This must be a nightmare. Wake up, Ned," he said, slapping his own cheek. "Wake up!"

I was speechless.

Ned Harrison was Dan Brown before Dan Brown. Blood Thunder was his most famous character. His Dirty Harry, his 007, his Harry Potter, his Sherlock Holmes. He'd written many books since the Blood Thunder series, but none came close in popularity. He wrote the series way before I was even born, so it had been a long time since he'd had that kind of commercial success.

I liked the Blood Thunder books, but some of his later books were way better. *A Pair of Small Hands* was one of my all-time favorite books. I should have recognized him from his book jacket—that moustache was unforgettable, but he *was* at least twenty years older now.

"Man, my dad read me all of your books growing up," Cisco said, trying for sweetness but just sounding like a jackass. "They should be movies, man! They'd be huge! You gotta make them movies!"

"I don't make movies," Ned boiled, staring at Cisco.

"You know, I think you should do a prequel like they did with *Star Wars* or *Star Trek*. I would love to play a young Blood," Cisco continued. He really didn't have a clue. "You could call it *Young Blood*. Did you see Captain Marvel? I could do it justice, man."

"This has got to be a bad joke," Ned said, collapsing in the middle of the floor like an empty laundry bag.

"Bluuud Thundah," Cisco annunciated, perhaps by way of an audition. Ugh.

Silence.

"Oh man," Cisco continued, really working himself up now, "Eve would be an awesome young Violet. Look at her. It's like type casting 101."

Eve cocked her big head to the side and smiled a bit uncertainly. I would kill her if she ever tried to lay a hand on Violet—at any age.

"Hey!" Milan snapped. "What about *me?*"

"You're not Violet. You're more of a Rebecca. Right, Ned?"

"Get dressed," Ned ordered from the floor, his voice lowering instead of rising this time. "I'm flying you out of here. Now."

"That's fine with me, writer man," Chaz said, quickly untangling himself from some sheets and looking around for his clothes. "I totally get that we are in your space, Mr. Harrison, and I am more than happy to evacuate so your creative juices can flow." Chaz kicked the sheets in Jonah's face.

"Hey!" Jonah snapped, looking at Chaz like a wounded dog.

"Hey what? Get dressed. Get your little girlfriend dressed. We're getting outta here!"

Jonah looked at me. I looked away. I was furious about being left in the rain like an old beach towel. I got the sinking feeling our "relationship" wasn't going to survive our rescue.

"Excuse me, Ed," Milan turned to Ned while buttoning her shirt, "but aren't you even slightly relieved that we're not dead? I mean, that's pretty harsh, mister! I don't care if you have enough money to buy a thousand crap islands. Do you have any idea what we've been through?" She was on the verge of tears.

"Apologies," Ned said, softening ever so slightly at her tears.

"Just get me out of here," she cried, scrambling for her clothes. Cisco offered his help with her shirt. "I don't need your help!" she snapped at him.

"Whoa," Cisco stopped, holding up both hands in mock surrender. "What's your problem?"

"Oooooh, Eve would make *such* a good Violet," Milan screeched, imitating Cisco.

"For real, Milan? You're mad at me about that? We're finally getting out of here, and you're mad at me? Besides, you don't even know what Violet looks like. Believe me, you'd rather be Rebecca."

"Thanks a lot!" Eve barked. Milan smiled at Cisco.

"Oh, shut up, all of you!" Ned said. Then he paused and took a series of deep, deliberate breaths. I could almost hear him practicing oms.

"I need to sleep," he said, lifting himself off the floor. He was much calmer. "We'll leave in the morning after I rest and refuel the plane."

"Can't you just radio for help, Ned?" Joe asked. "We'd really like to go. I'm sure you understand."

"No, no, no. I cannot radio for rescue," he mocked. "You think I want the paparazzi here? I will fly you back early tomorrow."

He started methodically gathering up all the clothes and sheets and blankets off the floor. He looked at a few of the scattered books and growled. I started stacking the books, ashamed at having been a part of this group of narcissists. Of wanting to be a part of them.

"I see you've been enjoying my hospitality," Ned said with mock serenity, looking at the mess of empty soup cans and liquor bottles.

"Dude, we didn't know you lived here. I mean, we thought we were gonna die here. Do you not get it?" Cisco asked.

"You call me 'dude' again and you will die here," Ned said, walking out the front with the blankets and clothes. Then he threw everything outside onto the dirt.

"Now get out," he said. And we did.

He's Like God with a Moustache

Joe spent what was left of the night giving us the back story on Ned Harrison. Not that anyone but me was listening. They were all too excited about leaving. Cisco's tongue was so far down Milan's ear canal I was positive she didn't hear a word. And besides, now that we were going back to civilization, they could all resume their lives of careless self-involvement. Why would they care about Ned Harrison? He was nothing to them but an eccentric pilot.

Jonah had been extremely apologetic about leaving me in the rain. He said he tried hard to wake me up, but I was too drunk. And when he tried to lift me up, I apparently objected. Whatever. Bygones and all that sort of thing. He was stroking my hand as Joe narrated the story of Ned's career.

Apparently, in 1982, Ned's novel *A Pair of Small Hands* won the Pulitzer Prize. There was lots of controversy around the book because a graduate student (with whom Ned had supposedly had an affair) claimed that the novel was entirely based on her private diaries. Ned alleged that the girl had freely given him her journals to use as research. The suit was finally dismissed, and all the controversy helped the book become a bestseller. It was rumored the girl was paid to go away, and the book went on to become a major motion picture.

Joe said the film was disastrously bad. Like *The Love Guru* or *Killers* bad. We're talking *Ishtar*, people. Millions of dollars lost, careers ruined. Considering it is one of my all-time favorite books, the fact that I had no idea that it had even been made into a movie spoke volumes about its sucking value. Ned blamed the director and "Warren," who played the lead, for misinterpreting his masterpiece and shutting him out of the process. Ned not only became a recluse afterward, he never allowed another one of his books to be turned into a film. So that explained why the Blood Thunder novels never made it to the big screen. It also explained why he was less than happy to discover Teen Hollywood camping out at his secret writing sanctuary.

"He made enough money writing books to buy an island?" Milan asked on a brief kissing hiatus. "Not that this place would be worth all that much."

"Easily," Joe answered.

"And he never does screenplays or adaptations?" Cisco looked shocked.

"No."

"What a waste."

"Is he married?" Eve asked.

"I don't know, Eve," Joe answered. "Haven't we moved on?"

"I was just asking," she protested. "Anyway, he's old, old."

"Well, it's reassuring to know there's an expiration date for your paramours," Joe said.

"How much time does he spend here, do you know?" I asked. I was fascinated.

"No idea."

"Is he working on anything now?"

"I don't know, Francesca," Joe said. "I'm not his publisher."

"Well, you seem to know a lot about him."

"Everybody knows what I just told you guys. You're just too young to pay attention to anybody over the age of thirty," he paused. "Except Eve."

"Ha ha," Eve mocked.

"Why don't you ask him if you're so interested?" Jonah asked me, giving me a playful push.

Was he jealous? He sounded a little jealous.

"Oh sure, he seems like such a welcoming guy," I answered. "And besides, do you not get that he's like a literary God? I mean, he's a genius. I'd be too intimidated to talk to him."

"He's a talented man," Joe agreed.

Cisco was rolling away with Milan behind a bush. Now

that they were certain there wasn't a plum role in it, they really couldn't have cared less about Ned.

"Maybe I should be a novelist," Chaz said stretching his arms like a cat. "All this up and close personal time with y'all has sort of zapped my interest in celebrity." He yawned. "Not much to it really. I mean, without an audience you're all about as interesting as Francesca."

"Hey," Jonah snapped. I liked his protective side.

Chaz snorted.

"Anyway," Jonah said, squeezing my hand, "after tomorrow this will all be a bad memory. I'm ready for steak and a baked potato with butter and sour cream. What about you, Fran?"

"I'd like a big plate of spaghetti with parmesan cheese."

"I gotta piss like a racehorse," Chaz said by way of excusing himself and making it clear he wasn't interested in our company.

The rest of us talked about what we were going to have for dinner the following night in an attempt to drown out Milan and Cisco's mating soundtrack.

It wasn't until daybreak that everyone finally drifted off to sleep. I couldn't shut my head off. I was too anxious and exhausted to relax. I decided to go for a long walk by myself. Since we would be leaving in a few hours, I wanted to digest the whole experience. I didn't know what would happen between Jonah and me, or between Cisco and

Milan, or with Joe, Eve, Chaz, or even Ned. I didn't know if my father would forgive me for fictitiously killing him. All I knew was that we were going home and from this point on my life would never be the same.

The Man behind the Paperback Curtain

By the time Ned came out of the house that morning we were aching to leave. We were all hungover, and nobody had slept well. Whatever affections we'd developed for one another over the last few days suddenly didn't feel so binding. We were leaving, and our former intimacy had a stench of embarrassment about it.

Ned sauntered outside wearing a robe, carrying a mug of coffee, and smoking a cigar. He had curly gray hair on his chest.

"Why aren't you dressed?" Chaz asked him anxiously.

Ned didn't say anything. He studied our eager faces with a sinister smile on his face.

"Oh God, can I have one?" Milan asked.

"What, a cigar?"

She almost nodded her head right off her neck.

He took a slow, deliberate puff and exhaled.

"It's a Gurkha, honey, $750 a smoke."

"Just a puff? I'll give you a BJ. That's gotta be worth half?"

"Jesus, Milan!" Cisco yelled. "Knock it off."

Ned shivered in disgust.

"When are we leaving, Ned?" Joe asked.

"We're not," Ned answered, exhaling again. He didn't look like he was kidding. "The plane needs a little tuning up. Just a few days and we should be good to go."

"A few days?" Joe balked. "Is this some kind of a joke?"

"No joke," he said, bringing the coffee mug to his lips.

"I thought you hated us?" Milan asked. "I thought we were in your space?"

"I do and you are," he answered. "But now that you're here, I see no reason to dash off so quickly. And you should enjoy these last few days of anonymity. You have no idea the craziness your disappearance has caused. It's all anybody talks about."

"Really?" Milan squealed with delight.

"Mm-hmm," he nodded. "Getting you all back to Tambo is going to be a media mess."

"Then radio in, Ned," Joe demanded.

"I can't do that, Joe. I don't want anyone here. It's out of the question."

Milan immediately began yanking her hair out.

"What is this about, Ned?" Joe asked. "Are you telling me you're going to hold us hostage here because you're press shy?"

"I'm not holding you hostage," Ned shook his head. "Like I said, I need to work on the plane."

"And?"

"And," he continued, "I think I may have overlooked an opportunity here. I may have misjudged you. I'd like to get to know you all better. I'd like to observe your species out of its natural habitat. And what better way? I mean, there has got to be a reason you are here, right? I don't believe in random events. I think you were sent to me."

"Are you out of your mind?" Joe asked. "I'll have you arrested, Ned. Where's the goddamn plane?"

"You think I'm letting *you* fly *my* plane?" Ned asked Joe, laughing. "You're responsible for all of this," he said, looking at us and opening his arms. "When the FAA figures out what you've done, you'll never see the inside of a cockpit again. And then not sending an ELT. And then letting the signal fire die out. And you were supposed to be the chaperone here? It won't look good, Joe."

"Who told you all of that?" Joe asked, his eyes darting around to each of us before landing on his son. "You little prick!"

"I didn't say a word!" Jonah protested.

"Well, I wouldn't believe anything he says," Ned laughed. "All those pharmaceuticals addle the young brain." He took a short puff on his cigar and exhaled.

"You told him about the drugs?" Jonah asked. I thought his face was going to explode, it was so red.

Joe shook his head.

"Well, somebody did. Who?" he asked, staring at Milan.

"Oh, please, like I care enough to remember anything about you."

"Now, don't fight," Ned interrupted. "It won't be too long. Just until I find my angle and get some more texture. I definitely think it will be worthwhile."

Texture? What the hell was he talking about? There was no way. Now that we knew we could get off, we were desperate to leave. It was like when you have to pee and you can hold it for only so long as you know there isn't a bathroom within sprinting distance.

"Look, I'm going to prepare a nice brunch." Ned was heading back into the house. "You just relax. I picked some scallions from the garden, and I collected a bunch of eggs," he sang cheerfully.

"Jesus, he's like Annie Wilkes in *Misery*," I said loud enough for him to hear. "What's he going to do to us?"

"You're a reader and a writer, Francesca," Ned laughed. "I like that. I think you also cook, right? Why don't you help me prep?"

Everyone turned and glared at me.

"How does he know you write…and cook?" Eve asked me. Her accent was back. "What's going on?"

I shrugged. "Don't look at me."

"Where are you from?" Ned asked Eve.

"La Jolla."

"Ahh," he chuckled into his mug.

"I demand to be taken off this island!" Eve ordered, in high Queen Elizabethan form.

"Sweetheart," Ned said, "unless you want this image on the cover of the *New York Times*," he said, pulling a crumpled piece of paper out of his robe pocket, "I don't think you're in a position to be making a lot of demands."

He threw the paper at Eve. She scrambled to open it.

"Oh God!" she gasped, covering her mouth in horror.

It was the photograph I'd taken of Eve's rash with my phone. She looked like a monster.

I instinctively reached in my back pocket and felt that my phone was gone. Oh my God. All of my "texts" to Jordan. And it wasn't just their secrets I'd recorded—Milan being prostituted out by her father, Eve and Peter McArthy, Jonah's drug addiction, Joe's infidelity. It was all the horrible things I'd said about every one of them...about Jonah! Ned must have read everything. I was dead meat.

"Who are you?" Eve shouted at Ned. "How did you get this picture?"

Ned started humming "Saturday Woman," Peter McArthy's most popular song, as he headed back inside.

"You said I could trust you!" she screamed at Joe. "How could you?"

"Eve," Joe said calmly. "I didn't say a word. You have to calm down."

"*Liar!*" she shouted. "I hate you!"

"Francesca?" Ned said. I jumped. "Would you care to help me in the kitchen?"

• • •

"Who's Jordan?" Ned whispered, casually massaging my Droid between his thumb and forefinger as he ushered me into the cabin. There was a small printer on the kitchen table along with a Ziploc bag filled with electronic cords and plugs.

"Give it to me, please," I begged.

"Who is she?"

"She's my best friend."

"So you're the girl who wrote the winning essay, right? You don't look like your picture in the paper, Francesca. Your hair is much redder."

"You stole my phone."

"I did, indeed."

"But it was dead. How did you read my texts?"

"I recharged it," he laughed, holding up a battery pack. "It's amazing how these things work."

"But it was damaged."

"Eminently fixable," he smiled.

"So you recharged my phone and then read my private correspondence?"

"Francesca," he said, ignoring my accusation, "you'll be surprised at the media attention you've gotten. AOL home page and everything. You're a celebrity, too, now, you know.

It's the biggest story since Michael Jackson died. It's all anybody's talking about."

I looked at my feet. I didn't want to be a celebrity. Not this way. I wanted to ask about my dad, if everyone knew my winning essay was a sham, but I couldn't bring myself to ask. It seemed so selfish after I'd inadvertently exposed everybody's secrets.

He waved my phone in front of my face like bait. "This is deliciously good," he said.

"Please," I begged.

"Why did you write all of this down?" he asked, scrolling through my phone. "There are hundreds of pages of material here."

"Material?"

"Why write it down?" he asked again.

"I just did it to chill out. It calmed me down. It wasn't meant to be read. Please!" I pleaded.

"You wrote it down because it made you feel better to see their flaws. It's the same reason you read tabloids. To judge them and relish your own sense of superiority." Ned shook the phone at me. "Really, it smacks of condescension and judgment. It's great stuff."

"You're wrong! I'd never let anybody see what I wrote. I would never betray them."

"But you already have, Francesca. Don't you see that?"

"Don't do this."

"It's perfect," he laughed to himself. "You're a good writer. You do an excellent job of capturing their pettiness, their complete lack of spiritual generosity."

"But you're taking things I wrote out of context. You don't understand."

"It's perfect."

"Perfect for what?" I asked, hearing my voice vibrating with panic as I sensed him coming to his point.

"My next book," he said with a laconic shrug. "A sort of *Lord of the Flies* meets *The National Enquirer*."

"You cannot be serious."

"No good?" he questioned himself with absent concern. "Well, something along those lines anyway."

"You stole that girl's diary to write *A Pair of Small Hands*!" I accused. "You're a fraud."

"I'm an artist," Ned corrected me calmly. "I turn the mundane into the spectacular. Experiences aren't owned; they're simply interpreted. Some people do it better than others. I take what's in front of me and turn it into art."

"You're a thief and a plagiarist."

"You say tomato…"

I looked down at my feet, as Ned's face was making me sick.

"You know, Francesca," he smiled, lifting my chin with his finger, "you're tied to an important circle of people by their secrets now. That's something you should treasure. Don't take it flippantly."

"Why would I treasure it? I didn't plan it. I'm not doing anything with the information." I paused. "And neither are you." My last statement came out sounding more like a question than a command.

"They really should have known better," Ned crowed, ignoring my attempt at authority. "You're not one of them. It's never safe to confide in outsiders. No matter the circumstances. Outsiders find it impossible not to hint, if not reveal, secrets and the sources. It makes them feel special."

"But I'm not like that. I would never do that!"

"You say that because you think you're friends with them. That you're a group. But you're not. Once you leave this place, you'll feel differently. They don't care about you."

"What do you want from me?"

"Aside from a certain point of view, I want details," he answered. "What happened with the plane? Why didn't Joe radio for help? What were you all surviving on before you found my cabin? I'm also confused about the hostility between Joe and his son. Why is Jonah so angry? His character doesn't come across clearly."

"That's because he's not a character, he's a *person*," I cried, stunned by Ned's unapologetic malevolence.

"I'll need more on Jonah's drug abuse. Milan's too," he went on. "And, my God," he laughed, "that business about McArthy is deliciously salacious. And your fibbing about your dad's death is enchanting. And I love a virgin narrator. It's all so right. It takes me right where I need to be."

I crawled inside myself and died a little. Everyone back home knew about my essay, then.

"Also, Francesca," Ned said after a minute. "The last entry is from yesterday. Then your phone kicked off."

"And?"

"And I need to know what happened after," he said. "Did the great Squiggy Small and little Eve Larkin get together? So scandalous! I got the feeling things were going that way. What happened with you and that, that boy?"

I recoiled in horror as he continued.

"The sooner you help me, the sooner I can fly you and your *friends* out of here."

"Give me my phone, Mr. Harrison," I demanded.

"Sure," he said, tossing it to me. "Call me Ned."

"Thank you," I said, washed in relief. "Ned."

"It's all backed up on my laptop. And I sent a copy to my email account in the States, so don't get any funny ideas about messing with my computer. I won't take kindly to that."

"You have Wi-Fi here?" I asked, panicked.

"Satellite. So," he said, knocking on his laptop. "Let's have it."

"Why would I tell you anything?"

"Do I have to spell it out for you?"

"Please."

"There's a great novel here, and you're going to help me tell it," he sighed as he took off his glasses and began cleaning them with his robe.

"But you're a famous novelist. What do you need me for? Just make it up."

"Nah," he belched. "I haven't written anything worthwhile in twenty years. I'm all dried up. Revealing the events through *your* eyes, in *your* voice, is what's going to make this book work. It'll have a dash of Tom Wolfe about it." He had a faraway look. "My agent's going to go b-a-n-a-n-a-s."

"Your *agent?* Are you for real? I'm not telling you anything."

"Then let's share your little journal with your friends and see how much they really like you after all, shall we?" Ned said, standing up. "Nobody likes a mole, Francesca."

"But I'm not a mole! You stole my phone."

Ned laughed. "I'll give you an hour to think about it. You either help me out and your secret's safe with me, or we tell them what you've done."

I stared down at my phone as I spoke. "I don't need an hour to think about it," I said flatly, surprised at the conviction in my own voice. "I'm not helping you."

"You'll find I'm not a very patient man, Francesca," he said, grabbing my phone right out of my hand and walking out front. I was chasing after him, pleading with him to stop. He tossed the phone to Cisco. Naturally, he dropped it.

"What's this?" he asked.

"It's Francesca's phone," Milan answered.

"I think you'll find the contents interesting," Ned said, stopping to look at us before heading back inside. "I know I did."

Cisco was holding the phone up to his face.

"Read it!" Milan said.

"I am," Cisco said.

"Out loud!" she yelled.

"I can't," he said after a long pause. "I can't."

"You can't what?" she asked laughing. "Read?"

Cisco didn't say anything.

"Oh my God," Milan whispered, turning bright red. We were all mortified. Cisco looked like he was going to cry.

"Is he kidding?" Chaz spoke with the urgency of a child.

"Illiterate?" Ned chuckled. "And you were going on a literacy tour when the plane disappeared? Ironic. Poetic almost."

"I'm not illiterate," Cisco whispered softly. "Just dyslexic. Severely dyslexic." He put the phone down and walked away. I hated Ned, but all I could think of was getting my phone before anyone else. Just as I made a jump for it, Eve snatched it up and started scrolling through my texts to Jordan. She didn't say anything for a long time. She didn't even look up. Eventually she handed the phone to Milan. I knew Chaz was next. And then Jonah.

"Francesca," Ned called from the patio. I nearly jumped out of my skin. "You're welcome to come in and help me prep brunch. I think you might find the ambience a bit more welcoming inside."

"Come here, Fran," Jonah called, narrowing his eyes on Ned and holding out his hand to me. I took Jonah's hand for what I knew would be the last time.

How Harriet the Spy Came to Worship Chaz Richards

L isten to this!" Milan said, squinting as she read from the tiny phone screen:

> Jordan:
> I just saw the terrifying contents of Milan Amberson's purse. I get the drugs and Frosted Flakes, but what do you think she does with the superglue and latex glove?

"Oh, ha ha," she faux chuckled. "You're such a wit, Francesca." She looked up at me and continued reading.

> Milan's gonna put out an album. Word of advice: Didn't work for Lindsay, ain't gonna work for you. But she's sooooo pretty it almost doesn't matter.

"Lesbo bitch," she said, not even looking up from the phone. She was scrolling frantically. I could see Eve laughing to herself. That was about to end.

I have to wave compliments around to get Eve to do stuff. Like dog biscuits.

Milan chuckled and continued.

I was standing outside their circle, listening to Milan read the words that I had written. Eve's mouth was a tight line and her eyes were angry. Milan continued reading. It was torture.

Jonah is an egomaniac masquerading as a leader of men.

Milan raised her voice.

As far as I can tell, the only thing he's ever led is an AA meeting.

Milan laughed. "That's rich, 'the only thing he's ever led is an AA meeting.' Now that's funny, isn't it, lover boy?"

"Is that what you think of me?" Jonah asked, pulling his hand away.

"No! Please. I wrote that the first night we were here. I didn't even know you then. I didn't know any of you then."

"And you think you know us now?" Chaz sneered. "You don't know anything, Francesca. You're just a silly little girl."

"Shut up, Chaz," Jonah said. Was he defending me? I racked my brain, trying to remember all the awful things

I'd written about him, about all of them. Milan kept reading aloud.

> I think Jonah actually thinks he's Jesus. Seems he's more the spawn of Mel Gibson than Squiggy Small. I hate everyone.

"Please," I begged. "I wrote that the first day we were here." I felt desperately apologetic and morbidly humiliated.

"See," Chaz said, looking at Jonah. "I don't know why you're defending her. She's obviously not worth it."

"Just leave it," he barked.

"Jonah's right, Chaz," Joe said, "let it go."

"Oh, listen to this," Milan purred, interrupting Joe.

> J:
> Joe's day: Crashes plane, forgets to send distress signal, takes beautification nap while rescue plane flies overhead.

Milan glanced at Joe before shooting me a look.

"But that was right after the plane missed us because you let the fire go out," I jumped in. "I was mad. I didn't mean it! I was venting."

"It's OK, Francesca," Joe said calmly. "You're right. It's OK."

"Oh, this is funny. Listen," Milan kept reading.

Chaz's man boobs are only slightly smaller than Milan's Silicone Sallies.

"Jealous, jealous," Chaz tisked, looking at me and pushing up his big sisters.

I cringed as Milan read the next entry.

So pathetic to build your career on gossip about people who either despise you or don't know who you are. And who's he kidding with that hairdo? It's as fake as Eve's English accent.

"Well," Chaz said without a beat, "you'd have to be pretty stupid to build your tween fantasies around Jonah Baron."

"Chaz!" Jonah interrupted firmly.

"What does that mean?" I asked, looking at Jonah.

"It doesn't mean anything, Francesca," Jonah said, glaring at Chaz. "But I can't imagine that you'd want to carry on with me seeing as I'm such a hypocrite."

Chaz laughed. "Touché!"

"Jonah," I cried, "please. You have to understand I was writing everything down as the days went by. You guys were never supposed to read it. Nobody was supposed to read it. I don't feel that way about you. I don't feel that way about any of you now. Everything changed."

"Why don't you give her phone back?" Joe finally said. "It's not her fault."

"No way. This is way too much fun," Milan said, scrolling backward and reading. "Listen to this."

Do you think Cisco would let me lick his armpit?

"Oh, gross, man!" Milan laughed. "You couldn't pay me to get involved in that gnarly pube party."

I was *mortified*. And then:

Cisco can't spell SOS. I mean, please explain? Are his parents cousins or something?

"That's mean, Francesca," Milan announced, suddenly discovering her empathy gene.

"Just because I'm dyslexic doesn't mean I'm dumb," Cisco said, looking at me like a wounded puppy.

"Oh God. I know you're not. I didn't even know about your reading issues, Cisco. Don't you get it? That was the first day we were here!"

It was obvious that nothing I could say was going to change their new perception of me.

"Look," I said, trying to collect my thoughts. "Forget being mad at me for a minute. Ned stole my phone, and everything you're reading is backed up on his computer."

"So what does he want with it?" Milan asked me. "Blackmail? He's going to sell it to the press if we tell anyone where his dumb island is? Like anybody cares."

"He's going to use it as material to write a book," I said, taking a deep breath. "And he wants me to tell him everything I know. He also wants to know everything that happened that I didn't write down. He said that if I cooperate he'll get us out of here quickly."

It took about five minutes for everyone to fully absorb this bit of information.

"So tell him," Milan said with indifference. "Why should you be any different from everybody else?"

"It was an accident, Milan! I would never tell him anything deliberately. Never. You have to believe me."

"How could you be so *stupid?*" Eve glared at me. It was stupid. I had no answer for her.

"You tell him I farted and you die," Milan said casually, still scrolling through my texts.

I looked at Jonah. He was shaving a piece of wood with a knife and wouldn't even look at me. I could tell by his expression that "it," whatever "it" was between us, was over.

"I'll just go in there and trash his computer," Cisco finally suggested.

"He emailed the files to himself in the States."

"He has Wi-Fi here?"

"Satellite."

Everyone stopped to absorb.

"But who cares about this stuff?" Milan finally said as

she continued scrolling. "Joe's an inept douche, I take pills, Jonah's a poser, Eve likes gray pubes...yada, yada...there's nothing so newsworthy here. I mean, who cares?"

"Speak for yourself," Eve snapped. "Not all of us are OK with having had our vaginas plastered on the cover of *The National Enquirer*. Some of us actually have private lives we'd like to keep private."

"Just because your vagina isn't cover-worthy, don't go all crazyweed," Milan chortled, walking over to Eve and whispering really loudly in her ear. "But that rashy picture of you will get good play. That's what you're worried about. Admit it."

Eve didn't say anything.

"Seriously, Eve," Milan continued, turning and continuing to scan through my phone. "What difference does any of it make? These are funny. And anyway, who are you protecting? Your ancient, *married* boyfriend who dumped your flat ass? His wife? His kids who are probably older than you?"

I was so grateful to Milan for diffusing the situation I wanted to kiss her.

"But the fire," Eve whispered, big eyes swimming with tears. "The dog. Everyone will know."

"Who gives a crap? Think about all the stupid shit Paris and Britney have done."

"Or Vanessa Hudgens," I ventured.

"Or Mel Gibson," Joe added.

"OJ, man," Cisco said. "OJ! OJ killed his wife, Eve. You think anyone's gonna care about a dog?"

"Or Kobe Bryant," Chaz laughed.

"And Amy Winehouse or Kate Moss," Milan added. "Or Bill Clinton!" she screamed, obviously delighted with her political knowledge.

"Or Eliot Spitzer," Joe added.

"Who?" they asked in unison.

"Never mind," Joe said. "That's not the point. Milan's right. The only power Ned has over us is if he thinks we don't want the information leaked. Let him write his book. *Confessions to Gordon from Francesca*," Joe snorted. "He should be ashamed of himself."

"Jordan," I corrected, suddenly feeling insignificant.

"Whatever."

"I've been around long enough to know that any press is good press," Joe said. "Milan is right."

"Of course she is," Chaz said excitedly. "It's all just information. Nobody's held responsible if it turns out Jennifer Love Hewitt is in fact a man or if Mary Kate eats nothing but I Can't Believe It's Not Butter spray from the can. It's all speculation. That's the fun."

"For you, perhaps." Eve said, "It's your job, for God's sake."

"Now come clean, Drama Queen," Chaz said. "This is nothing but an opportunity for you, sweetheart. You're lucky to get a mention in *Golf Digest* these days. A little scandal would serve you almost as well as a spray tan. If Ned's book is a success, you benefit."

"Chaz is right, Eve," Milan said.

"That's not the kind of publicity I'm looking for," she said in disgust. "I'm a real actor." Her accent was back in force.

Chaz rolled his eyes.

"The tabloids are another form of theater," Chaz continued. "You've got to know how to work the stage."

"I don't want to be Audrina Patridge, for God's sake," she moaned. "Nobody respectable *works* the tabloids."

"Really, Angelina?" Chaz snorted. "Or Jennifer, or Reese?"

"They don't work the tabloids; you guys hunt them down."

"Look, Sunshine. How do you think the paparazzi know where they'll be, with whom, and at what time? We get calls. Who do you think makes those calls?"

"You mean to suggest *they* work with you?"

"Well, you didn't hear it here, Einstein, but duh. Try as I might, I can't just miraculously be at all the right places all the time, can I? I'm not a superhero."

Eve looked as shocked as I was.

"Is that true?" she asked Cisco.

He nodded, clearly in on the game himself.

"Almost always," Milan admitted. "I mean, a lot more so since I'm unemployable, but there was always some of that going on."

"It's a necessary relationship," Chaz explained.

Eve didn't say anything.

"And people love a redemption story," Chaz said. "Ned's book can only help your careers, which, frankly, could all use a little nip and tuck," he cackled, clearing his throat before continuing. "Don't tell me you all came on this GLEA tour because you actually care about people less fortunate than yourselves. Please. It was a PR stunt for each and every one of you.

"So," he said, standing up now, "why not look at this as a gift from the publicity gods? On the one hand," Chaz said, extending his left hand like a scale as he spoke: "Pulitzer Prize–winning author Ned Harrison airs the dirty laundry of Hollywood's teen elite, or," he said, unfolding his right hand and lowering the scale, "five faux-Hollywood do-gooders teach hungry African kids reading skills." Chaz shifted his hands up and down in mock deliberation before dropping his right arm entirely. "Hmm, I wonder which one I'll read first?" he asked. "And *you* can't even read, for God's sake," Chaz snorted, unable to resist the dig at Cisco.

"I can read," Cisco protested again. "Just not that good."

"Whateva," Chaz said. "Any way you slice *that* story, it ain't comin' up sexy. Especially when you're a Goodwill Ambassador, for God's sake. You may as well cop to it. As a confession it's brave; as a secret it's a career-buster."

Chaz was making sense. There was no questioning his media savvy.

"Trust me," he said. "I get the most hits on the people who fall the hardest. Why do you think I love Milan so much? She's always so dusty, and then she emerges all squeaky-clean from rehab twice a year, and it's such a thrill."

Milan made a pretty little curtsy.

"Nobody wants to hear about people who never screw up," Chaz continued. "They're boring. Dakota Fanning, b-o-r-i-n-g. Amanda Seyfried, b-o-r-i-n-g. Emmy Rossum…"

"B-o-r-i-n-g!" we all sang together.

"People want a train wreck," Chaz agreed happily. "And you guys are the Express. Choo-choo," he chuffed smiling as he made a gesture of pulling a train horn with an evil grin.

"So what do you think we should do?" Milan asked.

"Nothing. Thanks to Fran's lack of discretion," Chaz glared at me, "the cat's out of the bag on all of us all now, right? So let Ned try and piece together a novel based on Fran's phone entries. It'll take him years to write a decent book. In the meantime, as soon as we get back, we'll send out our own press release to every paper and tabloid detailing everything that happened here. As long as we beat Ned to the punch, he's got no novel. Think of David Letterman. It's all a matter of how the information is revealed. It's all about maintaining control."

We all agreed. Chaz was right.

"Now, Francesca, my dear," he snapped his fingers. "It's well past lunchtime, and I'm starving. Go in there and get me something to eat. Cleaning up your mess has left me famished, Frances. Absolutely famished."

Dirty Laundry: The Spin Cycle

I'm not a catering service," Ned snapped, looking up from his computer after I'd made my request for food and drinks. He was angry that I'd decided against throwing my friends under the bus for the thrill of his lofty authorship.

"Tell me what's going on out there," he demanded, licking his writerly chops.

I didn't say anything.

"I honestly can't imagine who you think you're protecting, Francesca."

"I just can't do it."

"You Americans with your simple sense of loyalty and camaraderie," he mumbled. "It's quite ridiculous, you know."

"Maybe," I shrugged. "English people don't believe in loyalty and camaraderie?"

"We do," he sneered. "We're just better judges of character."

"Right. Like the Massacre at Amritsar?" I asked.

Ned looked at me and burst out laughing. "Bravo,

Francesca. Bravo." His smile lit up his face like a candle in a jack-o'-lantern.

I smiled back, secretly thrilling that my passion for the History Channel finally had its moment. I could tell Ned was surprise and impressed.

"You're obviously an extraordinary girl," Ned started. "You're educated, you can write, you're funny."

"You think so?" I asked. I was loving the compliments. It would take someone as eccentric as Ned Harrison to think that I was the special one in a group of marooned celebrities. Despite his being an evil plagiarist, I enjoyed the fact that he appreciated me.

"I do, I do," he pressed, lighting a cigar and fingering some marbles and keys in a little bowl next to his computer. "Think of the larger picture, Francesca. Think of your career."

"What do you mean?" I asked, sitting down across from him. I'd never really given my career a lot of thought.

"I can help you along," he suggested. "We could even write the book together," he exhaled.

I shook my head.

"Or, if you don't want to be involved," he puffed casually, "I'll write you a glowing reference for university? Whatever you like. Oxford, Harvard, Cambridge. You can write your own ticket. We can help each other out."

A letter of recommendation? Was he kidding?

"Thanks, but no thanks," I said.

"What then? What do you want?" His face was pink with frustration.

I paused to think if there was actually anything worth trading my morality on.

"Just something for us to eat and drink," I said.

"Tiresome," he mumbled, looking back at his computer screen now. I was invisible.

I started to sweat. It was fine to have a sense of pride, but we couldn't eat it for dinner, and the idea of going back to coconut juice was just depressing.

"Could I just have a few cans of soup?" I asked. "You can't starve us."

"I need you to tell me more about them, Francesca!" he shouted, pounding his fists on the table. "Fill in the blanks. What I have here is good, but it's not enough. I'm frustrated. I feel cheated."

"You feel cheated? How do you think I feel?"

"It's not about you, little girl, don't you see that?"

"I do. Very clearly." I stopped to collect my thoughts. "So you're going to hold us hostage until I cave in?"

"Enough with this hostage nonsense," he quickly said, holding up his hands. "You're all free to go. And as soon as I tune up the plane, I'll fly you out. But that could take days…weeks even," he said without a hint of irony.

"I don't know anything else," I pleaded, weakening at the prospect of a night without food. "Nothing happened last night. And do you honestly think they would tell me anything else at this point? It's like you said, they don't trust me," I lied. "But I'll try again, OK?"

He looked at me pointedly and looked back down at his laptop.

"If there's a will, there's a way, Francesca. If there's a will, there's a way." He gestured to a bottle of water and a huge bag of nuts before looking back at his laptop. "Take them and go. Go."

I grabbed the stuff and went back outside.

• • •

"For the love of God, shut up, Eve," Milan finally said after a half hour of listening to her complain about her ruined career at the hands of Ned Harrison. "You have no career. So it really doesn't matter about your yearnings for men with saggy balls. *Nobody* will care…and if they do, it will only serve to remind them that you still exist. Remember what Chaz said."

"I just feel like I'm the only one who really has something at stake," Eve whined.

"Hello, the guy knows Cisco can't read," Milan said, kissing Cisco sweetly on the cheek. "*That's* embarrassing."

"I can read," Cisco sulked.

"Oh, he'll end up being the poster boy for some literacy program. It'll just make him more famous," Eve sulked. "And the same is true for Jonah. I'm the only one who can't parlay my dirty laundry into something," she paused, searching for the right word, "something *more*."

"So what? You think your secrets are more outrageous than ours?" Jonah asked.

"A little," she admitted.

"OK," Cisco finally said, "I can raise you."

"Yes?" she asked, placing her hands together and pressing them to her lips in hopeful prayer.

Cisco paused to think. Thinking was a stressful verb for Cisco. One could almost hear the exercising of the limp brain muscles.

"I don't *always* recycle," he finally said.

"Oooooh," she purred in mock revelation. "Scandalous!"

"All right," he admitted. "I never do…unless someone is watching."

"Whatever, Cisco."

"I eat steak at home. Sometimes even veal."

"While we appreciate your admissions of hypocrisy," Eve said, shaking her head, "it just doesn't feel on par with having an affair with the most famous man in England and then setting his pied-à-terre on fire. You know? Just not the same."

"I wax my chest?" he threw at us like a fly ball at a Little League game.

"Again," Eve said, "really unappealing but not entirely newsworthy."

"It's newsy-ish," Chaz yawned, sucking lazily on the information guarantee.

"I had a nose job," Cisco finally blurted out.

"Whaaaaaat?" Milan shrieked. "You are grossing me out, man."

"Yes!" Chaz said, pumping a fat fist into the air. "I knew something about you was different after your Disney Possum days."

"Well, there it is," Cisco said, casually popping a nut into his mouth.

I knew once Cisco confessed, someone would try to top him. They were a competitive group, and they didn't like being one-upped.

"I had a boob job," Milan offered.

"That's no secret, jingle bells," Chaz said. "Try again."

"I put Ex-Lax in Kirsten Dunst's mojito so she'd miss her audition for *Naughty Corner*."

"Jesus Christ," Eve said.

"You did that?" Joe laughed.

Milan nodded. "I don't regret it either. It's the best role I ever had. And she would have gotten it back then. Oh, I also *accidentally* pushed Kristen Stewart off the set when we were filming."

We all looked at her in disbelief.

"What?" she shrugged innocently. "She was upstaging me."

"Aren't you guys like best friends?" I asked.

"We were," she sighed regretfully.

"All right," Eve cleared her throat, "You know those naked pictures of Avery Printz? The ones that came out last year that she so passionately denied being her?"

We all nodded.

"They weren't of her. They were of *me*." She was smiling this perverted little half grin I'd never seen before.

"Nooooo!" Chaz gasped. I thought he might take off, he was so amped.

Eve nodded.

"How?" I asked.

"Peter's son David was dating Avery at the time, so when the pictures he'd taken of me leaked to the press, he convinced David to lie and say they were of her. We kind of have the same complexion."

"Poor li'l Ave," Chaz laughed. "Her whole girl-next-door persona was destroyed after that. Why would David agree? It's so wrong."

"I think Peter kind of forced him into it," she shrugged. "You know, he gets a *really* good allowance."

"Sweet Jesus," Chaz cried. "So Peter lets Avery take the fall to protect his own ass…and yours." He swallowed a fistful of nuts. "Hmm, like father, like son, I guess."

"I gather she dumped David shortly thereafter?" I asked.

"Yes," Eve said, clearly enjoying her confession. "I guess it is pretty disgusting," she admitted.

I knew this was my moment to come clean. I was fairly certain that Ned was the only one who had bothered reading *all* my texts. Milan and the others would have only read what I'd written about them. And besides, once we got out of here they would all know the truth. I took a deep breath.

"My dad isn't dead," I said. "He just had an affair. I lied about him dying. I lied to get here. I wanted to win the essay contest."

They all stared at me with their mouths hanging open.

"What?"

"You lied about your dad dying?" Jonah asked, looking at me with horror.

"Yes. He left my mom and is having a baby with his girl-friend." I paused. "I was really mad."

"That's cold, Francesca," Cisco said.

"I know," I stammered.

"Who would do that?" Milan looked at me like I was the one who pushed my best friend down the stairs. I mean, in the scheme of things, my crime didn't seem *that* heinous.

"I never thought I would win the contest," I admitted. "I entered on a whim. Once I'd won, I didn't know how to get out of it. It was too embarrassing."

"But why did you lie to me?" Cisco asked.

"And me?" Jonah added.

"I don't know. I guess I liked being a part of something. Being fractured made me feel like I was more interesting."

"Now *that's* pathetic," Eve grinned.

"I know," I said.

It was quiet for a few seconds before Joe spoke.

"I was in a porn movie," he said, hanging his head but raising his eyes with a sly grin. "A few actually."

I was so grateful that he got the attention off me that the shock of his admission nearly didn't register.

"Whaaaaaaaat?" We all gasped. Jonah looked like he might faint.

"It was 1974," he said, taking a deep breath. "*The Double Dutch Bus, Double Dutch Two*, and *Little Head Riding Good*."

We all burst out laughing. It was really hard to imagine Joe as a young person…let alone naked…let alone having sex.

"Impressive!" Chaz exclaimed. "But how is it possible that nobody ever discovered it?" Chaz continued in disbelief. "Nothing gets by me. I'm a Google god."

"I had a nose job too," Joe added without a beat.

We were on the ground hysterical now. Joe was all right looking, but he had a big nose. A really big nose.

"I hope you sued your doctor?" Milan chortled.

"No. I asked for this," he smiled, touching his honker. "My agent suggested I might do better as a character actor. I used to look more like him," he said, pointing at Jonah. "And once I got the part on *Small Secrets*, I was glad I'd done it, if for no other reason than that I knew nobody would ever recognize me from my *previous* career."

"And what was your acting name?" I asked, trying not to laugh.

"Joe Jangles."

Needless to say we were all laughing so hard by this time that we had to take about ten minutes to collect ourselves. Jonah was laughing hardest of all, so it came as a particular surprise when he cleared his throat to speak.

"I think I'm gay."

"I *knew* it!" Chaz clapped immediately as he stood to do a little victory jig. "I *knew* it! There was no way I was buying that you were straight."

Chaz looked around awkwardly before sitting back down trying to wipe the smile off his face and bury his less than polite reaction. "Sorry," he bowed his head. "That was rude."

"Wowza," Cisco mused. "That's some hypocrisy, man. Jesus won't like that."

I was stunned.

"You're gay?" I finally said.

"I think so," he nodded apologetically. "Yes."

"And I'm the bad guy?" I said.

"I'm sorry. I wasn't sure. I'd hoped. I thought maybe…"

"You lied to me, Jonah. You told me you liked me! That you wanted to be with me!"

"It did seem like a bit of a stretch," Chaz whispered to

Milan, who nodded in agreement. I ignored them and kept talking.

"And then you made me feel guilty for betraying you because I kept a stupid diary? Are you kidding me?"

"I didn't do it to hurt you, Francesca. I really didn't."

"I was just a convenient beard?" I asked. "Shack up with the virgin so you can continue being a big, Christian fraud? Who cares about my feelings, right? Very Jesus-like. Very nice."

"At least it explains why he didn't want to sleep with *me*," Milan whispered to Cisco.

"I really am sorry, Francesca. It's not what I want for myself. I just can't pretend anymore. If I were straight, you're the kind of girl I'd want to be with. I really thought it would be different with you, but it was the same. I'm just not, not attracted…to girls. But if I were, you'd be it."

"Gee, thanks soooo much, Jonah," I squawked. "I'm so honored that you'd like me *if* you liked girls! You'll pardon me for not swooning over the flattery. Do you even believe in God? Is the whole Christian thing a fake too?"

"I love God," Jonah said softly. "I just don't know how he feels about me anymore." Jonah's voice was quivering.

"Unbelievable," I said, glaring at him.

"That's enough, Francesca," Joe said, standing up and walking over to Jonah. "I know you've had a bad week, but this isn't about you."

"Well, there's a surprise," I snapped.

"Francesca!" Joe looked at me and gestured to Jonah, who had his head between his legs. He seemed to have shrunk about three inches.

"Well, don't cry," I said, finally recognizing how hard it was for him to have made that kind of confession. Still, though, I was getting tired of being treated like a used Kleenex. Joe walked over to Jonah.

"I just wish… I wish… if only you'd told me…" Joe said, kneeling down next to Jonah.

"I never thought I'd tell anybody," Jonah mumbled quietly. "Including myself. I was scared. I'm a fraud," he laughed with a sort of self-disgust.

"You're a kid, Jonah. You've been told who you were supposed to be since you were eleven years old. Give yourself a break."

Jonah suddenly lifted his head and looked directly at Joe.

"So you're good with my being gay?" he said, his voice sounding suspicious, almost accusatory.

"I'm relieved," Joe said. "I want to help you in whatever way I can. You never would let me help you in the past. There were so many walls around you. If one came down, another one went up to replace it. At some point I just decided you really wanted me to leave you alone. So I did." Joe stopped for a second. "But I've always loved you. You're my son. You'll always be my son."

"Aww," everybody but me meowed together. I wasn't there yet.

"Look, Dad," Jonah said, wiping his tears and collecting himself. "I appreciate what you're saying, but I just can't help but feel like your acceptance is a little predatory."

"Predatory?" Joe asked, jerking back with big, confused eyes. He looked hurt.

"I mean, now that I'm gay, you want to be my daddy? Just because I'm flawed doesn't mean I need you. I don't need you."

"I know you don't need me," Joe said, smiling sadly. "And *I* don't think you're flawed, Jonah. You do."

Jonah placed his head back between his knees and took some long, deep breaths. Joe studied him for a minute and then continued.

"I think you're an incredible young man, Jonah, and I'd like the opportunity to know you better. That's all," Joe said, holding up his hands. "No ulterior motive."

"Because I don't need anyone," Jonah started, but his voice betrayed him. Tears were pooling on the dirt beneath him.

"I know that," Joe said, nodding his head.

"OK," Jonah looked up, not even bothering to wipe away the tears that spilled over his flushed cheeks. "Thank you. Thanks."

"Please, don't thank me," Joe said, choking on his own emotion. "We'll try again, huh?"

Jonah nodded, swiping away the wetness with his forearm. I got the sense their relationship was well on its way to repair.

"Come here, son," he said, holding out his arms. Jonah burst into tears as he made himself small in his father's embrace.

"I love you, Jonah," he said, tears streaming down his face. Jonah looked so young and innocent. It was like somebody had stripped off his protective coating.

"I'm so sorry," he cried, heaving into Joe's shoulder. "I'm so, so sorry."

"You're OK, Jonah," Joe reassured him. "It's all OK."

"Mom will kill me. My career is over now," Jonah said, trying to calm down.

"Hardly," Chaz bellowed. "You'll be huge. Huge! The gays *love* a new recruit…especially a closeted choirboy. My God, it'll be glorious. I'll get you on the cover of *Newcummers*, and you'll never look back. Trust me, honey, the gays are soooo much more loyal than the Jesus people. And we're obsessive. I saw Madonna sixteen times on her last tour. Sixteen times! I flew to twelve different cities in two weeks. Twelve cities in two weeks! Oh God," Chaz put his hand on his chest dramatically, "I just had the best idea. You'll do a reveal on *SNL*. You'll be the Ambiguously Gay Christian."

"That would be so fuuunnny," Milan giggled.

"*Newcummers*?" Jonah shivered.

"I'm joking, Jonah," Chaz explained. "We're talking

People, *Vanity Fair*, *Entertainment Weekly*, *GQ*. They'll all be drooling to get the exclusive. Adam Lambert who?"

"Why don't you be his manager?" Milan suggested to Chaz, half-joking.

"It's not a bad idea," Joe said, still hugging Jonah. "You'll certainly need a new team, as it were."

"I'll do it!" Chaz said, clapping.

"Umm," Jonah stammered, breaking his embrace with Joe.

"But he's a blogger, not a manager. He has no experience," Eve protested.

"If he does half the job for Jonah that Yvette Clarkson's done for you, he'll be fine," Milan said. "He's got the passion."

"And I'm so over blogging," Chaz said. "Please, Jonah. It will be such fun."

Jonah looked at Joe, who smiled at his son approvingly.

"We'll see," Jonah finally said. "What about my fans, though? There's just no way I'm not going to come off as a hypocrite and a deceiver. A sinner."

"You're allowed to change, Jonah," Joe said. "Being famous at such a young age is hard because it doesn't allow you to grow. Don't let anyone put you in a box. Don't let anybody or anything define what or who you are."

"The new Joe Jangles Hallmark Collection," Chaz announced. "Available at a stationary shop near you."

We couldn't help busting up again. Joe as a porn star *almost* trumped Jonah as a gay man.

"You know," Chaz suggested to Jonah. "I think your going Jewish would be a nice touch too. The Jews love a gay as much as a whitefish bagel platter."

"This has all been super-touching and everything," Milan said. "But since we're all 'out' now, as it were, why not just have Francesca go in there and tell Ned what he wants to know so we can blow this joint today. What do you guys say? What are we waiting for?"

"Me?" I squawked.

"I'm down with that," Cisco said, looking at Milan with pride.

"It's fine with me," Joe answered. "Quite honestly it'll be a relief to stop worrying about somebody exhuming my past."

Chaz nudged Jonah.

"Yeah," Jonah said, looking a little less convinced. It was one thing to tell us he was gay, quite another to make it a public confession.

We all looked at Eve, who was curled up in a tight ball of indecision wrapped in a ribbon of social pressure.

"I don't know," Eve started. "We could really regret it after."

"Excuse me!" I said. "I'm not telling Ned anything. No way. If you all want to unload your skeletons, feel free, but don't do it here…to Ned. Wait until we get back, like Chaz suggested. Use it to your possible advantage."

They were all staring at me.

"And I'm most definitely not telling him anything," I went on. "I feel bad enough about what happened. I am not going to be that person for the rest of my life. Screw Ned. Let him spin a fictional yarn out of those scraps. I have a better idea."

"Well?" Jonah asked, gently taking my hand by way of an apology. It didn't feel that much different from when I thought he was straight.

"Well," I said, pleased with myself, "why don't we just steal the plane? It's so simple."

"In cartoons," Joe scoffed. "There's nothing simple about it, Francesca."

"But you know how to fly. It's so obvious. We should just steal the plane when Ned is sleeping."

Everybody looked at Joe.

"I can't fly a seaplane," he said.

"It can't be that different from a regular plane."

"We can't all fit," he added.

"You could go alone and get help," I suggested.

"I've got no float training," he said defensively.

"You can figure it out, Joe."

I felt like we were in a verbal tennis match.

"I don't know a thing about water rudders," he said anxiously. "I can't read water conditions, and there are no brakes on those things."

He looked around at us and continued.

"And no runways or landing strips."

"That didn't stop you before," Milan said, reminding him of our graceful arrival here.

"That's very clever, Milan."

"Well, you're really not having a movie star moment here," she said.

"I'm not Vin Diesel, for God's sake," Joe yelled, defending himself.

"What the hell's a Vindweezel?" she asked.

"But really, Joe," I interrupted, "all you have to do is land on the water…close to a populated area. You can bail the plane and swim, right? It's not like you have to dock it."

Joe started biting his nails. I'd never seen him do that before.

"No way," he shook his head. "It's too risky."

"But I don't understand why." I was begging.

"Look, I still don't know where the hell we even are. If I head out in the wrong direction I could run out of gas in the middle of the ocean."

"We'd be no worse off than we are now," I suggested.

"Speak for yourself," he coughed nervously.

So that was it. Joe was scared. He was scared to fly again.

"Dad," Jonah said, "I think you can do it."

"I think I can, son," was what Joe was supposed to say. "I can't do it," is what he said instead.

"But why not?" we whined, collectively irritated at his blah de vivre.

"The ignition key. I need the key!" he announced, sounding pleased that he'd finally stumbled on a real obstacle.

I reached into my back pocket and pulled out the key I'd swiped from the little bowl on Ned's table.

"What's that?" Joe asked in disbelief.

I held the key in front of him.

Joe didn't say anything.

"Dad?" Jonah asked. "Is that the key?"

Joe looked at Jonah and reluctantly opened his palm.

"I'll go with you," Jonah said.

"Absolutely not. It's too dangerous." He paused for a minute. "I'll go alone. But somebody better make damn sure Ned's distracted until he falls asleep."

"I'll take care of that," I said.

"How?"

"Trust me. I can do it."

"Fine then," he sighed, looking at me and standing up slowly. "At least you'll all have somebody other than me to blame if it doesn't work."

I was elated. I was saving the day. My plan was going to work.

You Show Me Your Pontoon,
I'll Show You Mine

So your *boyfriend's* a poof, right?" Ned asked, thrilled that I had come around. Dinner was over, and Ned was sitting in front of his computer like a greedy child waiting for a piece of cake.

"No," I said, irritated at Ned's perspicacity. How did he know? Was it that obvious to everyone but me?

"He seems like a poof to me. You sure?"

"Umm, yeah," I said, pretending not to giggle. I was trying my best to smother my anger and channel my inner actress. "I'm 100 percent sure."

"Ahhhh," he smiled wickedly, searching my face for signs of deception. "No longer a virgin then?"

"No," I shook my head.

"I see."

"He wasn't a virgin anyway," I added. "Not really."

"You mean since he converted?"

"I mean since he slept with Miley Cyrus. Can I have something to drink?"

"Jonah Baron slept with Miley Cyrus?"

I nodded again. I was having fun. Ned got up to get two glasses and filled them to the rim with tequila.

"When?" he asked, pushing the glass toward me.

"About a year ago. She gave him venereal warts. And he's like OCD so it was really, really hard for him. He feels dirty all the time."

He cringed as he downed his drink.

"And weren't you concerned about it being catching and all that?" he asked, typing with one hand while refilling his glass with the other. There were drops of tequila dangling from his moustache like a terrier after a trip to the toilet bowl.

"Oh, he had it treated a long time ago. Keira Knightley made him take care of it."

"Keira Knightley?" Ned asked. "Are you telling me Jonah Baron slept with Keira Knightley?" He stopped typing.

"He's slept with like everyone. He's a sex addict. He uses sex to express emotional needs through physical contact."

Ned was quiet for a minute.

"And I'm going to help him with that," I said, breaking what was becoming an uncomfortable silence. "I'm going to help him get better."

Ned nodded. He was making me nervous.

"Mmm hmm. What else?" Ned asked. "What about him and Joe? Have they reconciled?"

"God, no," I lied. "They hate each other. Joe denies even

being Jonah's real father. You know, that's the underlying reason why Jonah is a sex addict. Hardcore abandonment issues," I added meaningfully.

"And what about all the religious mumbo?"

"A ruse. Jonah's an atheist."

"Of course he is," Ned started laughing. "What else, Francesca? Does Milan Amberson have a PhD in biochemistry? Is Cisco Parker a transvestite? Is Eve Larkin Joe's illegitimate daughter from his affair with Michelle Pfeiffer?"

I didn't say anything.

"I don't like being lied to, girl. Do you think I was born yesterday?"

"Um, no, sir," I stammered, trying to slow my heart rate down. "Really," I added lamely. "It's true."

"Go on and get out. I'm done playing games. Out!" he yelled, pushing me out the door.

• • •

"Good job, Francesca," Chaz said, standing over me like a schoolyard bully. "It went really well, I gather?"

"What happened?" Jonah asked.

"He didn't believe me. I think it would have been better if I'd gone with the story about Milan."

"Duh," Chaz shouted, shaking with anger. "It's *always* better to go with the story about Milan."

Milan nodded. "When in doubt…" she pointed to herself.

"So what happened?" Jonah asked.

"Does it matter?" I felt mortified at my failure.

"It's OK," Eve said, coming to my defense. "She tried. And besides, as long as he doesn't notice Joe's gone, there's still hope. Let's see what happens."

I couldn't believe Eve was defending me. Maybe this whole experience had forced us to evolve—as individuals and as a group. Nobody was screaming or accusing. The general state of hostility and defense was disbanded. It felt like everyone was on the same team. Then again, maybe it was just useful to have a common enemy.

"I hope my dad's OK," Jonah said quietly. "I kind of feel like I pushed him into doing something he wasn't comfortable with. Maybe it would have been better to just wait it out."

"He'll be OK," I said without confidence, knowing full well that I'd be responsible if something happened to Joe. Chaz stood up and started pacing.

"The guy's a pilot. He'll be fine. Just keep your voices down and relax."

"But what if he gets lost?" Milan asked. "It's so dark. How is he going to see?"

"Shhh," Chaz hushed her. "It's called radar. He'll be fine."

"Who the hell does Ned Harrison think he is?" Eve asked. "Can't he be incarcerated for holding us hostage?"

"He's not holding us hostage," Chaz quipped. "He's just

not facilitating our rescue. And besides, people with Ned's kind of money don't get incarcerated for anything but murder or tax evasion."

"Still…" Jonah started.

"Look," Chaz interrupted him. "It's not his fault we're here, just that we're *still* here. It'll be complicated to prove anything. He could claim we were trespassing."

"What if he, like, tries to kill us all or something?" Milan suggested. "I mean, once he realizes Joe left with the plane, he's gonna be so pissed."

"Keep your voice down," Chaz whispered.

"Let's just hope for the best," I said. "There's still plenty of time. He's only been gone about two hours, right?"

"Two and a half," a sullen voice said, as a drenched male figure in a transparent, hooded poncho made its way toward us.

"Joe?" we all shouted.

"Shhhhhh!" Chaz snapped, trying not to attract Ned's attention.

Joe was soaking wet, limping and cradling his left arm.

"You're still here? Why haven't you left?" Chaz whispered.

"I have left. I'm back now." Joe was chewing on something tough. He had a wild look in his eyes.

"What do you mean you're back now?"

"I told you I couldn't fly a seaplane."

"What the hell happened?"

"I couldn't see a goddamn thing is what happened," he said. "The water was choppy as hell. It was like trying to get a parade float off the sand."

"Sshhhhh!" we all hushed him.

"Seaplanes?" he scoffed. "What a ridiculous idea."

"Where's the plane?" I asked.

"Which half?"

"Oh my God."

"So Ned's gonna know you messed with it?" Cisco asked.

Joe started hysterically laughing.

"Most likely," he said, spitting something akin to tobacco out of his mouth.

"What happened?"

"Well, I managed to lift her up and level out, but then her nose hit the water hard and we doubled over."

"And then?"

"Then the left wing snapped off."

We gasped.

"And then," Joe continued calmly, searching for the details like it was a joke he had heard years before but couldn't remember how to word the punch line, "I managed to jump out before the fuselage rocketed back to the beach and flipped over." He did a little hand gesture to mimic the rolling over of the plane.

"It was dramatic. I wish somebody had been there to see it. It could be worse. At least the cabin is docked, right? I mean, she's actually right back where I started out from…only upside down now, with her pontoons in the air."

"And wingless," I added.

"And wingless," he confirmed.

"So that plan of yours isn't going to work after all, Francesca," he said with satisfaction.

"What are you wearing?" Milan finally asked.

"A poncho from the first-aid kit. And here," he said, throwing a bag filled with what looked like dog biscuits on the ground.

"What is it?"

"Dehydrated food. Jerky."

"Oooh, jerky," Chaz said clamoring for the bag.

"What happens when Ned sees his ruined plane?" Eve asked.

"He'll be mad as hell," Joe said.

"I just thought of something," I said.

"Great," Chaz said, tearing off a piece of beef jerky with his teeth. "Another nifty idea from Nancy Drew."

"Maybe when you crashed Ned's plane," I continued, ignoring Chaz, "the black box sent a signal?"

"I don't think sea planes have black boxes," Joe answered.

"But it might have had one," I said, ever the newly hatched optimist.

"Maybe. But the range is limited. Somebody would have

to be looking for the plane to pick up on a signal. Nobody is looking for Ned's plane."

It was quiet for a minute.

"How do black boxes work?" I asked.

"I don't know," Joe answered.

"What do you mean, you don't know?" Chaz asked him scornfully.

"I mean, I don't know," Joe said. "I don't know exactly how they work. Black boxes."

"You don't know how they work?" Chaz snapped again. "Maybe I'll be a pilot *and* a novelist. Neither job seems to require a particularly large area of expertise."

"Add acting to that list," Milan laughed.

"Touché," Chaz said, giving Milan a high five.

"Speak for yourself," Eve jumped in. "The kind of acting *we* do," she said, looking at Joe and Cisco, "isn't easy. It takes years of training. Studying. Method."

"Weren't you like five years old when you made your first movie?" Milan asked.

"Three."

"Right. And weren't you a model before you became a Possum?" Milan asked Cisco jeeringly.

"Yeah, but I took classes."

"Ooooh, classes," Chaz mocked.

"Let's not get at one another's throats again, OK?" Joe interrupted.

"My only point," Chaz continued, "is that none of us can do anything really useful. At least Francesca can cook. And I guess Milan can slaughter poultry."

It was quiet for a few minutes before Eve cleared her throat to speak.

"This experience has been humbling. It's almost like none of us exist without an audience."

"Or people to boss around," Milan added.

"Or deceive," Jonah added thoughtfully.

"Yeah," Cisco mused. "Or have sex with."

"Hey!" Milan piped in.

"I mean, you know, having lots of people available to have sex with, no matter how I behaved," he stammered. "Not that I want that now," he added, looking at Milan lovingly. "I just got used to not having to work too hard for anything. You know, just showing up has always been enough."

"I don't mean to interrupt the psychological healing process," I said, "but back to the box. Let's go see if we can find it in the plane. Maybe we can do something with it?"

"Like decorate it?" Milan laughed.

"It's better than sitting here all night," Chaz said. "Let's go. Maybe there's more jerky…"

Flight of the Living Dead

It must have been six o'clock in the morning. The sun had just come up. Of course, we hadn't found the black box. We did flip the plane right side up. It was hard work. Then we took turns eyeballing the interior, hoping the black box would appear on one of the little passenger seats like a mint on a hotel pillow. We didn't even know where to look. Chaz was right. We were a useless bunch. It was a stupid idea.

Everyone but me was asleep. Joe was in the copilot's seat with his mouth half open and a pool of saliva dripping out the side of his mouth. Milan was splayed out on the floor of the plane, while Eve was curled up in a ball in one of the passenger seats. Chaz was just outside the plane, buried in a foot of sand to ward off the cool night air. Only his arm and mosquito-bitten, domed head were poking out. Jonah was next to me, banked up against a pontoon and fast asleep on his belly. I looked at his delicate features with tenderness. His beautiful almond eyes were caked with pus. We all had some ferocious strain of pink eye to compliment the head lice. I felt itchy. I felt filthy. I felt hopeless. I felt like we were never going home.

I began to panic. The plane was ruined. What if Ned's radio died and we were stuck here forever? What if nobody ever came for us? What if everyone just forgot we ever existed? God knows, the filthy, stinking, bug-ridden group next to me didn't look like celebrities. I didn't even know what the word meant anymore. We could have been any random group of survivors of a plane crash. Modern-day victims of a Herculaneum or Pompeii, nameless faces, frozen in time, buried in sand…waiting to be rediscovered and discussed in two thousand years. Maybe the island would become a tourist site where the curious could come trade theories on who we were and what we were doing here before buying a coffee and a postcard at the gift shop. I shivered, trying to shake off the vision. I almost jumped out of my skin when Jonah spoke. It was like the living dead.

"Did you hear that?" he mumbled, not moving.

"Hear what?" I asked, straining to hear anything but my racing heart beating in my skull.

"It sounded like a horn or something."

I stood up and pried open my sticky eyelids to greet the vision ahead. It was real. I saw a huge ship in the distance. It was heading straight for us.

"Holy shit!" I screamed. "Wake up!"

Jonah sat up and wiped the sand out of his hair.

"Holy shit."

Chaz was working his way out of the sand as Eve, Milan, and Joe wormed their way out the little plane door single file.

"What do we do?" Eve asked, waving her little, frantic hands over her head. "What if they don't see us?"

"They're heading straight this way," Joe announced, looking serenely ahead like he was acting the part of a seasoned old sea captain. The rest of us started waving like lunatics. The ship sounded its horn in response.

"It sees us!" Cisco yelled. "I think it's coming for us!"

All of a sudden, we heard the blades of a helicopter. As the ship turned slightly south, I saw the miraculous. There must have been six boats and three helicopters seeming to appear out of thin air. We stared in disbelief as our five-day silence was punctured by the sounds of massive machinery.

"Francesca must have been right about the black box," Joe smiled. Milan grabbed me by the waist and started twirling me around in circles.

As the helicopters got closer, we were able to see that the first one was the South African Red Cross, followed by a STAR chopper (not the magazine but the Specialized Trauma Air Rescue), AmbuStat, something called SAfm, Afrikaans, and, incredibly, one with a BBC logo. The last helicopter slowed overhead as individual paparazzi hung from the landing gear with cameras like little spiders hanging from a web.

"Look, it's a helicopter just for *Star* magazine!" Milan sang.

"And the BBC!" Chaz yelled as he pointed above.

They were passing over us now, circling in search of a place to land. The boats were still a good mile off.

"They can't land here," Joe called out over the noise, shielding his eyes from the sandstorm the choppers were causing. "Run to the landing strip!" We were covering our eyes and ears as we headed up the beach, crouching down low like they do on TV.

"Is that guy wearing a *People* vest?" Eve asked, stopping in place as she strained to make out the logo on one of the newsmen.

"Yeah!" I screamed, grabbing her hand to pull her along. "C'mon."

"And *EW!*" Milan hollered gleefully, running toward the cameras like a child to her mother.

Eve's hand slipped through my fingers. Suddenly she was running in the opposite direction.

"Eve!" I shouted after her. "What are you doing? Where are you going?"

She was running as fast as she could, which wasn't all that fast in the sand.

I yelled to Cisco, who was directly in front of me, and pointed to Eve, who was running the other way.

"What's she doing?" he asked.

I nodded, and he headed after her.

Just then the sound of a loudspeaker cut through the cacophony of horns and swirling blades.

"Jonah Baron, your Lord and Savior has not abandoned you."

Jonah stopped short as a man from the *Christian Examiner* dangled overhead with a microphone. "God bless you, Jonah Baron. God loves you, Jonah Baron."

Through the screen of sand I made out Jonah's terrified face. All of a sudden he was running in the same direction as Eve. Joe turned around after him.

"Don't, Jonah! Don't!" I heard Joe screaming.

The helicopters hovered in confusion as Milan and Chaz ran to meet the press and as the others ran for cover. I stood in the middle, blinded by sand, confused, excited, not knowing where to go. I decided to follow Milan. (When in doubt, go with Milan.) She was guiding the *People* helicopter to the runway in a state of delirious ecstasy. Chaz was skipping behind her, waving his hands in the air. The boats had come in, and a fleet of officials, medics, journalists, and photographers were coming up behind us. I knew they were there to help, but I felt hunted and terrified as they screamed for us.

By the time we got to the landing strip, the Red Cross helicopter had just landed. Ned was standing there, a hundred yards away, his face twisted in a fit of rage.

For a few minutes, after the last helicopter landed, it was quiet. Milan and Chaz stood holding hands. I was standing a few feet behind them, frozen in fear.

Suddenly, I felt Joe's hand on my shoulder. I flinched.

"It's OK, Francesca," he said, pushing me forward. "It's OK."

I felt a sort of release as I turned around and saw he was with Eve, Cisco, and Jonah. They looked serene. Cisco put his arm around Jonah.

"Are you ready?" he asked Jonah kindly.

Jonah nodded and stood tall.

"This is so cool," Milan cooed, squeezing my shoulder.

"How bad do I look?" Eve whispered to me, girlishly tucking a piece of hair behind her ear. I leaned over and wiped a strip of crust off her eyelid.

"Not bad at all," I lied. She smiled.

There was an eerie silence as the strangers stared at us like holy miracles. They searched our faces. "Is it really them?" we could almost hear them collectively thinking. They looked shocked and disbelieving. People were crying. Nobody thought we were still alive.

We waited for the circus to begin, but it was another moment until one lone figure came forward from the first helicopter. It was a girl, and she started running toward us.

"Francesca!" she cried. "Francesca!"

It was Jordan!

"She's hot," I heard Cisco say as I ran hard to meet her, and we locked in an embrace.

"What are you doing here?" I asked.

"Your texts," she cried. "They all came through the day before yesterday. Like two hundred pages at once. We thought you were dead, Francesca," she sobbed. "I thought it was a joke, but it was your words. I knew it was you."

"I don't understand," I cried, burying my head in her neck to hide my face from the photographers who had begun to surround us.

"We took my phone to the police, and they thought it was a prank!" she explained. "My mom finally convinced them it wasn't a joke, and they traced the texts to Ned Harrison's computer. Ned Harrison!"

"So when Ned charged my phone, the texts automatically sent to your phone?" I was stunned.

She nodded tearfully.

"*All* of them?" I asked in disbelief.

"Did you really make out with Cisco Parker?" she whispered as I saw my mom, Emily, and my dad come running toward us. My family.

I burst into tears.

"Well, did you?" she asked, laughing through her tears. I looked over Jordan's shoulder and saw Cisco smiling at me as the paparazzi and news crews descended around them.

Epilogue

It Does Have Its Perks

There's nothing like being presumed dead to make your family realize you're the greatest thing to come along since YouTube. Emily can't get enough of me since meeting Cisco Parker, and my mother was so grateful I was alive she seems to have had a complete personality makeover. "Worrying is like praying for something bad to happen," is her latest saying. Now *there's* an aphorism I can get behind. Maybe I should thank her new boyfriend, Larry, but I think it has more to do with my surviving five days in Africa with Milan Amberson.

As for my dad, well, it turns out, other than Jordan, he remains the only person I can really talk to. As I see it, if he can forgive my fictional lapse into patricide, I can forgive his falling in love with somebody named Chandra. She's not my favorite person, but she makes a kick-ass cannoli, and it's near impossible to hate the mother of a fat baby boy named Archie…with bright red hair!

Ned was right about one thing. I am a kind of celebrity now. I mean, I'm no Beyoncé, but once my phone diaries were released to the general public, I couldn't even buy a bag of Skittles without being recognized. Going back to high school was out of the question. Thank God.

My mom and dad actually agreed on something for a change and allowed me to take the GED and accept the job offer at *Seventeen* magazine in New York. Courtney Gallagher thought I'd be an asset to the magazine, and, without tooting my own horn, she was right. I'll be starting night classes at Columbia next fall, but in the meantime, I'm writing a monthly column and I'm in charge of all the celebrity bookings. Let's just say I came to the job with a lot of connections, and, at the tender age of eighteen, I'm the youngest member on staff. I've even got an assistant. Toot, toot!

The thing is, correct as Ned may have been about my notoriety, he was wrong about my friends on the island blowing me off after our rescue. None of them did. Not even Chaz, who is now the manager for the biggest gay pop sensation since Elton John. Jonah's album, *Coming Back from Coming Out*, sold over twenty million copies world-wide, placing it just between Britney Spears's *Oops!...I Did It Again* and *The Best of Bob Marley*. Not bad for a guy who was worried about his career. And Joe, who wisely managed to kill *Hoggalicious Two* from being released, was on hand when Jonah accepted his Grammy for Best Single, *Love the Sinner, Hate the Sin*, a duet he recorded with Milan Amberson. I guess she knew what she was talking about after all. Sometimes, it is all in the mix.

Eve went home to live with her parents in La Jolla for a year. She's decided not to act anymore…at least for now. She wrote a script about a young intern who discovers his sense of self after a scandalous affair with an older female senator. The buzz has been great, and there's talk that Cisco may play the lead.

As for Ned, well, things didn't turn out well for him. His island, with the help of the Hollywood Historical Society (and backed by some people you know), will be the location for a new reality TV show about a boot camp for aspiring teen actors. For the price of a small luxury vehicle, spoiled hopefuls from all over the world are flown to *Camp Hollywood Savage* to reenact our experience for three days (no phones, prepared food, or bottled water) before beginning a rigorous four-week training with a crop of seasoned agents, acting coaches, and other industry insiders. A percentage of all proceeds go to *The C. Parker Foundation*, a program that builds schools for young women to raise literacy in Africa.

About the Author

Sloane Tanen is the author of eight books, including the bestselling *Bitter with Baggage Seeks Same: The Life and Times of Some Chickens*, *Going for the Bronze*, *Hatched: The Pig Push from Pregnancy to Motherhood*; the children's titles *Where is Coco Going*, *Coco All Year Round*, *C is for Coco*, *Coco Counts*; and the young adult picture book *Appetite for Detention*. Sloane is a painter whose work has been exhibited in a number of shows and can be found in private and corporate collections. She received a BA from Sarah Lawrence College and holds graduate degrees in literary theory from NYU and in art history from Columbia University. She lives in Berkeley, California, with her husband and two sons.